The
Marigold
Chemise

SHERYL WESTERGREEN

Fulton Books
Meadville, PA

Published by Fulton Books 2022

The Marigold Chemise is a work of fiction. Unless otherwise indicated, all the names, characters, businesses, places, events, and incidents in this book are either the product of the author's imagination or used in a fictitious manner. Any resemblance to actual persons, living or dead, or actual events is purely coincidental.

ISBN 978-1-63985-390-8 (paperback)
ISBN 978-1-63985-391-5 (digital)

Printed in the United States of America

Silk charmeuse is known as the "Ferrari" of silks. One side is softly muted crepe, and the other side is classic shimmery satin. It drapes beautifully and is often used for lingerie.

Part I

Lucida hurries along Via Giulia. She is late and dreading the harsh words of her father. Lately, she has been visiting the studio of the Salvatori family, famous painters on the Via Margutta, and if her father becomes aware of her secret visits, his punishment will be swift and severe. Her dear friend Alessia had convinced her to sit for a series of paintings. Initially, she resisted, largely due to the fear of her father's disapproval. But when Alessia presented her with the most sensuous marigold-colored garment she had ever seen for her to pose in, she could not resist. The chemise had thin delicate straps and a diamond-shaped panel at the waist, softly hugging the female form.

"Isn't this the most beautiful thing you have ever seen?" Alessia had asked. "A patron gave it to my father, and he passed it to me. The fabric is rare silk charmeuse."

Caressing the chemise, *camicia da donna*, between her palms, Lucida began to feel foreign sensations.

"Please, my friend," Alessia had pleaded. "I need to make paintings that are not of Bible myths or stiff portraits of the self-important rich. I want to show beauty and power. You are the only one I can count on, and the marigold chemise will be perfect for the compositions. Please. The paintings are just for me, for my work. No one will see them."

The seduction had begun. The marigold chemise had begun to work its magic as they planned the series of work. Alessia is the artist, so she was contemplating composition and palette, but Lucida found that when she donned the marigold chemise, she naturally moved her body to the perfect degree that suggests an intimacy with the viewer. They decided on five paintings, each with a unique composition of Lucida posing in various stages of exposure.

She pleads with the saints that she will arrive home before her father and that in the chaotic household, neither her mother nor her siblings will take note of her arrival. She will slip in through the servant's entrance and pretend that she has been gossiping with the cook.

The Galvani family resides in a palazzo on Via Giulia, Rome, a beautiful street just off the Tiber River lined with wisteria and plane trees. Lucida's father, Luigi, is a physician. He is serious and strict, in direct contrast to his wife, Eugenia, who is sweet and scatterbrained. Lucida is the eldest at fifteen, followed by Brigida at thirteen, Luigi Junior at twelve, Giovanni at ten, and baby Beatrice is ten months. An assortment of pooches, stray cats, and birds tended by the house staff in the small garden completes the household. By nature, Eugenia is incapable of order and calm in running the household. Everyone loves her, and she is generous with her laughter and affection, relying on Luigi to discipline their brood and maintain some semblance of order when he is home.

Safe! Lucida is able to venture undetected from the kitchen up the stairs to her room. She quickly sheds her outer cloak and sinks onto her bed to review her afternoon in private. Alessia is brave to pursue this series of paintings, but the Salvatori studio is so busy, a veritable hive of industry, that it is possible that no one will take notice of the work, not bothering to peek beneath the drop cloths. In her mind's eye, she sees herself working with Alessia as they experimented with the first pose. They settled on a seated position with Lucida propped against cushions draped with lengths of cloth across the divan. Deep ultramarine blue, titanium white, and a hint of scarlet set the stage. The marigold chemise was the centerpiece with one strap off the left shoulder, exposing her breast. She can feel her heart rate quicken like the little birds who land on her window ledge each morning, their tiny breasts pulsating wildly.

After just one afternoon enfolded in its softness, the marigold chemise has beguiled her. She hasn't experienced anything like this before, a feeling of being intensely alive and vibrant.

Lucida is aware that her father has been pursuing conversations with his friends and associates about a suitable future husband. The custom of the time being is that girls from better families will marry at about sixteen to a man of about thirty since he will already be established in his business. It is a business arrangement. Her family will pay a dowry to his, consisting of money and household objects, while he usually gives her betrothal jewelry before the day of marriage.

She has never questioned her future. She assumes that she will have a life like her parents, a nice palazzo, some children, and a place in society. Until today, she hasn't envisioned the actual marriage or the man who will be her husband. As much as she fears her father's disapproval, she trusts him to procure a suitable match.

Brigida bursts into Lucida's room, laughing at the puppy wiggling in her arms and giving her sloppy kisses. "Father is home for the evening meal. He has to go back to the hospital later, so hurry to the table."

Everyone gathers, and after a blessing by their father, the kitchen servant serves the fish, bread, olives, and wine. It is the custom for Luigi to inquire about the activities of his offspring during the evening meal. A hired tutor, Ariston, arrives every morning to teach the four older children a curriculum designed by Luigi to prepare them for daily life. The boys will then advance to more formal study. This evening, he begins with Lucida. "Lucida, what did you do today after Ariston left?"

"I went for a walk in the Borghese with my friend Isabella and then came home to study my lessons."

"*Allora*." He holds her eye a few seconds longer than usual and moves on to Brigida.

Do I seem different? It cannot be. It is just my imagination, Lucida thinks to herself.

The following morning drags on with lessons. Normally, Lucida is sharp and animated, setting a fine example for her younger siblings as they study Greek, Latin, basic mathematics, and the writings of the great intellectuals of ancient Rome, such as Cicero. Ariston, their tutor, is a young Greek freedman. It is common in the times for the Roman higher class to hire Greek slaves or freedmen to teach their children. Luigi set an ambitious curriculum for his progeny, but he wanted their afternoons to be free for play and adventure. Ariston rebukes Lucida for her inattention and promises to report to Luigi if her mind wanders again tomorrow.

She barely registers his warning but replies, "Yes, Ariston, tomorrow will be better."

Finally, lessons are complete for the morning, and Lucida calculates that if she skips the lunch their cook serves them, just taking a slice of bread, she can avoid her mother and slip out. She hears her mother gossiping with one of her friends, and the rest of the brood are happily laughing and eating in the nursery. Cook ignores her as she grabs a slice of bread and rushes out the back entrance.

She pulls her cloak and hood tight against the chilly November air and quickly makes her way to the Salvatori studio on Via Margutta. Alessia is waiting for her, easel and paint at the ready for the canvas. Oil paint and turpentine are pungent, permeating everything in the room. A few windows are propped open, allowing some circulation, but the air is close and to Lucida, inviting. She slips behind the curtain and dons the marigold chemise with a shiver, settling into the pose and taking care to place her limbs carefully on the markers Alessia has left.

Alessia works swiftly, using a burnt sienna for her underpainting, layering in the planes of the body, the cloth, and the divan, establishing the darks and lights. Once again, Lucida feels herself drawn into a dreamlike trance, registering sensations unknown to her until now. She senses that there is a certain power in these sensations but is not sure she can trust it.

"We've made excellent progress today. I am pleased. You can change now." Alessia is gazing down at Lucida and sees that she has startled her from her reverie.

Lucida blushes, embarrassed to be caught daydreaming. "You know my father would not approve of me posing for you like this. If he learns of this, there could be trouble."

Alessia sighs deeply. "But you promised me. I need to prove to my father that I am ready to establish myself. These paintings will do that. They will show him I deserve to have my own voice. Please, please keep your word to me. Father will be discreet. No one will know."

"Don't fret, my friend. I will be back tomorrow. I want to help you. I like posing for you," Lucida replies, her eyes beginning to fill.

Spring brings wisteria cascading violet along the streets, and Alessia has completed five powerful paintings portraying Lucida in the marigold chemise, compelling the viewer to be enchanted. The final day of posing arrives, and Lucida is behind the curtain, dressing for departure. In a flash impulse, she decides to keep, really to steal, the chemise. Once her dress is on, the chemise is hidden. She makes a hasty goodbye to her friend and hurries out to Via Margutta. All the way home, she rehearses various methods for concealing her treasure, finally settling on a small box at the rear of her wardrobe usually meant for extra hair adornments no longer in fashion. She will wrap it in a muslin to protect it.

Horse drawn coaches fill the streets, and the air is full of clopping hooves, shouting and competing aromas of dung and *fornos* baking bread. As she turns on to Via Giulia, she nearly collides with a coach and is thrown against the wall fountain, rudely bringing her into the present. Shaking, she makes it to her doorway and is greeted by the arguing of Giovanni and Luigi Jr. Luigi Jr. doesn't want to let his younger brother come with him to meet his friends. Lucida has no time for this pettiness and warns Luigi that she will report him to their father. She is uncharacteristically stern because Luigi backs down for once and pushes Giovanni out the door ahead of him.

That evening, Father asks her to stay behind after the meal to speak with him and Mother. She is sure Brigida will be eavesdropping, always the little pest. Luigi and Eugenia sit close; Eugenia's hand tucked inside his. They seem excited, as if they have a secret between them. Lucida briefly wonders if there will be another baby but discards the thought. They would have included the entire family for that kind of news. Eugenia regards her oldest daughter with great affection and anticipates that Lucida will be thrilled with their news. She has become a beauty and quick of mind, a daughter to be proud of.

"Your father and I have been speaking with some of our friends about a suitable match. We feel that it is time for us to proceed in arranging your marriage. Signor Niccolo Bianchi has agreed to a meeting next week for an introduction. He is established in his family's banking business and is ready to take on a wife suitable to his society."

Lucida cannot respond. She has been expecting this, of course, but it feels too fast, especially given her secret life these past months. Well, she really doesn't have a choice, does she?

Finally, she is able to utter a meek, "Of course, Mother and Father."

It doesn't even occur to her to ask about his character, his looks, or his family. In a kind of trance, she asks to be excused to her room.

Luigi and Eugenia are puzzled. They had expected her to be enthusiastic.

"Maybe she isn't feeling well. I will talk to her tomorrow, Luigi." Eugenia kisses his cheek.

"Very well. This is the best match for her," Luigi says. "I want her to be secure. The Bianchis are stationed solidly, and Niccolo seems the type to treat her well."

Lucida barely reaches the door of her room when Brigida pounces and invites herself in.

"I know what is happening. Is he handsome? What palazzo will you have? Can I be the maid of honor? As soon as they get you established, it will be my turn. I can't wait. A few more years, and I will be prettier than you, and I will have an even better match." Brigida is bouncing around like a puppy; she is so excited.

She pauses, regarding her sister with a skeptical eye. "By the way, why have you been disappearing every afternoon? You can't always be walking in the Borghese with Isabella. It has been too cold. Have you been sneaking to see that Albergo boy we met at church last year? I know he is sweet on you, and I saw you flirt. Father would be angry. His family are only bakers. They are nice, but he is not suitable for you. Mother doesn't notice that you are gone every afternoon, but I could let her know."

Lucida sighs. She knows where this is going. "Okay, which piece of jewelry do you want to keep your mouth shut?" Anything to get rid of her. Brigida leaves with the ruby ring gifted to Lucida by their grandmother. "Don't let Mother or Father see you wear it," Lucida warns.

Lucida locks her door and pushes a heavy chair in front of it for extra security. Off comes her dress, and before the mirror, she luxuriates in the marigold chemise, asking it, "Where will you take me?" Surrendering to the comfort of her bed, she stops herself from dozing off and gets up to find the box in the back of her wardrobe. Reverently, she rolls the chemise and wraps it with a length of muslin, tucking it into the box.

The next afternoon, the warm spring air invites a stroll. By habit, she finds herself on Via Margutta. The wisteria is in full bloom now, violet lining the way. Alessia appears before her, out of breath and pale as porcelain.

"Oh, Lucida. Oh, Lucida! I was coming to find you," she stammers.

"What is it?" Lucida asks, a slow dread beginning in her heart.

"Last evening, Father visited my corner of the studio. He walked right over and pulled the drop cloths off the paintings before I had a chance to stop him. We argued and argued. He agreed that I have come into my own with my work. He thinks that the paintings are powerful but is afraid they are scandalous. Then he had his boy go fetch a dealer, Signor Ruel, who arranges private showings to certain collectors. Lucida, I am afraid that he did see you visit me in the studio. He knows we are friends, but it never occurred to him that you were posing. Signor Ruel is having the work delivered to the framers shop tomorrow. He is sure he can sell them all in just one showing. There is nothing I can do to stop him. My father needs the money and is in full agreement with him. Certain collectors will pay very well for seeing you in the marigold chemise."

Now it is Lucida's face that is pale as porcelain. She feels that she may faint and supports herself against her friend. Passersby give them strange looks. The blood begins to return to her brain, and she struggles to regain control of herself. Her family must never discover that these paintings exist.

Alessia and Lucida had played together in the Borghese and remain friends, but the nurse had accompanied Lucida, and the parents never socialized in the same circles, so maybe a word would never get to them that their daughter had posed for a group of scandalous paintings—painted by a young woman no less—regardless of how talented she is.

They determine that it would be best if the two of them are not seen together for now. If Alessia has any news for her, she will leave a note in the crack between stones at the wall in the Borghese where they had played together as children. Lucida walks there frequently, so it will be easy for her to check.

Orazio Salvatori is standing in Alessia's corner of the studio. The five paintings are lined against the wall. He is proud of his daughter's work. The work has matured, become more confident. Her friend is a beauty, and sensuousness exudes from her. The marigold color seems more powerful to him than when he employs it in his own work. He can't decide which painting is the most provocative. Despite any misgivings, he intends to override Alessia's objections and have Signor Ruel make him some money. The commissions from the church are slow in payment, and his household seems always on the verge of debt. He hears Signor Ruel arriving and makes haste to wrap the paintings for transport.

Lucida's mind is blank with dread as she makes her way to her favorite church, the Santa Maria in Trastevere. She needs to collect her wits, light a candle, and pray for guidance. There are a few elderly women gathered near the entrance, but they ignore her, and she makes her way toward a pew near the front.

Her favorite view is of the apse mosaic, showing the Coronation of the Virgin. She is seated on Christ's right hand, surrounded by saints. Today the light is softly streaming in shafts of gold through the apse's windows.

Kneeling, hands in prayer, she asks for forgiveness for her rash behavior and for divine assistance in keeping her secret. After a time, she begins to feel herself relax a bit and decides to light a candle with another prayer for strength and foresight.

The route home over the Ponte Sisto and on to Via Giulia is one she has navigated hundreds of times, and she feels a little more settled with each step. She has a new future waiting for her. She will step into her role of wife to a successful businessman with confidence.

Eugenia is waiting for her daughter when Lucida arrives home. She invites her into her sitting room so that they can have a private conversation. Lucida breathes deeply and reminds herself that she has invoked divine protection, so there is nothing to be afraid of.

"I have been troubled all day, my dear. Are you feeling well? You hardly seemed yourself last night when your father and I gave you the exciting news about meeting Signor Bianchi." Eugenia leans forward with loving eyes and cups her hands around Lucida's.

"Mother, I was just tired last evening. Isabella and I have been taking long walks in the afternoons. Maybe I overdid it. Tell me what you know about Signor Bianchi."

The afternoon has arrived for Lucida and her parents to meet with the Bianchi family. The coach takes the route toward the Piazza Navona to the palazzo of the Bianchis. It is a splendid palazzo, much grander than the Galvani's. The servant shows them to the elegant drawing room complete with murals and baroque furnishings. Niccolo steps forward to greet Lucida, bowing slightly over her hand. Their eyes meet, and Lucida perceives approval in his. On her part, she is pleasantly surprised. He is a classically handsome man, and she senses a strong yet kind character. The parents hover but pretend not to. They are invited to be seated, and the four elders are happily gossiping between planning the future of the couple. Niccolo and Lucida steal an amused glance.

So this is my future, Lucida muses. *As long as they don't discover the paintings, I foresee happiness for myself.*

Signora Bianchi invites Lucida and her mother to tour the palazzo and garden, commenting on various family pieces passed down through the generations. She is warm, similar to Signora Galvani, but her manner demonstrates that she rules her household with a firmer hand. Presently, they are joined by the men.

Niccolo moves to stand next to Lucida and addresses the parents. He would like to formally ask for her hand, and if she agrees to the marriage, he would prefer that Lucida be involved in choosing the wedding jewelry. Everyone is stunned by this request as the custom would be for him to make the choices and decisions.

Yes, this will be a good match for my Lucida, thinks Luigi.

Lucida is silently echoing her father's thought. Acceptance to the marriage is given, and they agree to a September wedding. There is much to be done to prepare. The air is happy with anticipation at joining the two families. No dark clouds on the horizon.

That evening, alone in her room, Lucida dons the marigold chemise. She allows herself to put aside her dread of discovery and relax into dreaming of a happy future. She will have beautiful children in a palazzo full of laughter, and her marriage to Niccolo will be strong and happy. Every time she wears it, she feels the magic of the chemise. It strengthens her, makes her feel more alive, and is wakening her passion and determination.

Overnight, the Galvani household is abuzz with chatter of the wedding. Eugenia is thrilled, but she is going to have to rely on her household staff and her sister to keep her on track with organizing. Fortunately, Luigi is accustomed to taking charge and making decisions.

Signor Ruel is a stout man with a hearty laugh that belies a scheming and rather unpleasant nature. He runs an art gallery near Piazza Navona, featuring works of reputable artists, landscapes mostly. They are pleasant, some allegorical. This provides a modest living for Signor Ruel although he always keeps his antenna alert for work that can be sold discretely to a discerning group of gentlemen—much more lucrative than landscapes.

When Signor Salvatori has sent a word for him to come at once to his studio, Signor Ruel isn't sure what to expect as the studio is mostly dedicated to works of a religious nature sponsored by the church. He greets the artist in his usual jovial manner, inquiring about the purpose of his urgent request. Signor Salvatori is eager to show the work.

"Come, signor, I have a surprise for you."

He leads him to Alessia's corner of the studio. Five large canvases are covered in drop cloths. With a flourish, he removes the cloths, allowing them to pool on the studio floor.

Signor Ruel catches his breath, his heart beating rapidly, and his round cheeks flushing. Before him, he views a young beauty wearing a chemise of a stunning marigold color, posing in a languid manner. Her eyes and body are demanding to be noticed, inviting an unchaste speculation on the part of the viewer. Each of the five paintings features a different pose: one lounging against cushions, breast partially exposed; one with her back bared, a slight turn, exposing some breast with her head turned to implore the viewer; one with a direct frontal view, legs spread with the marigold draping over her upper thighs; another lying on her side, the marigold chemise pulled high on the legs and her hand cupping one of her breasts; and finally, one posed on a bed with lush linens, the model sitting propped against cushions with her hand on the bed next to her, as if inviting the viewer to join her.

The palette shifts a bit from painting to painting, but the intense marigold of the chemise on the young woman is the star of the show. Confidence in the execution of the work exudes such a quality that one cannot help but be drawn strongly to the paintings.

"Could Salvatori have created these paintings?" muses Signor Ruel. "When did you do this work?" he inquires.

Salvatori stands firmly between the paintings and the dealer. "I did not paint these. This work is my daughter's, Alessia."

The art dealer is stunned. "Your daughter? Why would you allow her to work like this? I am surprised you let her assist with your work. Painting is man's work. Women aren't artists."

"Nevertheless, it is her work. Are you not impressed?" responds Salvatori. "Perhaps I should contact another dealer who appreciates the quality of my daughter's work."

Signor Ruel is mentally calculating. He receives invitations from time to time to bring some special work to a gathering of wealthy men who convene each week to discuss business and enjoy a meal and drink. There is some sort of entertainment, like music, a poetry reading, an exotic dancer, or some fine art for sale. He knows the men well enough that he has no doubt the work would be well received.

"I can arrange to have the framer pick them up tomorrow." The art dealer stands just as firmly in front of Salvatori. "I will present them at a private gathering this month, and I know they will all sell. Do we have an understanding?"

Salvatori is torn. He understands the nature of this private sale, and he wants his daughter to receive artistic credit, but he worries about her reputation…and he wants the proceeds for the sales.

"The name of the artist must be unknown. There must be anonymity, and you must agree that no one will know they were created in my studio. I will receive 75 percent of the sale."

The haggling continues with the final agreement of 60 percent for Salvatori and 40 percent for Ruel. The deal is sealed with a handshake and an agreement to keep the artist anonymous. Cash for Salvatori will be collected discretely; Ruel's boy will pass the payment to Salvatori at a prearranged time on the street. Salvatori is fairly certain that no one on his staff is aware of Alessia's work as they have been so busy, and her corner of the studio is cordoned off with dividers. He will have to rely on the discretion of Ruel's framers.

Alessia arrives at the studio later that morning with a heavy heart. Her father greets her exuberantly. His anticipation of receiving funds from the sale of his daughter's work has contributed to his excitement despite his misgivings over fears about his daughter's reputation. He doesn't even consider Lucida's reputation. He isn't aware of who she is other than a friend of his daughter's. He hasn't paid any attention.

Signor Salvatori relates the details of his arrangement with the dealer Signor Ruel.

"Daughter, I believe I have secured an excellent venue for the sale of this work. The money will help our family just when we are in great need. You are a good daughter, and the work is quite stunning. I am sorry that we need to be discrete, but you know what happens when a girl's reputation is tainted. We can't risk that for you. You can begin working on the new commission for the church today. Start the underpainting, and I will check on it this afternoon."

Alessia is livid. She cannot speak. She turns and quickly exits the studio, rushing on to Via Margutta and nearly knocking over an elderly woman out to do her shopping.

"*Scusami, ti prego perdonami,*" she mutters.

She keeps up her hurried pace all the way to the Borghese. Collapsing on the bench near the wall where they played together as children, Alessia catches her breath and attempts to calm herself. She is so hurt and angry at her father. How could he do this to her? He has put Lucida and herself both at risk, and her own ambition has contributed to this mess. She doesn't see how she will ever be acknowledged as a great painter. It is hopeless. She must warn Lucida. Alessia scribbles a note to Lucida and stuffs it in the crack in the wall.

"Meet me near the entrance to the park off Santa Maria del Popolo. I will come each afternoon at four to see if you have received this note."

As a small rebellion, she decides that she will not return to the studio that afternoon and turns toward the family home, determined to tell her mother that she is not feeling well and to take her to her bed. She is fuming, the anger swelling from her heart in great waves.

The marigold is likewise associated with the sun—being vibrant yellow and gold in color. The flowers are open when the sun is out. The mari-

gold is also called the "herb of the sun," representing passion and even creativity. It is also said that marigolds symbolize cruelty, grief, and jealousy.

The Galvani household has been abuzz with wedding preparations, and Lucida has allowed herself the luxury of daydreaming in her marigold chemise of her happy marriage to Niccolo. The private moments are the highlight of her days, and when thoughts of someone discovering the paintings intrude, she refuses to let them darken her horizon.

It is a lovely afternoon, the sun not too punishing, perfect for a stroll to the Borghese. She should check the wall to see if there is any word from Alessia. Families are beginning to emerge at the end of siesta for the traditional *passeggiare*. She admires the azaleas and the carpet of early blossoms covering the ground. The pistachio green of the first leaf buds on the trees is one of her favorite sites and makes her want to do some sketching when she returns home.

She approaches the wall and discretely makes her way to the crack, standing in front of it and searching with her fingers behind her back. Yes, there is a note. She cups her right hand around it and strolls away from the families for some privacy. Alessia has asked to meet her. This means she has some news. Fear of the reality of her situation comes rushing into her heart. She struggles to calm herself and regain control. She doesn't know for sure what news Alessia will bring when she sees her tomorrow. Maybe if she sketches before the evening meal, that will distract her.

The evening seems to stretch on forever with chatter of the wedding dominating the dinner conversation. Luigi and Eugenia are planning a party to celebrate the engagement. Shall they entertain at home or at one of their favorite *ristorantes*? Who should be on the guest list? On and on it goes with Lucida struggling to appear excited and engaged.

The next morning is no better for her. Ariston scolds her for being distracted and threatens again to speak to her father. She is happy, though, that her father has insisted that she continue her lessons rather than have her stop because of the wedding, as many fathers would have done. She loves learning and is proud of her intelligence. How could she have allowed herself to get into this predicament?

Finally, it is time to leave to meet Alessia. The streets are still fairly quiet, as the siesta is just ending. Shopkeepers are beginning to prepare to reopen their shops. She loves the Piazza del Popolo with the Porta del Popolo's central arch. It is recently completed, a grand gate built on the orders of Pope Pius IV Medici. The outer face has statues of Saint Peter and Saint Paul on either side of the arch and a huge Medici coat of arms above. Luigi had marched the children to the gate numerous times during construction, lecturing them about the architect, Nanni di Baccio Bigio, who modelled it on a Roman triumphal arch.

She begins to climb the steps to Viale D'Annunzio, the street just behind Via Margutta, toward the entrance to the Borghese. Alessia is waiting for her at the top. They embrace, happy to see each other.

"Lucida, the paintings are gone. The dealer, Signor Ruel, has collected them to be framed, and they will be sold at a private gathering. Father has made Signor Ruel agree that the artist will remain anonymous, so I will receive no credit. No one knows that it was you who posed. Perhaps one of the staff would have seen you visiting me, but they don't know who you are. If they are sold privately and discreetly, there is little chance they would be displayed publicly. I think you may be safe from discovery. I pray that you are. But, Lucida, I am so angry at my father. He wants me to go back to just helping him with his commissions. It will be hard for me to have time for any work of my own. Those paintings were my best work so far. Is it wrong for me to want recognition? People think women aren't real artists. It is not fair, and it is not right, but there isn't anything I can do about it. I don't think I can forgive my father. I should pray about it, but I don't want to."

Lucida is partly relieved knowing that there will be a private sale, and perhaps no one will suspect that she is the model in the paintings. But her heart goes out to her friend. Alessia deserves recognition. Her paintings are better than many of the male artists. It is truly not fair. She puts her arm around Alessia to comfort her.

"You have got to keep up your own work, Alessia. I know that your father is proud of you. I think you should wait a little while and then keep speaking to him about doing your own work. You know he needs the money for the paintings, so that might convince him. We need to figure out a way for you to get acknowledged for your work. Let's not give up."

"You are right, Lucida. Thank you for knowing how important this is to me. You are a true friend." They kiss goodbye, promising to meet again next week, and go their separate ways.

Signor Ruel has arranged for the paintings to be shown at the next meeting of the businessmen. Finally, the evening arrives. He and his assistant work all afternoon transporting the framed paintings and arranging them at the rear of the dining room where the men will be meeting. Each painting stands on an easel draped in a cloth. Unveiling them will be the dramatic highlight of the evening.

There are ten men this evening. They arrive one by one, greeting each other enthusiastically. Mingling near the small bar set up at one end of the room, they inquire after each other's business affairs and families. The atmosphere is jovial and relaxed. They look forward to the comradery of these evenings.

Signor Bianchi has been the unofficial leader of the group of men for some time, and he invites the men to the dining table. Waiters begin with the gustation: a salad of mallow leaves, lettuce, chopped leeks, mint, arugula, mackerel garnished with rue, sliced eggs, and marinated sow udder. The meal continues with succulent cuts of kid, beans, greens, a chicken, and ham. Dessert is fresh fruit and vintage wine. The men eat heartily and raise a toast to the chef in compliment of a delicious repast.

As they are enjoying the wine, Signor Bianchi announces the entertainment of the evening. He has not yet viewed the paintings and is looking forward to what Signor Ruel has arranged for them. He signals to the waiter to have Signor Ruel brought in.

"*Gentiluomini*, tonight we are in for a special surprise. Signor Ruel, the art dealer, has brought for us five new paintings available for purchase. He assures me that they are unique, very special. The artist has asked to remain anonymous at this time, which only adds to the allure of the these works. Signor, let us have a view."

Signor Ruel steps forward and begins to unveil the paintings one by one. Chatter in the room ceases as the men move closer to the work. The art dealer sees that they are enchanted, mesmerized even. His greedy mind begins to calculate how he can get the men to bid against each other to own a painting. Slowly, the silence is broken by the men's comments.

"These are extraordinary. There is great skill here. The artist, he must be someone we have heard of or maybe he is from Firenze. The woman is a beauty and so *sessuale*. She draws us to her."

"Signor Ruel, are they all for purchase for the same price?" inquires Signor Bianchi.

"*Si, si,*" Signor Ruel replies.

His crafty eyes survey the men. Voices raise as the men declare they wish to purchase a painting. They are all highly interested. It begins to dawn on them that there are five paintings and ten men.

"*Gentiluomini*," Signor Ruel begins, "let us be fair. We will allow the purchase to the highest bidders of each work."

Consent for bidding is agreed upon quickly. They are all eager.

Signor Bianchi is studying the paintings. He must have one. But which is his favorite? He studies the woman posing in the paintings. Does she look familiar? He can't decide. He determines that he will purchase the painting with the woman seated on a bed of lush linens, her gaze direct and her hand on the bed beside her, as if beckoning him to join her. Yes, that's the one.

Signor Ruel begins the bidding. He can't believe how high the numbers are going. Voices are raised in excitement. The competition is a game for the businessmen. Finally, five of the men are new collectors of Alessia's work with the remaining five clamoring for Signor Ruel to bring more of the artist's work. Signor Bianchi has purchased his favorite. He will have it hung in his private study. He thanks Signor Ruel for a successful event, and the evening winds down with

Ruel collecting payments and arranging for the works to be delivered to their new owners. Signor Ruel is quite satisfied with himself. He can't help but puff his chest in pride and his heart with greed.

The next morning, Signor Ruel orders his boy to bring a note to Signor Salvatori. It directs him to meet that afternoon just after the siesta at the Antico Caffè Greco, where they can have a private conversation. He determines that he will bring the money to Salvatori himself, no use trusting his boy to hand it off since it is by far more than both men expected. Plus, he will now need to cajole the artist to have the daughter produce more work. Signor Ruel is beside himself with excitement and greed. He knows his standing with Signor Bianchi and the others has vastly improved.

Signor Ruel's boy is waiting for Signor Salvatori when he arrives at his studio on Via Margutta. Salvatori receives the note, hastily reading it and directing the boy to return his response to Ruel. He scribbles that he will be at the Greco at 4:30. Signor Salvatori ponders what Signor Ruel may be planning. He is aware that the dealer is sly and greedy, and he thought that the boy was supposed to deliver any proceeds from the paintings. He has so much work to do that he decides he will have to put off thinking about Ruel until their afternoon appointment, especially since Alessia has convinced her mother that she is not feeling well and can't come to the studio to assist him. He is proud of his daughter's talent and has misgivings about her not receiving credit for her work, but he can't conceive of a way to change that. He has always been close to her and hopes that she will soon return to the studio where she belongs.

Signor Ruel is waiting at a table nestled in a corner near the back of the café. Signor Salvatori is immediately aware of the art dealer's excitement as he invites him to sit. He has already ordered them an *aperitivo* of Campari.

"Signor, you will not believe our success. All the paintings have been purchased. The men were in a competition to own them, bidding up the price. There were ten men and five paintings, and they are pleading for more work from the unknown artist. Here is your share." He pushes a leather satchel toward Salvatori, urging him to look inside.

Salvatori pulls the weighty satchel to his chest and peers into the opening. The satchel is stuffed with lire, soldi, and dinero. There are more coins than he usually sees in a year's time. He is stunned into silence, his mind twisting and turning.

Signor Ruel watches him closely and is crafty enough to give the artist time to calculate what the heavy satchel will mean for him and his family. He continues, "Your daughter needs to produce more work. We will make a fortune."

Salvatori emits a heavy sigh. He is grateful for the money, but he is also repelled by Ruel's greed and unsavory nature. He needs to ponder the wisest way to manage the art dealer's proposal.

"I will send my boy with a message when I am ready to discuss this with you," he tells Ruel, ignoring the obvious disappointment covering Signor Ruel's face. Taking the satchel of coins, he exits the Greco and makes his way back to the studio.

The new painting is discretely delivered and installed in Signor Bianchi's private study. It is the one room in the villa that Signora Bianchi does not preside over. Since the beginning of their marriage, it has been understood that the door remains locked as Signor Bianchi's business papers and books are not to be disturbed in any way. Signora Bianchi doesn't mind. She has enough to occupy her energies in running the household, and Signor defers to her in matters of interior design. It is a satisfactory arrangement.

This evening, the Bianchis are entertaining a business associate and his wife, Signor and Signora Ricci. They spend a leisurely meal, enjoying cappelletti stuffed with breast of pigeon, which have been cooked in a good capon stock made a beautiful marigold color by the addition of saffron, followed by fish with fresh herbs, and accompanied by a white wine of the Glera grape and a melon tart to finish.

San Gimignano, not far from Rome, is famous for saffron. The town's towers were built using wealth generated from the saffron trade. The reddish strands transform into seductive marigold color when added to a dish.

The conversation is pleasant, with gossip and the news of Niccolo's betrothal to Lucida Galvani. The Riccis are excited by the prospect of the good match and are complimentary of Lucida. They have known the Galvani family, Signor Galvani being a respected physician, for many years. One of their daughters, Isabella, had been a childhood friend, and they commented that they had recently seen Lucida walking near the Borghese with a young woman they didn't recognize. They both noticed that Lucida had become quite a beauty.

Signors Bianchi and Ricci retire to Signor Bianchi's study following the meal to discuss a business matter and the ladies to the drawing room to gossip and speak of the new fashions.

Signor Ricci enters the study, furnished richly in dark wood and emerald upholstery, a distinctly masculine room. He settles into one of the leather chairs and notices that there is a new painting installed on the opposite wall. He takes in the painting, unable to peel his eyes off the beautiful woman in the marigold garment, inviting him to join her. He is speechless as he finally shifts his gaze to Signor Bianchi.

"Where did you find this astonishing painting? Who is the artist?"

Signor Bianchi explains that the art dealer Signor Ruel had brought five paintings to the business meeting last week and they were all sold.

"The artist has requested anonymity. I have no idea who it is. Perhaps someone from Firenze."

The men stand in front of the painting, studying and appreciating it. Signor Ricci comments that the girl in the painting seems familiar, but he can't identify who it might be. Signor Bianchi agrees that he had the same thought.

"An artist's model with classic features, I don't know."

They proceed to discuss business until it is time to rejoin their wives and say their goodbyes for the evening.

Orazio returns to his studio following his meeting with Signor Ruel. There is much work to be completed, but he is unable to calm his mind, swirling with conflicting impulses. He needs to be alone to contemplate the best path forward. There is no one that he dares to confide in. His decision must be made carefully and in solitude.

The chatter of his assistants is grating on his nerves, and he uncharacteristically shouts at the men to be silent. Then on second thought, he orders them to leave for the day. He doesn't notice the quizzical glances between them; he is so wrapped up in his inner turmoil. As they gather their belongings and file out, the silence he needs takes hold.

He empties the satchel with the coins clanking on his desk table. Lire, soldi, and dinero form an impressive puddle. With a deep sigh, Orazio begins to sort the coins. The amount is enough to cover his current debt and support his household for another month. This is unheard of in his experience. The Salvatori family has forever been under financial strain, and even though they always manage, the lack of financial ease is always present. Orazio would love to provide his wife and children with a better life and ease the strain on his soul.

Another thought occurs to him. How will he account for being in possession of such an influx of funds? The holders of his debt accounts will be surprised that he can pay them in full instead of negotiating for leniency. His dear wife will be pleased for a fatter household purse, but she is astute and will inquire about the source. Shall he fabricate, telling them that he has received more commissions from the church? Does he want to begin a web of duplicitous stories, especially to his wife? Orazio has always considered himself to be a good and honest man, forthright in his dealings with others and particularly with his wife, who is always in his heart.

His mind's eye brings Alessia into focus, his talented firstborn. Part of Orazio wishes that she had been a son, but he stops himself from moving along that train of thought. It would be easier, but that is a betrayal of her and her real abilities. Being a woman in these times is a real liability, and that is no fault of his or hers.

His eyes drift closed, and he sees the powerful paintings she has created. If he is honest, he knows that he does not have the instinctive talent Alessia has been blessed with to create those images. Her use of the marigold color, the way she has mixed the paint and used the model is superb. Really, it is a shame that she will never be given credit due or reap the financial benefit. Well, that can't be helped. On the other hand, the added stream of income to the Salvatori purse is very tempting indeed. And why shouldn't the family benefit from their God-given talents?

There would be more funds to fatten the family offering to the church, wouldn't there be?

It is growing dark now, and as the studio twilight begins to dim, the beginnings of a plan are bubbling up from Orazio's unconscious. He doesn't move to light the room but remains still, staring off into the room, his arm resting near the pile of coins.

What if Alessia were to begin a series of new paintings during the siesta? The assistants never fail to take their siesta. What if she worked on the Sabbath when they weren't around? Then she could spend a few hours working with the assistants on the church commissions. It would seem normal to the assistants. Perhaps he could make her corner of the studio more private and secure, away from prying eyes.

He could begin to speak at home about the possibility of more church commissions coming his way, couldn't he? That would prepare his dear wife to expect an improvement in their purse. Perhaps she would inadvertently share the news with her friends and, of course, the gossip would spread to his debt accounts.

Orazio begins to feel a little ease in his mind as the plan takes shape. He is starting to feel tired and hungry and decides that he should head home. He scoops the coins into the satchel and moves them to the secret compartment in the floor beneath his desk table for safekeeping. As he steps out onto Via Margutta, the sounds of the street engulf him, and he greets neighbors and friends, "*Buonasera, buonasera.*"

Alessia has been avoiding the studio and her father, feigning illness. She has taken to her bed, refusing the meals her mother tries to temp her with, only sipping on some weak tea. She feels that her spirit is broken and fears that her normal *gioia della vita* will never return. Except for Lucida, there is no one who understands how she is feeling. And Lucida is soon to be married and will have her new life. It is doubtful that she will have time for her friend.

The light is fading quickly now, and she listens to the sounds of the street. The rattling of carts and shouts of greetings. Normally, the colors of the streets and all the activity are vivid in her mind's eye, and she enjoys creating little scenes, imagining them on canvas, the shadows and highlights, the vibrancy of the colors. Now everything is dull and vapid.

She startles as there is a firm tap on her door. It is not her mother's gentle knocking.

"Alessia, I need to speak with you now. It is very important. I am coming in."

Orazio does not wait for a response as he enters her room and makes certain that the door is latched. He pulls up a chair to sit near the bed and lights the bedside candle. The light engulfs Alessia's face, the flickering of the candle highlighting the contours of her expression. Orazio's heart gives a little lurch to see his daughter so sad, her normal happy expression erased.

He begins speaking softly and slowly, relaying the news that all the paintings have sold and for a higher price than either he or Signor Ruel imagined.

"Alessia, the gentlemen who were in attendance were outbidding one another, and they are very eager to have more work. The sum I have collected will pay our outstanding debts and support the household for at least another month."

Alessia's intention to shut out her father is strong, but in spite of her strength, she can't help feeling intrigued. She wills her expression to be flat.

Orazio is determined. He already has a plan in mind, and so he begins to fill in the details to his daughter.

"We will make a more private place for you in the studio. You can work on the new paintings during the siesta and maybe other times when the assistants are not there. If you continue to help me with the commissions, no one will think anything of it. You will be able to develop this body of work. We can make a lot of money."

Alessia looks deeply into her father's eyes. "Of course, I will be receiving credit and recognition of my talents and money, right?"

The squirming twists Orazio's heart. *Well, there is no help for it,* he tells himself. Better to be direct. His daughter is strong and smart.

"Alessia, *caro,* you know that is not possible. I wish things were different, but they are not. We will have to keep the artist's name anonymous. Already, the men think that the artist is a man from Firenze, someone they have not heard of. A new talent. Signor Ruel agrees that this is the best course. The secrecy will add to the demand for the work. We will need to be discreet. We don't want suspicion about more income. I will begin telling your mother that more commissions from the church are coming. She will be happy with a larger purse. I will inform her that I am now giving you a salary for all your work in the studio, that you are now old enough to be earning money for your future. I have deeply contemplated this. You will be able to keep painting your own work and earn some money. It is for the best. What do you think?"

"I will think about this and speak to you tomorrow. I need to rest now." Alessia turns from her father and closes her eyes, dismissing him.

Orazio sighs, blows out her candle, and leaves the room. He is tired and hungry and not at peace with himself.

In ancient Rome, a marriage would have been called justae nuptiae, justum matrionium, *or* ligitimum matrimonium. *Romans believed a nerve ran directly from the fourth finger of the left hand directly to the heart. Due to this, wedding rings are worn on this finger, a tradition that continues to this day.*

Niccolo and his parents have been busy implementing plans for him and Lucida and their new life together. Niccolo wants to purchase their new home and surprise Lucida and her parents before the wedding. They are negotiating a price with one of his parent's neighbors who is moving to a larger palazzo. This palazzo is more modest than that of his parents but is well suited to a young couple and still with room for a family.

The bride and groom have chosen the wedding jewelry. As was the tradition, there is an iron one and a gold one. The first of these is worn at home while the second is worn in public to impress people. Iron is chosen as the material as it is meant to symbolize strength and permanence. The gold is a symbol of wealth. The symbol common on the rings is that of two hands and a heart—two hands and hearts joining. Lucida had requested the flowers behind the hands in the design to be marigold in color. The jeweler had wondered at the unusual request, but he complied to please the customer. Niccolo is proud and pleased that Lucida voiced her desire. She will be the perfect wife for him. Later that day, he returns to the jeweler and commissions a necklace in the marigold color as a special present for Lucida. He is grateful to their parents for making such a perfect match and allows his mind to dream of their perfect future together.

The Bianchis have invited the Galvanis to their villa to discuss the arrangements for the engagement celebration and the wedding. There is much to be done, and everyone is anticipating all the events with pleasure.

The two families have begun to feel more relaxed around each other, enjoying dinners at the Galvani household and meeting all the children. Niccolo has only one sibling, an older sister, Martina, who lives in Firenze and is preparing to work with her father on opening a branch of the Bianchi business there. He loves the exuberant household with children laughing and playing and imagines himself as a happy father. He prays that he and Lucida will be blessed with a large family.

Niccolo wants to consult with his father on the cost of the palazzo and the wedding jewelry. He wants everything to be perfect, and he trusts his father's judgement. The Galvanis won't be arriving for another hour, so he calculates that there is time for a father-and-son conversation. His step is light and energetic as he descends the staircase from his bedchamber to his father's private study.

He knocks on the door and announces his presence. There is silence, so he knocks again and waits. Still, no response. Curious, he thought that his father had arrived home and gone directly into his study, as is his habit. Without thinking, he opens the door, surprised that it is not locked. The room is rather dark as it is nearing evening and no candles are lit. He looks around, always intrigued by his father's private study and a bit intimidated. He wonders if he will also have such a room as a married man. His eyes are slowly adjusting to the dim light as they settle on a large painting. The painting has not been in the room before, and he is sure that his father did not mention that he had made a new purchase. He moves closer to the painting, but he is unable see it clearly in the darkened room. Looking around for a candle, he can make out a large candlestick on one of the side tables. He fumbles a bit but manages to light the candle, moving closer to have a look at the painting.

Niccolo's eyes adjust further, and he sees that the subject is a lovely young woman in a marigold chemise seated on a bed, her hand beckoning the viewer to join her. He is entranced. He is debating with himself if he should quietly exit his father's study when the door opens, and his father enters the room.

"Niccolo, what are you doing in here? You know this is my private study." His face is stern as he addresses his son.

31

Niccolo is embarrassed at being caught in the study uninvited. He stammers his explanation. "Father, I came to discuss the wedding jewelry and the villa. I want your guidance. You didn't answer my knock, and the door was unlocked, so I entered to see if you were working. I am sorry."

Signor Bianchi softens. "It is all right, my son. Let us discuss the matters of jewelry and the villa. We have time before the Galvani family arrives."

"Father, did you purchase a new painting?" Niccolo inquires. "It seems very different from the other work in our home."

"Yes, son, the art dealer Signor Ruel brought five stunning new works to our business group meeting. The artist wants to remain anonymous, but we think it may be someone from Firenze. The work is irresistible, and all five pieces sold at more than the dealer was asking. This was my favorite. Of course, it is only for my study and my eyes. Your mother would not approve. You understand? You are about to be a married man. In fact, I think you are ready to join our businessmen's group, don't you think? You will be taking on a larger role in our company and, of course, earning a larger purse to give your new bride and family the life they deserve."

Niccolo's head is spinning—the seductive painting, the invitation to join his father's business associates in their meetings, more responsibilities at the company, and his upcoming nuptials. He is really launching into mature adulthood. He will make his father and mother proud and his Lucida as well.

The father and son light some more candles in the room and move closer to the painting, absorbed in the seduction of the work.

"Father, do you think the model in the painting looks familiar?" Niccolo asks.

"Yes, I thought so as well. The girl is a classic beauty. They must have beautiful women who are willing to model for artists in Firenze," his father replies. "Well, we better get to the matter of the jewelry and palazzo."

They settle in, and Signor Bianchi brings out the drawings of the new palazzo and the accounting of the costs for them to peruse. The palazzo will be a gift from the parents to the new couple. Niccolo is responsible for purchasing the wedding jewelry. He tells his father that he has commissioned a necklace of marigold color as a surprise for Lucida in addition to the rings.

Signor Bianchi privately congratulates himself on raising a good son. He seems to be coming into his own and will become a strong businessman and a good husband and father. He sighs with contentment as he and his son extinguish the candles and leave the study.

Alessia's night has been restless, tossing and turning and falling in and out of her slumber. She dreams of herself in the marigold chemise, running through the streets of Rome in her bare feet in the middle of the night. Like an angel, she floats over the cobblestones through Trastevere and up the hill toward the Janiculum. The Janiculum overlooks the city and was once used as a defense lookout. It is also home to the Palazzo Corsini, built for Cardinal Domenico Riario.

Halfway up the hill is the Tempietto, completed by Bramante in 1502 on the place where it is believed that St. Peter was crucified. Alessia loves this little temple. Above the sixteen Doric columns is a classical frieze and a delicate balustrade. Although the scale of the temple is tiny, Bramante's masterly use of classical proportions creates a satisfyingly harmonious whole. She has visited the Tempietto often, always gaining strength and confidence with each visit.

In her dream, she becomes the angel of Tempietto, floating through the columns and then alighting on top. From this vantage point, the angel in marigold can view the River Tiber and the beautiful monuments of the city. Bramante visits her soul, swelling her heart with respect for beauty and proportion, whispering that she must continue her work no matter the obstacles.

Sunlight streams through her chamber window, waking Alessia from the dream. She lies very still, trying to keep the beautiful dream with her. The household is beginning to stir with activity as her parents and siblings prepare for the day. She has to make a choice. Either she can decide to feign illness for a while longer, or she can rise and join the rest of the household. The dream remains with her, and she knows that its message is clear. She luxuriates in a long stretch, puts aside her bedcovers, attends to her toilette, and dresses for the day.

The maid is serving the family café and bread as they sit around the table. Orazio greets Alessia fondly, and her mother comments that she is looking better, more like her natural self.

"Yes, Mother, I do feel better today. I will join Father at the studio as usual. It will be good to get back to work. With the new commissions from the church coming in, there is much to do," Alessia speaks with confidence.

"Well, take a break midday and return home for lunch before siesta. You need to eat and regain your strength. Orazio, make sure you bring her with you," her mother directs.

Orazio and Alessia gather their cloaks and satchels and make their way to the Salvatori studio. Neither of them says a word. They are contemplating Orazio's plan individually. Orazio is relieved that his daughter has agreed to return to work, and he intuits that it would be wise to allow Alessia to broach the subject in her own way. He silently prays that Signor Ruel will not show up today demanding answers.

"Father, I feel the need to stretch my legs and get some fresh air before we start work for the day. I am going to take a quick walk up the hill to the Borghese. I won't be long," Alessia speaks quickly and hurries off before her father can object.

She needs to leave a note for Lucida to meet her the next afternoon at their usual place. Her thoughts are swirling in her brain, fast, like a child's toy top. She is going grasp this opportunity to make her own work. Perhaps someday she will receive credit, but for now, she must follow her heart and brush wherever it will lead her. Will Lucida agree to sit for her again? With her upcoming marriage, she understands that her friend may not be able to agree to more sittings. That means she will need to find another model. Shall she keep with the theme of the marigold chemise or start another idea? She will look through her props today and decide. Her mind begins to conceive of various new poses and compositions she could experiment with.

The garden wall comes into view, and quickly she composes a note to Lucida and slips it into the designated crack in the wall. She has missed the scent of the oils in the studio and hurries back down the hill and onto Via Margutta. Her heart swells as she pushes the heavy wooden door and makes her way up the stairs to the studio.

Orazio has already begun arranging partitions, tables, and easels in one corner of the studio along one of the large windows. He decides that he will provide Alessia with a few more feet of space. She will be working hard, and he figures there will be at least five new paintings for her to start working on. He has instructed his workers to build the stretchers. The studio is alive with pounding and the scraping of furniture rearranging.

He sees that Alessia has arrived and calls out to her. "Come, come. I am arranging your new workspace. I think the partitions will give you some privacy to work, and I've given you a little more space too. What do you think?"

The anger that had been brewing at her father begins to dissipate despite her misgivings. She can see that he is enormously excited and wants to please her.

"Thank you, Father. Yes, I think this space will work nicely for me. What is all of the pounding?"

"It is the workers building the stretchers for your new work. They can be ready to stretch the canvas tomorrow."

Lucida returns home from the gathering at the Bianchis pent up with a tangle of energy. Sleep is impossible, so she allows herself to slip into the marigold chemise as she luxuriates in sweet fantasies of her soon-to-be new life. She has grown fonder of Niccolo as they began to know each other; her feelings are beginning to blossom into love. The marigold chemise awakens new sensations of passion and delight. In her mind's eye, she engages in visions of a perfect life full of love and happiness. Slowly she drifts to slumber, neglecting to put away the marigold chemise in its wardrobe hiding place.

In the dream, she sees Alessia floating above the Tempietto, an angel in the marigold chemise. The angel is strong and sure, and it seems to Lucida that she and Alessia merge as one in the magical marigold chemise.

The little wren on her windowsill chirps her awake, but she resists. She wants to cling to the dream to not forget it and ponder its meaning. Glancing down, she sees that she is still wearing the marigold chemise, and the images in the dream are solidified for her. She will make her way to the Borghese today to check the crevice in the wall in case Alessia has left a word for her.

Morning lessons speed by. Everyone is in a happy mood in anticipation of Lucida's wedding. Brigida begs her older sister to let her tag along on her afternoon walk.

"Please, please, Lucida, let me go with you. You will soon be married and no longer living with us. Please."

Lucida weighs her request. She is kindhearted, and despite Brigida being an overall pest, she is fond of her little sister. She relents, thinking that she will have to find a way to distract Brigida when she checks the crack in the wall for a note.

They gather their cloaks and begin the walk to the Borghese. Brigida jabbers away, gossiping about her friends. She asks if they will be meeting Isabella, but Lucida tells her no. She was just planning to get some air by herself. She prays to herself that they will not run into Isabella and get into an uncomfortable conversation.

They arrive at the entrance, and Lucida suggests they go to the old playground first. Brigida bounces around the playground as if she is still a small child with Lucida watching and laughing. Meanwhile, she slowly backs toward the wall in front of the crevice and quickly retrieves Alessia's note. Slyly, with one eye on Brigida, she turns away and reads the note. Alessia is asking that she meet her at their usual place this afternoon, and it is almost time.

Thinking quickly, she calls out to Brigida. "Sister, you enjoy yourself in the playground. I am going to run down to San Lorenzo in Lucina to light a candle. I want to pray for a little while. I won't be long, then we can go have a gelato together."

Lucida hurries down the hill to meet Alessia. Brigida is already bored with the playground. She muses to herself that she finds her sister's sudden urge to light a candle and pray suspicious. Why doesn't she pray in their neighborhood church? And why did she not ask Brigida to join her? *Why don't I follow her and see what she is up to?* she thinks.

Brigida is fast on her feet, and soon, she is following Lucida at a discreet distance. She sees that Lucida does not veer to the right toward San Lorenzo but instead is walking in the opposite direction. Shortly, Brigida sees that her sister is embracing a woman that she does not recognize. They are engaging in an intense conversation, and Brigida notices that Lucida passes a note to the other woman. They are gesturing but are keeping their voices low and private. After a time, they embrace goodbye, and Lucida turns to make her way back the Borghese. Brigida swiftly turns and practically sprints, retracing her route back to the playground. Fortunately, she is much faster than her sister, as Lucida saunters back up the hill with a heavy heart and her thoughts in a jumble.

"Did you light a candle and pray?" Brigida inquires.

"Oh yes, it is such a lovely church. I haven't been there in so long. Are you ready to find some gelato for us to enjoy?" Lucida lies to her sibling.

Alessia has informed Lucida that her paintings have all sold at a very high price and that her father has arranged with Signor Ruel for her to create more work, even though the artist will have to remain anonymous. She implores Lucida to sit for her for just one more series, and then she will find a new model. She wants to seize this opportunity so badly. If she works quickly, Lucida will be finished sitting for her before her wedding. Lucida is torn, and she tells her friend that she needs to take the night to contemplate. They arrange to meet the next afternoon, and Lucida promises to have her decision ready.

Lucida and Brigida choose gelatos from the Borghese Park vendor and savor the sweet treat, sitting on a bench near the path and gazing at the couples and children in the charge of their caretakers strolling and enjoying the afternoon.

Brigida is uncharacteristically subdued as they make their way through the noisy streets to the Galvani residence. Lucida is so distracted by her meeting with Alessia that she does not note her sister's silence. She can't wait to be home and in her room for privacy and the space to contemplate her decision.

Once in the door, Lucida barely greets her mother and siblings as she rushes to her room and secures the door. Her little wren friend is waiting for her at the window. She sighs and asks the bird for advice, "What should I do, my little friend?"

The wren only gazes back and then hops to the edge of the sill and propels itself to one of the higher branches of the parasol pine near her window.

There is still time before she will be expected for dinner, and she determines that a short nap will help to calm her nerves. Slipping off her dress, she dons the marigold chemise and relaxes on her bed for a rest. Soon Lucida has drifted into a deep sleep and the same dream of Alessia floating over the Tempietto in the marigold chemise and the two of them merging as one fills her consciousness.

She is awakened by Luigi's hearty greeting as he arrives home from the hospital and greets Eugenia and his brood. Laughter and squeals of delight from the baby Beatrice bring Lucida out of the dream and into reality. Reluctantly, she removes the marigold chemise and tucks it into its hiding place and readies herself for the evening meal. *Lucida*, she reminds herself, *you need to pay attention and be with your family. Questions will be forthcoming if your distress is apparent.*

Brigida is seated across the table from Lucida at the evening meal of fish, bread, and olives and fixes her gaze on her sister. She is certain that Lucida is being deceitful, and she vows to uncover her sister's secret.

Lucida excuses herself early with no explanation and secludes herself in her room. She is so torn that it is impossible to make a rational decision about continuing to sit for Alessia. She must not be discovered or the Bianchis may call off the marriage. On the other hand, she believes in Alessia and her talent and feels an obligation to support her friend. Besides, she does enjoy sitting for her friend, especially in the marigold chemise.

Morning lessons drag on, with Lucida summoning all her reserves to pay attention. Today they are working on the Coptic alphabet, and Ariston is assigning his pupils a short essay inspired by nature. When completed, they will each read their essays aloud. Ariston praises Lucida for her essay describing her wren and his habits. He reprimands Brigida and Luigi for their poor command of the Coptic glyphs and instructs them to stay after the lesson and practice. Brigida sighs in frustration and rolls her eyes at Lucida.

Following the midday meal of fish, cold meat, bread, aubergine, and rowdy conversation, the family prepares for their siesta. Lucida determines that she will sneak out and make her way to Santa Maria in Trastevere. She needs to pray and light a candle. She has a big decision to make and needs some solitude and spiritual reassurance before she meets with Alessia.

Once the sleepy silence has settled over the Galvani household, Lucida slips from her room, making her way to the street. Traveling the familiar route over the Ponte Sisto into Trastevere always instills confidence and calm in her heart. The narrow streets are quiet during the siesta as she enters the piazza and prepares herself for deep contemplation. She sees only an old woman bent and kneeling in prayer. Her favorite place in the church is on the left side near the front. It has the best view of the apse. Afternoon light filters through the windows, a holy tribute to the Virgin Mary and the saints. Lucida prays for guidance and wisdom. Once the feeling of calm descends, she lights a candle for protection and steps back out onto the piazza. She squares her shoulders, pulls her cloak close, and heads toward the Via Margutta and the Salvatori studio.

Brigida is a stealthy one. Her little chest puffs out in pride as she has now followed her sister over the Ponte Sisto into Santa Maria in Trastevere and through the winding streets to Via Margutta. Keeping a safe distance, she observes Lucida slip into one of the doors along the street. Carefully, she inches toward the door to read the nameplate: Orazio Salvatori, Pittore. Brigida is puzzled. What is her sister doing here? She doesn't think her family knows the painter. Afraid of being discovered, Brigida turns to rush home and sneak in before the siesta is over.

Lucida feels the force from her dream pull her toward the Salvatori studio. Strangely, she is not afraid of her choice and trusts that she is meant to help her friend. Her feet are light as she ascends the stairs to the studio. It is quiet as the workers are in siesta, but she has a sense that Alessia will be busy in her corner, not indulging in the siesta.

The friends greet with a warm embrace, Alessia quickly asking for Lucida's decision.

"My friend, I am with you. If we work rapidly, I can sit for sketches for the next group of paintings before the wedding. Everyone is so busy with the preparations that they won't notice my excuses for being out every day."

Alessia is ecstatic with the news and grabs Lucida's hands for a little jig around the studio. "Let's not waste any time."

She grabs her sketchbook and charcoal, instructing Lucida to take some quick poses for her. The friends work for an hour before they hear the workers returning to the studio for the afternoon session. Quickly they move behind Alessia's screen and plot their next session. They decide that it might be best for Lucida to steal out of the Galvani residence at siesta time to give them privacy to work and less chance of Lucida to be questioned.

"I want to have you pose in the marigold chemise again, Lucida. It is magical on you. I seem to have misplaced it, but I will search again. I'm certain it is here somewhere."

Lucida cringes inside. Well, she will just have to hide the marigold chemise long enough to then discover it when she returns to the studio tomorrow.

"I'm sure you will locate it, Alessia. I will help you search tomorrow. Yes, I agree. The marigold chemise is truly magical, and I can't wait to pose in it for the new paintings. Arrivederci."

Lucida floats on happiness and anticipation, making her way home. She better hurry as the streets are beginning to come alive at the end of the siesta.

The garden door is ajar, allowing the warm breeze to waft into the kitchen and gently disgorge scents of simmering pots. Cook and her helpers are chattering companionably, absorbed in their tasks as Lucida slips quietly in, hoping to avoid any family members as she makes her way to her room.

Eugenia and Brigida intercept Lucida before she can escape to her room.

"Where have you been, sister?" demands Brigida. "Mother and I want to get an early start to meet with the seamstress at Signora Fontana's for a fitting. Our gowns for the wedding are ready for a first fitting, and you were not in your room when I went to get you."

Her mother and sister gaze at Lucida intently, waiting for her response, Brigida suspiciously and Eugenia with concern.

"Oh, I am sorry. I didn't mean to worry you. I woke early from siesta and wanted some fresh air, so I went for a stroll along Via Giulia. I love our street and will miss it when I leave, and it is so pleasant during the siesta when it is quiet. I will hurry to freshen up, and then we can depart for the seamstress." Lucida wonders to herself how she can lie so easily. The lies just slip from her tongue as easily as melted gelato.

Signora Fontana has a commanding presence, good-naturedly shouting instructions to her seamstress team. The whole shop is a hive of activity and excitement. There are bolts and bolts of fabrics and trimmings surrounding the large tables the teams work at.

Signora Fontana's dear husband passed away, and she has compelled their business to thrive in his absence. Signora greets the Galvani women fondly as she orders one of her assistants to fetch the gowns for fittings. She leads them to the rear of the shop and parts the curtains to a fitting chamber.

"First, our beautiful bride," she announces. Lucida's wedding gown is a froth of silk, satin, and transparent chiffon and lace. The bodice is fitted satin embroidered with subtle white blossoms attached to a skirt that falls in cascades to the floor. The underlayer is satin and lace, and chiffon drapes in elegant swirls accented by satin bows. A chiffon shawl clasped with a bow envelops her bare shoulders.

Eugenia's eyes tear up as Signora Fontana slips the gown over Lucida's head and begins the adjustments. Lucida cannot believe how beautiful the gown is…a true baroque masterpiece. Even Brigida is silenced. The fit is close, so adjustments will be managed quickly. They discuss the headpiece and agree that it should reflect the embroidered blossoms on the bodice.

Marigold is Lucida's favorite color. She wants Brigida's gown to be marigold satin with bows referencing the bridal gown on the skirt and an embroidered bodice. They all agree that the color and style suits Brigida and her cheeks blush at the thought of all the wedding guests seeing what a lovely young woman she is becoming. Signora Fontana has suggested a lace gown for Eugenia in a pale golden color. Lucida's heart melts when she sees how elegant her dear mother looks in the gown. She intuits that Luigi will be pleased.

It has been a special afternoon, and the three Galvani women chat quietly as they enjoy the stroll back home, feeling content. Citizens have emerged from siesta, and the mild weather is enjoyed by all as they conduct business and converse with friends and neighbors.

The Galvani household settles into the afternoon siesta with the exception of the two eldest daughters. Lucida has carefully rolled the marigold chemise in the velvet drawstring satchel she uses to carry her sketchbook and pencil. If she encounters anyone, she will say that she can't sleep and wants to sketch the trees in the Borghese.

Brigida doesn't bother to settle in for a rest. She feels quite certain that her sister will be slipping out once again, and she is ready to tail her discreetly. She will get to the bottom of this mystery.

Right on schedule, Brigida, her ear to her door, detects Lucida's soft, tentative steps as she slips from her room, down the stairs, and out the back servants' entrance. Quickly, Brigida begins her tail, staying close to the side of the street so she can slip into a doorway if Lucida turns to glance behind her.

Lucida is contemplating how to manage "finding" the marigold chemise in Alessia's studio. Guilt enters her mind, but she suppresses it with a sigh and reminds herself that thanks to the marigold chemise, she is braver and stronger than she imagined herself to be.

Arriving at the Salvatori studio, she hesitates briefly to scan the street. Not seeing anyone, she enters and makes her way to Alessia's section of the studio. It is quiet; all the assistants must be on siesta. Bravo! Alessia has not yet arrived. Quickly, she removes the marigold chemise from her satchel and stuffs it in the cushion of the divan where she had posed. She hears Alessia ascending the stairs to the studio. Just as Alessia arrives, Lucida triumphantly pulls the marigold chemise from the cushion.

"Look! I found the marigold chemise!"

"That's strange. I thought I looked in the cushions yesterday. Oh well, I must have overlooked it. Well, go change, and let's get started. The first canvas is ready."

Lucida dons the marigold chemise, ready to begin the pose.

"Let's pose you on the divan. Curl your legs under you with your right knee exposed, and support yourself with your right hand. Yes, now extend your left arm as if you are reaching out to someone," Alessia instructs her model. She lets the right strap of the chemise slide down Lucida's arm, exposing her breast, and gently tips her chin up a bit. "Think about beckoning a lover to your bed. Let me know when your arm tires and you need a break."

Lucida allows the magic of the marigold chemise to take its effect as Alessia begins using a light wash of sienna to compose the body on the canvas. The atmosphere is charged with concentration. She only has a few hours to work before Lucida must return back home without being detected. They are both reluctant to end the session: Lucida because she loves the passion she feels in the marigold chemise, and Alessia is so thrilled to be working on this new painting.

"Alessia, would it be all right if I keep the marigold chemise with me tonight and bring it back tomorrow? I have grown to feel it is almost like a part of me."

"Of course, Lucida. Really, you must have it. It is my gift to you. Please accept it. By the way, I had a strange dream. I was wearing the marigold chemise, and I was like an angel flying over Bramante's Tempietto. The dream was instructing me to keep producing my own work."

Lucida is stunned. "Alessia, I had a similar dream flying over Bramante's Tempietto as if I was an angel, and then it was like the two of us had merged into one."

They both felt a chill run the length of their spines and locked eyes, not knowing what to say or think. It is time for Lucida to depart. She gathers her satchel, with the marigold chemise tucked safely inside, and makes her way to the street.

Once Brigida sees that Lucida has gone to the same place, the Salvatori studio, she quickly returns home and slips back into her room. She is confused but is determined to be patient and watchful. Certainly, the truth will make itself known in good time.

The wedding date is approaching with only two months before Niccolo and Lucida are to be wed in holy matrimony. Details are falling into place. They will be married at Santa Maria in Trastevere, where the Galvani family has worshipped for generations. The young couple has been meeting with the priest in preparation for their life as a married couple. Both families are pleased with the coming union and look forward to welcoming grandchildren into the fold.

Signor and Signora Bianchi have invited the Galvani family to their home for an evening of entertainment and dinner. They have engaged a troop of performers to occupy the children while the parents, Niccolo, and Lucida review the wedding plans and decide on any details that need to be finalized. Following dinner, there will be music by the madrigalist Giovanni Pierluigi da Palestrina of the Roman School. He will also be performing at the wedding and is dining with the families this evening.

Brigida, Luigi Jr., and Giovanni are herded into Niccolo and his sister's former nursery to wait for the performers. They are abuzz with speculations about the performance. Will there be juggling, music, acting, or their favorite, a puppet show? Little Beatrice is home with her nurse, but it won't be too long before she will be able to join her siblings on these special occasions. Everyone adores her, and they can't wait for her to be included.

Brigida remembers that she left her handkerchief in her mother's satchel and excuses herself to retrieve it. Luigi Jr. and Giovanni tell her to hurry. The performers will be arriving anytime now.

She makes her way down the staircase but realizes she is confused and can't remember which room her parents are meeting in. There is a door to her left near the foot of the stairs. Perhaps that is the room. Slowly she opens the door. No one is in the room, but Brigida is a naturally curious girl, so she quietly closes the door and waits as her eyes adjust to the dim light.

She sees that it appears to be a study with masculine decor, probably it belongs to Signor Bianchi, she determines. Brigida turns slightly to her right and notices that there is a large painting hung between two windows. Moving closer, she begins to examine the painting. Noticing a candle on the small stand nearby, she decides to light it and have a closer look. Holding the candle up, she sees that the painting is a portrait of a young woman in a marigold chemise. She is posed on a bed and looks as if she is inviting the viewer to join her. Studying the face of the young beauty, her heart catches and her breathing stops. That young woman is Lucida. She has no doubt. Visions of the nameplate on the building Lucida has been sneaking off to—Orazio Salvatori, Pittore—swim before her eyes.

What is the meaning of this? Why would Lucida be a painter's model? Why would Lucida allow herself to be painted in such a seductive manner? Brigida can make no sense of it. She recalls her mission to retrieve her handkerchief from her mother but decides that she should return to her brothers instead. Her head is spinning.

The performers have arrived and are setting up for a puppet show and music. Luigi Jr. and Giovanni are giving their rapt attention to the troupe and call out to Brigida to join them as the music begins. They are performing *Bacia il Coniglio Marrone* (Kiss the Brown Bunny), a play about a cockroach and a dog. The cockroach bets his friend, the dog, that he will be kissed three times in the next three minutes. Hilarity ensues. Luigi Jr. and Giovanni are rolling with laughter and are so absorbed in the show that they don't notice that Brigida is strangely quiet.

Dinner is being served. Signora Bianchi has paid special attention to the menu for this evening. Romanesco soup followed by pork and garum novus, blood cake, puntarella, quails and pomegranate, braised mutton, struffoli, prunes, and goat curd. To drink are prosecco, pitchers of Fronton Negrette, and Seduction, a sweet wine of the Pyrenees.

Luigi Jr. and Giovanni respond to inquiries about the puppet show, showing off and making everyone laugh. Signor Galvani expresses his appreciation to the Bianchis for the children's entertainment. He is an astute man and notices that his Brigida, who is normally loquacious, looks rather pale and has hardly uttered a word. *Perhaps she is not feeling well*, he thinks. He will mention it to his wife later.

The meal is delicious, and all are satisfied. Signor Bianchi suggests that the men retire to his study briefly while the madrigalist prepares for his performance and the women and children can join them in the drawing room.

Niccolo follows his father and Signor Galvani into the study where they light candles and prepare to relax for a few minutes before rejoining the women and children. Signor Bianchi compliments Signor Galvani on his lovely Lucida and relays how much he and Signora Bianchi are looking forward to having Lucida as a daughter-in-law.

Luigi states that he and his wife are also pleased with the match and are anticipating a fond relationship with Niccolo. He sighs with satisfaction as he congratulates himself on procuring an excellent match for Lucida. It is at this moment that he notices the painting behind Niccolo's chair.

"What a lovely painting, Signor Bianchi. Who is the artist?" he inquires as he moves closer for a better view. He sees that it is a portrait of a young beautiful woman wearing a marigold-colored chemise and in a rather seductive pose. His gaze rests on her face and freezes. The model looks exactly like Lucida.

"The artist has chosen to remain anonymous. We think he may be someone from Firenze. The art dealer Signor Ruel brought five of the most stunning paintings to our businessmen's group. They were all this same woman posing in the marigold chemise, and they all sold in a bidding war for a very high price. We have begged him to urge the artist to create more work. Niccolo and I thought that the young woman looked familiar, but we couldn't place her. Most likely, it is a model the artist uses in Firenze. You must agree that it is a stunning painting."

Luigi is at a loss for words but manages to agree. "Yes, it is a very stunning painting. We should go now to rejoin the ladies and children. I am anxious to hear the madrigalist Giovanni Pierluigi da Palestrina. I hear that he is superb."

The men retire to the drawing room where the ladies and children are waiting with the famous composer who is ready to begin his performance. He commands everyone's rapt attention.

Lucida and Niccolo are seated next to each other, and they steal loving glances as they let the music wash over them. Lucida can't believe that this famous composer will be performing at their wedding. The Bianchis really have a lot of influence. She will soon be joining this admired and influential family and allows herself to feel happy and self-satisfied.

The composer is praised amid applause, and he assures Niccolo and Lucida that he is honored to be performing at their upcoming nuptials. He thanks the Bianchis for the delicious dinner and lovely evening.

The children are beginning to yawn as the Galvanis depart amid fond embraces and appreciation for the exciting evening.

Luigi and Brigida independently mull the evening's discovery as the family walk home in the cool evening, admiring the moon and stars.

Alessia and Lucida have been working steadily. Lucida makes her way to the studio each day at siesta, posing in the marigold chemise. It is as if the garment has magical qualities that seep into her soul. With each session, she feels stronger, bolder, and more passionate. Because of the coming wedding, Alessia has been working on detailed sketches for five new works. She can complete the paintings without Lucida's presence, using the sketches as a reference. Lucida agrees to return for a few sessions if needed.

Signor Bianchi and most especially Signor Ruel are anxious to have the new work at the men's business meeting. The members who lost out on the bidding are eager to be collectors of this mysterious artist from Firenze.

Rumors about the paintings have begun to circulate among the men who encounter the fortunate owners of the paintings in business and social events. Niccolo has been approached by several young associates who inquire if he could arrange to have them view his father's painting. He thinks to himself, *Why not?* After all, he will no doubt be a member of the group soon, and with his additional responsibilities in the family business, he needs to practice deepening his business connections.

Niccolo decides to approach his father about the request that evening and asks for a moment with his father when they return home for the evening. They settle in front of the painting, admiring it in the glow of the candles. Signor Bianchi grants his son's request, thinking how proud he is of his son. He is really coming into his own and will soon be a partner in the business, someone to carry on when Signor Bianchi departs this world. He sighs with satisfaction. They agree that Niccolo should bring his associates to the Bianchi villa the next evening to view the painting and have a small refreshment and conversation.

Three of Niccolo's associates arrive the following evening, eager to view the painting, which is now becoming such a fascination, with young men competing to see who can view all five of the paintings first.

"*Benvenuto, benvenuto*," Signor Bianchi greets the men. "Niccolo is waiting in my study with wine for us to enjoy."

The men greet Niccolo who serves them wine, and they settle in to view the painting. There is silence as the men are mesmerized by the young woman in the marigold chemise who seems to invite them into her bed.

"Signor Bianchi, how fortunate you are to own this painting. The artist will no doubt become famous. You say that he is from Firenze?"

"That is the speculation. He has chosen to remain anonymous. I know not why."

One of the men steps closer to the painting, gazing intently at the face of the young woman. "This beauty looks so familiar to me. I can't place it. You know, she looks a lot like your fiancée, Lucida, Niccolo. You are lucky to be marrying her. She is so beautiful, and I hear she is intelligent as well."

Signor Bianchi and Niccolo also study the face of the woman intently.

"Yes, you are right. There is a certain resemblance to Lucida, isn't there? Well, they must have lovely young women in Firenze who model for artists."

The men enjoy refreshments, and as the conversation turns to business matters, Signor Bianchi notes that Niccolo takes the lead in discussions with more authority. *He is really going to blossom as he takes on more responsibility in the business*, he thinks as he sighs contentedly.

Luigi finds that he is distracted all morning as he makes his rounds at the hospital. Several times he has to ask a patient to repeat a response to his inquiry about their condition. He asks his assistant to take extra careful notes this morning, thinking that he will review them later, so as not to be remiss in attending to an important detail. He is relieved when it is time for the midday break and decides to take a longer route home to give his thoughts space to breathe.

How could the lovely young woman in Signor Bianchi's painting be his Lucida? *It is just not possible*, he thinks. She would never allow herself to be put in such a compromising situation. The image of the painting will not leave the screen of his mind. It seems to pulsate, the young beauty in the marigold chemise with his Lucida's face. He is almost in Via Giulia when he decides that he will approach his daughter for a private conversation that afternoon.

The midday meal is chaotic as Luigi Jr. and Giovanni are competing for attention with their antics and ignore their mother's instructions to quiet down. Normally, Luigi would not allow this, but he remains lost in his internal quagmire and doesn't even notice that his wife's attempts at restoring order are ineffective.

Lucida asks to be excused for her siesta and makes her way to her room. She wants to change before slipping out to meet Alessia at the studio. She figures that her brothers will keep everyone distracted, so it will be easy to slip out today. In record time, she has changed and is out the servants' entrance on her way for an afternoon of posing.

Brigida is about to step out of her room and hide in wait for Lucida to leave. She is becoming very efficient and confident in trailing her sister. After her discovery last evening in Signor Bianchi's private office, her head has been spinning off in myriad possibilities, and she is frightened for her sister. She has just stepped into the hallway when she sees her father approaching Lucida's door. He knocks softly, then with more force, he's calling his daughter's name. No response is forthcoming. After several more attempts with no response, Luigi opens the door and surveys the room. The bed has not been disturbed, and Lucida is nowhere to be seen.

Brigida softly steps behind her father, and she, too, observes the empty room. Luigi gets startled as he almost knocks Brigida over as he turns to leave. The father and daughter lock eyes for a very long moment. Brigida's heart is racing as she quietly addresses her father. "Father, I believe I know where Lucida has gone. Follow me."

The father and daughter discretely leave the Galvani residence and make their way toward Piazza Navona, the Piazza di Spagna, and Via Margutta. Brigida stops and takes her father's hand in front of a placard near a substantial wooden doorway—Orazio Salvatori, Pittore.

"Lucida is here. I am certain," she tells her father.

Luigi is stunned, uncertain of what to think or say. "How do you know this?" he asks.

Ashamed, Brigida admits that she has been following Lucida and has seen her with another young woman she doesn't know exchanging intense conversations and notes.

"Father, I am afraid for our Lucida. What if people find out that she has been modeling for a painter? Especially, what if the Bianchis find out that the painting in Signor Bianchi's study is of Lucida?"

"How do you know about the painting in Signor Bianchi's study?" Luigi demands as he finds himself becoming angry.

"I was looking for mother that night when we were at the Bianchis to retrieve my handkerchief, and I accidentally opened the door to the study. I was curious, so I entered and saw the painting. Don't worry, no one saw me."

Luigi consults his timepiece and realizes that the siesta is almost over, and he should return to the hospital. He is just about to instruct Brigida to return home and to not mention their discovery to anyone when Lucida steps out on to Via Margutta. She seems preoccupied and, in a hurry, walks quickly in the opposite direction, not seeing her father and sister.

"Brigida, my daughter, go back home at once, and do not let your sister see you, and especially do not say a word to anyone about this. I need time to think about the best way to manage this awful situation. I am going back to the hospital now. I will see you this evening."

It is a shame that some of the gentlemen at the business meeting were not able to purchase one of the stunning paintings of the beauty in the marigold chemise, muses Signor Ruel. He chuckles heartily as he reminisces over the bidding war. A number of the gentlemen have visited his gallery since that meeting, inquiring as to when there will be new works by this artist from Firenze. They wonder if they can order a commission, and one even offered him a bribe if he would reveal the name of the artist. *Well*, he thinks, *that is tempting, but maintaining the mystery around the artist is a clever business decision.* He makes a great show of taking their names, promising to contact them when the new paintings are ready to be shown at the business meeting. He reminds them that the business meeting is exclusive, not just anyone has the privilege of purchasing these paintings.

Signor Ruel scribbles a hurried note to Orazio, calling his boy to make haste in delivering it to the Salvatori studio.

> Signor,
>
> Please be advised that I will be visiting your studio tomorrow morning before I open my gallery. I am anxious to view the progress your daughter has made on the new paintings. I have had many anxious inquiries with offers of commissions as well. Our business deal is going to be even more lucrative than I imagined.
>
> Signor Ruel

Turpentine pierces her nostrils as Alessia cleans her brushes and tidies the workspace. She has been working on the new paintings at a furious pace, the work flowing freely from her heart. She is now far enough along and has enough sketches that this afternoon she advised Lucida that she doesn't need to risk returning to the studio to sit for her. Tears slip over her lashes as she relives their parting this afternoon. They embraced as she sent Lucida off with the marigold chemise hidden under her dress. She promises to leave a note in the wall with a time to come view the finished paintings before they leave the studio. She will miss her dear friend.

The assistants are preparing to leave the studio for the day, chattering and gossiping. Alessia can't quite make out what they are saying, and she doesn't normally pay much attention, but an interesting snippet makes its way to her corner of the studio.

"*Si, si,* I heard they had a bidding war, and only five of the men were able to purchase the paintings. They are scandalous, a seductress in a marigold chemise, I hear. A friend was invited to view the painting purchased by Signor Bianchi. You know, his son, Niccolo, is set to wed Lucida Galvani soon. Do you know Niccolo?" The group reaches the door, still gossiping away about the paintings.

Orazio startles Alessia as he enters her workspace, a bit of cerulean blue on the hand holding a note. "Signor Ruel is coming tomorrow morning to check on your progress. What is wrong? You look distressed."

"Father, I overheard the assistants talking as they were leaving. The gossip about the paintings is spreading. One of the paintings was purchased by Signor Bianchi. His son, Niccolo, is marrying Lucida Galvani next month. Do you know the Bianchis or the Galvanis? Father, Lucida Galvani is my dear friend. She is the model for the paintings. This is a *disastro*! What are we to do?"

Orazio is stunned. He has not been paying attention. He has been so busy with his work and with the mental calculations of a larger purse for his family that he didn't even consider the model, just assuming it was some working girl that Alessia knew. He doesn't know the Bianchis or the Galvanis, but of course, he has heard of the prominent families. This is a *disastro*!

"We need time to think, Alessia." He yells for Signor Ruel's boy to wait and scribbles a response to Ruel.

Signor Ruel, do not come to the studio tomorrow. I cannot meet with you. I need to complete my commission for the church. My

daughter and all the assistants are needed. We
will not be available for several weeks.

He watches Signor Ruel's boy scurry down Via Margutta with a
heavy heart. Hauling himself up the stairs to the studio, he prepares
to face his daughter.

The light is beginning to soften, illuminating the new paintings, slanted patterns distorting the image and palette. The work is
only one-third completed, and only the sketches show Lucida's face
in a recognizable manner.

Orazio gathers the sketches and begins to crumble them, stuff-
ing them into a satchel.

"Father! Stop! What are you doing to my work? Stop!" shouts
Alessia. She is furious and attempts to save some of the sketches, but
her father is much stronger and pushes her aside.

"We cannot risk your reputation or the Galvani girl's reputation.
You will both be ruined. I have been thinking about your immense
talent. You are a more talented painter than many men, including
your father. I have been hearing that in Firenze, the people are more
open to women using their talents. Perhaps this is the time for you to
leave the family nest and establish yourself as a painter. If we can find
you a husband, that would ease the way. My friend Signor Stratassi
has a brother who is a businessman. We may be able to make an
acceptable arrangement."

Alessia grabs the largest pallet knife on the workbench and
slashes all her canvases. She is shaking with fury at her father and the
world. Undried paint splatters on her arms and her torso, leaving her
splotched. She turns to her father, drops the pallet knife, glares into
his eyes, and storms out of the studio. Via Margutta is alive with the
passeggiata, families enjoying the dusk as they stroll, greeting their
friends and passersby. Our artist attracts curious glances as she storms
down the street, covered in drops of paint, face contorted with anger,
and in no mood to politely greet her fellow citizens.

Orazio circles the studio, frustration and anger caught in circles
as he paces, throwing the ruined canvases in the corner. The satchel
containing the studies of Lucida land on top of the pile. Finally, he

hurls a drop cloth over the whole mess and storms out of the studio, ignoring neighborly greetings.

His dear wife greets him as he enters their home. "Dear, what is wrong?"

"De nada, nothing, nothing. I had a disagreement with one of the assistants," he replies, embracing her with a quick kiss.

"Alessia arrived home a short while ago. Her gown is ruined with paint. Maid is helping her clean up. She seemed very distraught, but she refused to confide in me. Alas, she is more your daughter than mine." She sighs.

Alessia and Orazio steer clear of one another that evening. Alessia composes a note to Lucida, instructing her to meet at the north entrance to the Borghese the next afternoon. It's urgent! She slips out to deliver the note to their crack in the wall, her feet gliding along the cobblestones and her expression molded into pleasantness as she nods to her neighbors.

The wedding is fast approaching, with just a few weeks until the bride and groom are joined in holy matrimony. Details are falling into place, and both families are enveloped in anticipation.

Lucida finds that she cannot resist daily periods of daydreaming in the marigold chemise. This is the time of the day she most looks forward to. Just yesterday, she dozed off during one of these sessions. She had donned the chemise, experiencing the familiar thrill, and nestled herself under her covers, her chestnut hair fanning the pillow, turning herself over to the magic of marigold.

The dream begins with the same scene. She and Alessia merge into one as they float over the Tempietto in the marigold chemise. But in this dream, they glance upward and see storm clouds approaching. The winds begin to howl, tossing them as if they are specks of dust. Suddenly a chariot appears, and they find themselves as two angels in marigold being transported by four white horses, pulling the chariot over the storm and into the clouds. She notes that she is not fearful in the dream, but upon awakening, she feels unsettled as she prepares to join the family for the evening meal.

Everyone is chattering over each other as the maid serves them. They are having a seafood stew of tellin, oysters, octopus, and white fish along with bread. Eugenia is a bit rattled by all the details of the wedding. She always relies on Luigi to steady her, so she's a little annoyed that he seems distracted.

"Luigi, are you listening to me? We need to meet with the *ristorante* to finalize the wedding supper menu tomorrow," Eugenia implores.

"Yes, dear, I am listening. I cannot join you tomorrow. Whatever you determine is fine. Take Lucida with you or your sister." Luigi does his best to hide his annoyance.

He addresses his second daughter, "Brigida, bring your schoolwork into the study after dinner. Ariston tells me you did not do your best this week. We need to review it."

Brigida finds her father seated at his massive desk. There are papers and books stacked on each end of the desk, framing her father. He is absorbed in one of the household accounting books, so Brigida announces her presence by shutting the heavy door with a noticeable thud.

"Come, come, my daughter. Be seated," he says as he indicates the chair across the desk.

Brigida feels like a small child in the massive chair, feet dangling off the floor. She braces herself for his lecture on improving her studies. She knows that she is not as bright as Lucida, but prettier for sure.

Luigi sighs deeply, his face showing distress as he addresses his second daughter. "Brigida, the two of us now have a secret. I am afraid that I must insist that this secret remain between us. I know this is not how I usually instruct you children, but in this case, I see no other option. I am praying that no one ever discovers that it is Lucida in those paintings. The families must proceed with the wedding as planned. That is the best for Lucida's secure future. I believe you are old enough to understand. Meanwhile, you are to cease following your sister. She is not to discover that you have seen her. Do you understand? Can I trust you with this burden?"

Meekly, Brigida responds, "Yes, Father, you can trust me with our secret. What did Ariston tell you about my studies?"

Luigi shakes his head and motions for her to leave the room. Well, this is not what she expected. Of course, she will keep their secret, but she doubts she will be able to restrain herself from following Lucida. That is far too thrilling.

Ariston dismisses his charges for the day. He is saddened that this will be Lucida's last week for attending his tutoring sessions. He admires her quick wit and intelligence and admits to himself that he is a little sweet on her. Lucida is also sad that she will be leaving her lessons. This is the end of her formal education. Perhaps she can persuade Niccolo to hire Ariston for some individual sessions. He does seem to have an open mind about most matters.

Today the weather is fine, so she announces to her family that she is going to meet her friend Isabella at the Borghese for a stroll. She is unaware that her little sister Brigida is following at a safe distance.

The play area is full of children and their nurses, laughing and shouting in good fun. She makes her way to the wall and makes a pretense of enjoying the children at play. Her hand recovers the note, and she strolls away to read. The word *urgent* frightens her as she crumples the note and disposes of it.

She is almost to the north entrance of the Borghese when she spies Alessia seated on a bench just past the entrance gate. She feels a kindred spirit to her friend and will miss seeing her and working with her. A wave of melancholy washes over her as she moves to greet her friend.

Alessia glances up to see Lucida approaching and rushes to embrace her.

"Let us stroll, my friend," instructs Alessia as she links her right arm with Lucida's and moves her along the gravel path. Strolling along, she relays the snippets of conversation among the studio assistants she overheard and the quarrel with her father. She tells Lucida that maybe it really is for the best if she leaves her family and tries to work in Firenze and make a name for herself. There is a businessman, Pietro Stratassi, whose brother is a friend of her father's, and her father suggested that an arrangement could be made for a marriage. She just wants to paint and have her work recognized. If she has to marry to get away, so be it. That may be her fate.

"What do you think, my friend?" Alessia asks.

Lucida's mind is spinning out of control after her friend's revelations.

"The Bianchis are going to discover that I am the model in the paintings. And his father has purchased one? I cannot believe it. I am ruined. My family, I will dishonor them." Lucida is sobbing as Alessia directs her to a discreet bench in the park behind a laurel hedge for some privacy. Concealed behind the hedge, little sister Brigida is attempting to make sense of their conversation.

Orazio is determined that his daughter will marry and move to Firenze. He will miss her deeply but feels that he must implement his plan swiftly. Her mother is eager to have Alessia betrothed and begin her life as a woman, so thankfully, she is not creating obstacles to Orazio's plan.

He is to meet with the Stratassi family this evening. They are to arrive at the Salvatoris' home at 9:00. He has also invited his dear friend Giovanni Battista, brother of Pietro Stratassi, who agrees that Alessia and Pietro would be a good match.

The Salvatoris greet the Stratassis warmly. The maid offers refreshments as they settle in for discussion. They are discussing Orazio's latest commission when Alessia enters the room. She remains standing, giving the impression that she is in control of herself and this somewhat awkward situation.

Pietro has long admired Orazio's work and is humbled to be in the position of joining the famous painter's family. He has not given much thought to obtaining a wife, but his brother Giovanni has convinced him that it would be to his advantage to marry, especially to marry the Salvatori daughter. It would be advantageous to his career. He sees that Alessia remains standing. She looks a bit formidable to him but quite attractive. He decides to stand to greet her and moves forward in a gracious bow.

"I am honored to make your acquaintance. I have always admired your father's work, and I hear that you are a talented assistant to him."

Alessia offers her hand for the requisite kiss, gazing intently at him. "I am a painter in my own right, and Father has suggested that I establish myself in Firenze. It is time to make my work known. Now if you excuse me, I will leave it to my parents to manage this arrangement."

She turns to leave the room as Pietro is left speechless by the power of this self-possessed young woman.

Orazio, Pietro's father, and Giovanni Battista swiftly negotiate a dowry, and Giovanni offers a wedding gift of a palazzo in Firenze for the couple. Pietro and Alessia offer no objections, and the two are to wed in Santo Spirito in Sassia in Rome. Directly following the wedding, arrangements are made for them to travel to Firenze and settle into the palazzo.

Alessia refuses to allow herself any sentiment about this swift arrangement. She can feel her heart harden as she goes about the motions of preparing for the move to Firenze. Pietro will be an adequate mate. He is not demanding of her, and she feels no compunction about performing her marital duties, as she sees herself as a sensuous woman. In her opinion, it is the same as being a sensuous painter.

The young couple's belongings have been loaded into a cart for transport, with Alessia and Pietro making the journey on horseback. Their families gather to wish them a safe journey. Orazio is overcome with sadness, tears streaming, as he embraces his daughter and releases her to her future.

Lucida sleeps fitfully. Her thoughts turn to worry about her friend and about her own dilemma. She hasn't heard a word from Alessia since the day in the Borghese. *I need to speak with her*, she thinks and determines that she will make her way to the Salvatori studio as soon as she can. Once her father has left for the hospital and her siblings are in lessons with Ariston, she makes her way to Via Margutta.

Fumes from the oil paint embrace her as she makes her way up the stairs to the studio. It is quiet as the assistants are concentrating on their work, ignoring her as she makes her way to Alessia's corner. She cannot believe her eyes. There on the floor in a messy heap are Alessia's studies and canvases that has been ripped and shredded, paint smeared on the floor and furniture. The work is in ruins. *Where is Alessia?*

Lucida, in a state of shock, turns to leave. Orazio blocks her path.

"Where is Alessia? What happened to her work?" she stammers.

"She left for Firenze yesterday with her husband, Pietro Stratassi. They will be established in a palazzo, and Alessia will have her own studio. She deserves to be recognized for her work, and it will be easier for her in Firenze. We need to protect you both from scandal. I will never reveal that those paintings were completed by Alessia and that you were the model. The dealer Signor Ruel is the only one who knows, and I will bribe him with promise of more of Alessia's work from Firenze. He does not know who the model for the paintings is. I am destroying the sketches and her uncompleted work. You should go, and never return to this studio."

Lucida is unsure how she manages to walk from the studio to the sanctuary of Santa Maria in Trastevere. She kneels in her favorite pew, praying for her friend and for herself, asking for strength and guidance. Light from the apse's window falls across her cheeks, illuminating tears of sadness as she realizes how much she will miss her dear friend and the sessions in the marigold chemise. She lights a candle, asking for protection and wisdom from the saints.

The wedding date is fast approaching. Signor and Signora Bianchi invite Lucida and her parents to their villa to review the wedding arrangements and plan to surprise them with the gift of the couple's new villa. They have arranged with the workers to walk through. Niccolo wants to have Lucida involved in final decisions for renovations.

Joyful greetings are exchanged when the Galvanis arrive. However, Niccolo observes that Lucida appears to be a little pale and withdrawn, not her usual engaging self. Luigi, ever the astute physician, notices the change in his daughter as well.

Signor Bianchi invites everyone to join him in his study for a special announcement and signals to the maid to bring champagne for the toast. She pours the wine, and Signor Bianchi raises his glass, inviting everyone to do the same.

"*Per cent'anni* [one hundred years of luck to you], Lucida and Niccolo." He turns his attention to the Galvanis. "We have a special surprise. Signora and I have purchased a villa for the children to begin their new life together. It is nearby, and I have arranged for us to view it together. Come, come."

There are gasps of surprise at the announcement. The Bianchis are smiling with joy and pride, and the Galvanis are stunned. They did not expect this generosity. Signora Galvani finds that she is tearing up with happiness for her daughter. She will have a very nice life, and to start her new life with a villa is perfect. Her mind's eye is full of visions of a happy household full of children.

Signor and Signora Galvani are seated facing the wall that houses Alessia's painting. Of course, the men had all viewed the painting, but the Signoras Galvani and Bianchi had not, as they normally wouldn't be invited into the study, and strangely, neither of them pays any attention to the painting. Their thoughts are on the villa and the wedding. Luigi stares at the painting as he attempts to digest the news about the gift of the villa to the betrothed. Both he and Niccolo notice that Lucida is also staring at the painting and is becoming more and more pale.

Signor Bianchi takes command of the room and orders everyone to finish their champagne and move on to the villa. He is excited to show it off. "*Sbrigare, sbrigare,*" he bellows.

The group hurries to the street and follows Signor Bianchi to the villa being readied for Lucida and Niccolo. Soon they are greeted by the chief worker who will conduct the tour. The renovations are near completion, but there are still some decisions to be made. Everyone is impressed with the romantic style. The plaster has been refreshed in creamy white with ornate ceilings and decorative coves along the room perimeters. The floor terrazzo has also been refreshed and polished. It is lovely. Everyone exclaims their approval. "*Bella, bella.*"

"Please, parents. I would like to have some time alone with Lucida to discuss the final decisions for the renovation. We will meet you back home for the midday meal," announces Niccolo.

He gathers Lucida in his arms and inquires if anything is wrong. "You seem tired and distracted, my dear."

"I am fine, Niccolo. I am just a bit tired. I didn't sleep well last night. Do not worry," she reports, forcing a smile and more cheer in her voice. "I love the villa. It is perfect for us. What a beautiful surprise. Tell me about the decisions we need to make."

"I want you to choose which room will be our bedchamber. Let's go upstairs, and I will show you the rooms."

They ascend to the upper floor, which has six bedchambers. Moving through the chambers, Lucida is already making decisive choices. The largest room will be for the children's nursery and their school and playroom as they become older. The smaller ones will be for their bedchambers. There is a medium corner room that has light streaming through and a view of the garden and umbrella trees below.

"This will be our bedchamber, Niccolo. I love this room. It will be perfect."

Niccolo is beaming. "I knew that you would choose this room. You will be in charge of choosing the furnishings for our villa. I want it to have your special touch."

Lucida muses that she is very fortunate. If only no one discovers that she is the model in the painting, all will be well.

Lucida and the maid have been filling trunks with clothing, books, and childhood treasures. Her trousseau with handmade nightgowns and undergarments along with some new frocks are packed away in a special trunk. Lucida has slipped the muslin with the marigold chemise in among the garments. She has vowed to herself that she will keep it with her always.

Leaning on the windowsill, she watches her little bird friend hop along the garden vines, looking for berries and seeds. She will miss him. She blows a kiss, wishing him safety and joy to sing.

Voices drift up from the street. The men are here to cart her trunks to the new villa, and she hears her mother direct them up the stairs to collect them. Her heart beats faster as she anticipates her wedding tomorrow and her new life. May the saints protect her and keep her secret safe.

Luigi and Brigida have been closely observing Lucida. The wedding is tomorrow, and so far, there has been no discovery of the nature of Lucida's involvement with the paintings. The two have not discussed it, and Luigi is hoping that in all the flurry of activity around the wedding, it will be forgotten. Brigida is fearful of a revelation and her sister's reputation...and the implied reflection on her own. She wants a better match than her sisters. She can't help it that she is competitive.

Eugenia has suggested that they use Brigida's room to dress and prepare for the ceremony. The maid has arranged the gowns and jewelry and will assist them with their hairstyling.

Before she retires for the evening, Lucida raps on Brigida's door and asks to enter. She embraces her little sister, tears slipping down her cheeks. "I will miss you, my sister. We will visit often, but it will not be the same."

Brigida leans into Lucida's embrace while whispering in her ear. "I know your secret. Father knows your secret. We know about the paintings. You must never let anyone find out. It will ruin our reputation, and Niccolo will banish you from the Bianchi family. Go now, and we will never speak of it again."

Lucida freezes. How did they find out? She releases her embrace abruptly and flees from the room, not daring to look Brigida in the eye.

Alone in her room for her final night in her parent's home, she tries in vain to relax and get comfortable. She cannot imagine how her father and sister discovered her secret. She will have to be very brave and never allow the secret to spill from her lips, no matter how much a confession would give her some relief. Scenarios of discovery spin through her mind.

Finally, Lucida drifts into an exhausted sleep. Her dream transports her over the Tempietto. Alessia and Lucida drift above the clouds and into a replica of the Tempietto. They are seated together in the center on a plush divan, Lucida in the marigold chemise and Alessia studying her. As they glance about, they view the paintings lined up before them. They admire the work, taking strength from the images. As they focus on the paintings, they notice beings emerging from behind the paintings. There are grown children and younger children. They begin to circulate around the Tempietto, studying the paintings and studying Alessia and Lucida, smiling and gently touching the two women on their shoulders.

Two young women, who appear to be the oldest of the group, come to stand before Lucida and Alessia. Their images become startingly clear, and speaking together, they pronounce, "My dears, do not worry, we will protect and pass along your marigold chemise and the paintings."

Now the group join hands encircling the two women and slowly ascend through the Tempietto, disappearing from view.

Lucida is awakened by the song of her little bird friend making a racket on the windowsill. The sun streams across her bed and warms her face. Stretching herself awake through the fog of sleep and dream, she struggles to retain the dream, but it dissipates, and she is only able to recall being with Alessia in the Tempietto. She wills herself to remain perfectly still and commands her mind to bring the dream back to her consciousness to no avail.

Dreamed marigolds—a very good sign because it predicts a fateful meeting with someone who will be a loyal partner in life. Following a successful marriage, it will improve her situation in the society. In addition, these flowers portend a large fortune, honor, loyalty in love, the success of all undertakings, especially if you've seen a bunch of them. At the same time, wilted or dried marigold can negate the value of prosperous dreams.

Part II

The family compound is a merging of two villas, a large court-yard, and workspace for Alessia. The Arno River is just a few streets away, with bustling commerce and activity, making it a lively neighborhood. Martina Bianchi had finally convinced her parents and Niccolo that he and Lucida should relocate in Firenze now that their daughter and two sons were old enough to attend school. Schools in Firenze would provide the children with a superior education. Signor Bianchi is convinced that Niccolo could manage a new branch of the Bianchi enterprises. Martina makes it her business to know all the latest gossip and hears that there is a couple, Pietro and Alessia Stratassi, who want to purchase the villa next to theirs as an investment but unfortunately are shy of the necessary funds.

Shrewdness is Martina's forte. Her father often lamented to himself that it was a shame that she wasn't a male offspring. Martina convinces him that investing in the villa would be a wise move. Firenze is rapidly becoming more and more influential, and having property and expanding the business is a good investment in the future.

Servants arrive the month before to ready the villa for the young Bianchi family. Lucida is sad to be moving away from her family, but with promises of visits to come, she starts to become excited about the move. A new beginning for all of them and good for the children's education.

She loves being a mother, and she and Niccolo are happy together. When Niccolo describes the villa, he relays that it is part of a compound with a shared courtyard. The Stratassi family has a son and a daughter, the same ages as the Bianchi children, so the children will have ready playmates. She has convinced Ariston to join them to supplement the children's education and, if she is to be honest, to continue hers as well.

The Bianchi's carriage arrives at their new home. Lucida approves of the stately building. Ochre stone, *marrone* exterior window trims and shutters, and emerald vines are spiraling on the facade. Niccolo has to quiet the children; they are so excited. The servant has been alerted by their noisy arrival and awaits at the entrance.

Niccolo gallantly sweeps his wife across the threshold and gently deposits her on the stone floor. They tour the villa, hand in hand, the children bouncing around with delight. At the rear of the villa is a set of large glass doors that lead to the shared courtyard. They see a well-tended garden with small pools, statuary, and a variety of plantings. At the opposite end of the courtyard is a matching set of doors leading into the adjoining villa. Seated on a stone bench is a woman working with a charcoal on a large sketch pad. Hearing a commotion, she glances up. There across the courtyard is her Lucida. She drops the pad from her lap and runs with open arms to embrace her friend. Lucida cannot believe it. The two women begin crying and sputtering to each other.

"Is it really you? Do you really live here? Are you really the new owners?"

Niccolo is curious. "How is it that you two know each other?"

Pietro echoes the question.

Alessia and Lucida lock eyes. Before Lucida is able to compose herself Alessia laughs. "We played together in the Borghese when we were children. Lucida's nurse loved to bring her to the children's play area for fresh air, and my mother did the same. We became fast friends, but we haven't seen one another for ages. This is fate. Now we can enjoy each other and our children will be playmates as well."

Pietro, being very gregarious, is pleased that his audience has grown and declares that they must celebrate the reunion of Alessia and Lucida that very evening. It is warm, and they can enjoy a meal in the courtyard. He hollers to the servant to fetch the cook. When she appears, breathless from rushing to see what Pietro is demanding, he expounds upon her great talent in the kitchen to Niccolo and Lucida.

The cook blushes. "I will see to a special meal for you." As she rushes off, she is thinking that she will have to alter her whole plan for the evening meal.

"Tonight, we shall dine and raise a glass to our villa and our new friendship," bellows Pietro.

Although they are tired from the journey, the Bianchis are ener-gized by this new adventure and are delighted when they enter the courtyard at the 9:00 hour for dinner. The courtyard is ablaze with candles, and the Stratassis are lined up to greet them. Alessia directs the children to one end of the long table, and the adults settle them-selves on the other end. They dine on *menestra de carne* (soup with meat and cinnamon), *capretto arrosto in sapore* (roast lamb), *herba de campo cocta et cruda* (special green salad mix), *crostini all agliata* (bread toast with garlic), and *frictelle de poma* (fritele of apples).

Pietro pours the wine as he boasts about procuring the best Chianti from the *buchette del vino* of their neighbor. (The *buchette del vino* [small holes for wine] are foot-tall openings enterprising Florentine nobles built into the street-facing walls of their palatial residences in the Renaissance era.) He continues to dominate the conversation, bragging to Niccolo that his wife, Alessia, is a very tal-ented artist, insisting that they visit her studio tomorrow.

Lucida and Alessia exchange glances throughout the evening. Lucida wonders if Alessia is pleased with her marital match. Pietro seems so domineering, and Alessia seems more subdued than Lucida recalls. Finally, Alessia seems to revive and interrupts her husband to engage Niccolo in the conversation. Lucida takes the cue and relays a spirited story of their journey from Rome.

The children are beginning to tire, and their nurses are called to take them to their beds. Pietro proposes that he and Niccolo stroll for a bit so he can treat him to a tour of the neighborhood. At last, Lucida and Alessia are alone.

"Alessia, you must tell me everything. Are you happy with Pietro? Are you painting? Do you like being a mother?"

"My father quickly arranged the marriage with his friend Signor Stratassi once it seemed like my reputation would be ruined when the paintings of you might be attributed to me. He really gave me no choice. I was so angry that I destroyed the new work and my sketches. However, now I have my own studio, and I am working on some church commissions. I am receiving some good notice. Pietro is blustery, but he is proud of my painting, and he treats me and the children well. He is not the love I dreamed of, but I have made peace with that, and I love the children. They keep the household full of life, and with the nurse to help, I have time to paint. Tomorrow you can visit my studio. And what about your life, Lucida?"

Lucida sighs deeply. "I love my little family, and I am excited for our new life, but I will miss my family. Ariston is arriving soon and will be living with us to help with the children's education and mine as well. I miss learning, and Niccolo is encouraging me to continue. He will be busy establishing the new Bianchi branch here in Firenze. I have missed you, my friend, and I often think of our sessions with the marigold chemise. Those were special days."

The two friends chat away happily about their children and their households. Pietro and Niccolo return from their stroll. Everyone is tired, and they wish each other a pleasant night's rest.

The Bianchis settle into their new home. Niccolo is away for long days establishing the Bianchi branch of the business along with Martina who is second-in-command and finds himself flourishing as he makes decisions and directs the business without his father. The Bianchi and Stratassi children are forming bonds, and Ariston conducts lessons and study direction in addition to their schooling. The two families mingle frequently, enjoying the companionship.

Lucida has developed the habit of donning the marigold chemise when she finds some time to herself and letting herself slip into a reverie. She finds it empowering. One afternoon during siesta, when the household is quiet, she pulls a dress over the marigold chemise and sets across the courtyard to Alessia's studio. She knows that Alessia takes advantage of the siesta time to work.

Gently, she raps on the studio's door. When there is no response, she slowly pushes the door open. The aroma of oil paint and turpentine rushes to fill her nostrils, and she inhales deeply. Alessia is standing in front of a large canvas, studying the work. She is absorbed in her thinking, unaware that Lucida has entered her studio. Lucida remains silent, observing her friend for several minutes before she clears her throat, announcing her presence. Alessia turns and smiles deeply, stretching out her arms for an embrace.

"My friend, what a nice surprise. What has prompted this visit?"

Lucida quickly unbuttons her dress, letting it drop to the floor. The marigold chemise still works its magic. "Perhaps it is time to bring the marigold chemise back to the canvas. What do you think, my friend?"

Alessia turns to pick up a sketch pad and charcoal. "Here, do you recall this divan? I brought it with me from Roma. Settle yourself in."

It is as if no time has passed. Alessia sketches, deciding on composition for the paintings to follow, and Lucida relaxes into the marigold chemise, absorbing its magic.

The two friends establish a routine. Lucida visits the studio during the siesta, posing in the marigold chemise for Alessia. They experiment with sensual and passionate poses. Alessia remains true to the palette of the first paintings. Deep ultramarine blue, titanium white, and a hint of scarlet. Again, the marigold chemise takes center stage. The weeks pass. There are now five new paintings, more powerful than the first body of work. The women are both energized, deriving such pleasure from working together. The marigold chemise exudes energy, tantalizing them both to continue.

One afternoon, they line up the paintings along the studio wall and step back to admire them. Lucida in the marigold chemise, feet bare, and Alessia in her painting smock.

"I am pleased, Lucida. These are successful. Perhaps for the next paintings, I will change the palette and composition. We could pose you as if you are in nature. I will work on sketching some ideas. What do you think?" inquires Alessia.

"I like that idea. Let's go together to the Giardino Boboli and take inspiration from the statuary and fountains. Perhaps we can bring the children along for a treat," Lucida responds as they continue to study the paintings.

A distinct breeze crosses the threshold of Alessia's studio, interrupting the intimacy of the moment. Surprised, they turn to find Niccolo and Pietro coming through the doorway. The two men enter and immediately are aghast. There before them are five large paintings of Lucida posed seductively in the marigold chemise. Moments of charged silence ensue.

Niccolo approaches Lucida, grasping her biceps, holding her at arm's length, and locking his eyes with hers. "My god, Lucida. It was you in my father's painting. The one in his study." He moves his gaze to Alessia. "So this is how you two know each other."

Niccolo releases Lucida from his grip, turns abruptly on his heals, and leaves the studio, slamming the door behind him.

Pietro moves closer to the paintings, studying them closely, alternately glancing back at Alessia and Lucida, as if he cannot believe his eyes. Finally, he inquires, "What did Niccolo mean when he said it was Lucida in his father's painting?"

"I created five paintings in my father's studio on Via Margutta in Roma of Lucida in the marigold chemise. My father arranged for the art dealer Signor Ruel to sell them on the condition that the artist would remain anonymous although Signor Ruel knows that I am the artist. We needed the money for the family purse. Signor Ruel brought them to Signor Bianchi's business meeting, and they all sold for more than we expected. Signor Bianchi purchased one of the paintings for his private study. The others were purchased by prominent businessmen. Gossip began to spread, and my father was afraid for my reputation. We had a fight, and I destroyed the new work I had started with Lucida. That is when he made arrangements with your father to have us wed and me to move to Firenze with you. That is the truth." Alessia feels relief that the truth has been revealed and finds herself standing a little taller, more confident.

"So that is why you married me!" Pietro shouts, and now he turns on his heals, slamming the door after himself.

Silence permeates the studio. Lucida slowly retrieves her dress, gliding it over the marigold chemise. She turns to embrace Alessia.

"I will see you tomorrow, my friend." With a long sigh, she exits the studio, gently closing the door.

Lucida retrieves a shawl from one of the chairs askew near the dining table in the courtyard where they had dined the evening before. She noticed that the servants had neglected to remove the wine from the side table. She pours herself a generous glass and set-tles into a chair nestled beneath the lemon tree in the corner of the courtyard. She pulls the shawl tightly around her shoulders, slips off her shoes, and tucks her feet beneath her hips as she sips her wine, watching the moon rise higher on the horizon. She is grateful for the moment of solitude.

Niccolo has refused to speak to her, not even looking directly at her since the afternoon when he stormed out of Alessia's studio. He spends long hours at work, often dining with his friends. He contin-ues to be warm and engaged with the children when he sees them after siesta, but then he leaves the villa and does not return until late. He has been sleeping on the divan in his study, refusing to return to the marital bedchamber.

Lucida has adopted the Franciscan church of Santa Croce as her private place for solitude and praying. She particularly admires the Giotto frescoes in the south transept. After admiring the frescoes, she has the ritual of praying in one of the chapels that line the east wall of the church, lighting a candle and praying for guidance and protec-tion. She has visited the church daily since the day Niccolo stormed out of the studio two weeks ago.

The wine is making her sleepy, and her chin rests on her chest as she drifts into dreamland. In the dream, she and Alessia are back in the Tempietto on the Janiculum Hill in Roma. She is wearing the marigold chemise, and Alessia is in her painting smock. They join hands and lightly dance in a circle, their hair loose, heads thrown back in laughter. They sense a sudden breeze drifting in from the ceiling of the little temple. Ceasing their dancing, they turn to see the artist Bramante, the architect of the Tempietto. His eyes are intense, as he addresses the two women.

"Why are you afraid? Do not allow the foolish men to dwarf your talent and enthusiasm. Be strong."

Bramante's form dissipates, and Lucida and Alessia stare at each other in wonder. Alessia leaves the temple as Lucida watches her drift back down the hill. Alone in the center of the temple, Lucida dances in the marigold chemise, tears running down her cheeks.

The wine cup slips from her hand, clanking on the stone patio and startling her awake. She is still for a moment, attempting to retrieve the dream from her unconscious. *Tonight, I will sleep in the marigold chemise*, she decides.

Lucida strolls back into her home, her heart heavy and missing Niccolo. Her children are still awake, and she takes a moment to observe them from a distance as they engage in a game of chess. Antonio and Cristina have grown so fast. Cristina carries her father's expressions and gestures while Antonio resembles his mother closely. They have blossomed in Firenze and formed strong bonds with the Stratassi children, Piero and Lucia, especially Piero and Cristina who are always managing ways to be together. She saunters to the chess table and kisses the crown of each adolescent's head.

"Don't stay up too late. I am going to retire for the evening. *Ti voglio bene.*"

"We won't, just as soon as I beat Cristina." Antonio laughs. "Father came home a while ago. I think he went to his study."

Lucida makes her way to her room with her heavy heart. She determines that she will confide in Alessia tomorrow. She will relay the dream she had earlier and ask for her friend's advice on her marriage. She completes her toilet and dons the marigold chemise before snuggling under the covers. Sleep visits her quickly and deeply.

Song of sparrows stirs Lucida awake. She stretches her limbs, and her left arm lands on something firm. Turning, she sees that it is Niccolo, still sound asleep. Tears pool as she moves to snuggle against her husband. Peacefully, they lie for long moments, listening to the sparrows greet the morning.

Niccolo turns to cradle his wife, whispering in her ear, "*Mi dispiace, mi dispiace.*"

The family is gathered for their prima *colazione*, chatting as they enjoy their caffe latte, bread, butter, and jam. The strained atmosphere between Niccolo and Lucida has lifted, and everyone is lighthearted. They are interrupted by one of the servants. He brings a note to Niccolo. Everyone is at attention as Niccolo opens the letter. He reads and then looks up, silent.

"What is the news, Father?" inquires Antonio.

"It is my father. He has taken ill. I must return to Roma imme-diately before he passes. Lucida, I think you should stay behind to be with the children. Alessia and Pietro can help you with anything and keep you company. I was afraid that my father would not live long after he became ill. I will go to Martina, and we will arrange to leave at once. Lucida, please have the maid pack some clothing for me. Martina can arrange a carriage for us."

The family gathers close for an embrace before Niccolo departs to meet his sister. Lucida reminds the children that Ariston will be here later this morning for a session shared with Piero and Lucia. "Finish your breakfast and review your lessons to prepare. Do not disappoint Ariston. I do not want a bad report from him."

Lucida retreats to the garden, perusing the blooms and gather-ing some herbs for the cook as she digests the events of the morning. It is unfortunate that Niccolo has to depart so abruptly after he has returned to the marital bedchamber. *Well, the reunion will be all the sweeter when he returns*, she muses.

Signora Bianchi holds Niccolo and Martina close as soon as they dismount the carriage.

"Thank goodness you have arrived. I was so fearful that you would not be able to say goodbye to your papa. Come, he is resting with the nurse. The doctor just left. There is nothing more that they can do for him."

Niccolo and Martina move to their father's bedside. They are shocked at how shriveled and pale he looks, dwarfed by the bedding. Signor lifts his frail arm in greeting, reaching for Martina's hand.

"You must take care of your mother, my dears. I have every-thing arranged with the solicitors, and I trust you two will manage the business well. Trust no one but each other. Martina, I leave all my business ledgers to you. Please share and educate your brother. Niccolo, I want you to have the special painting that is in my study. The one I purchased from Signor Ruel at the business meeting so many years age. Now that you have your own study, the beauty is yours to enjoy. Pass it to your son, as I have passed it to you."

Signor Bianchi closes his eyes and appears to drift asleep. Signora signals her children to leave the room with her. They gather outside the door, crying as they embrace.

They spend the day comforting one another and reminiscing about Signor Bianchi, his words and deeds. As the day comes to an end, Niccolo and Martina retire to their father's study. They note that Signor Bianchi has stacked his business ledgers in impressive piles on his desk along with notes indicating the solicitor they should deal with after his demise. Lighting candles and settling in, they both focus on the painting. The beauty in the marigold chemise is beckoning to them. Martina had never seen the painting.

She studies it for a long time. Turning to her brother, she inquires, "What a beautiful and powerful painting. Doesn't the model look familiar to you? Do you know who the artist is?"

Niccolo sighs deeply as he debates confiding in his sister. Reflecting on how much he trusts and admires her and given his own need to unburden himself, he decides to confide in her.

"Martina, you are right. The model looks familiar because she is familiar. It is our Lucida. She modeled for Alessia, the daughter of Orazio Salvatori, the painter on Via Margutta in Roma. Alessia completed five paintings of Lucida in the marigold chemise, and her father colluded with the art dealer Signor Ruel to sell them at father's business meeting. When it became apparent that the artist and the model could be revealed, Signor Salvatori arranged a hasty marriage for his daughter to Pietro Stratassi and packed her off to Firenze. In a twist of fate, the villa you found for my family is the one inhabited by Alessia and Pietro. The two friends were ecstatic to be united, and our two families have become very close. Then one day, Pietro and I returned earlier than usual and decided to surprise Alessia in her studio and see her new paintings. Imagine our shock when we see new large paintings of Lucida in the marigold chemise lined against the studio wall. We both lost our tempers and stormed out. I would not speak to Lucida for weeks, and I only just apologized to her, and we reunited the evening before we received the news about Father."

"I see," Martina replies, keeping her expression carefully neutral. "You must mend any unpleasantness with Lucida. She is a good wife and mother, and we need to keep our family strong, especially with Father leaving us."

Niccolo finds himself feeling lighter now that he has shared his secret with his sister. He takes her hand, squeezing gently. "Thank you, dear sister. You are always so wise. Let us bid a good night to mother. I am weary from our journey, as you must be as well."

Dawn breaks over the Borghese and begins to pool lemon light through the open window in Martina's childhood bedchamber. She pulls a shawl around her shoulders and pushes the window wide open. Breathing in the fresh dawn air and savoring the familiar vista of cypress along the Borghese hills, she notes that an idea is beginning to form. *When I return to Firenze, I will flesh out this idea and most likely take the necessary steps to bring it to fruition*, she confides to herself.

There is a commotion in the hallway, so Martina opens her door to investigate. Her mother and Niccolo are approaching, advising her to hurry to father's bedchamber. The doctor has indicated that the time is now near for Father. The priest has been summoned and will arrive momentarily. They gather round Signor Bianchi and see that he has the shallow breath of a being near the end of his earthly chapter. He has turned inward, and it is apparent that he is not aware of his loved ones surrounding him. The priest arrives just in time to perform the prayers and last rites for Signor Bianchi as he slips peacefully into the world of the soul.

The following days are a blur of arrangements for the funeral, the visiting of family, friends, and business associates. They meet with the solicitor to go over the arrangements for Signora Bianchi and her offspring. Niccolo and Martina attempt to persuade their mother to close the villa and return to Firenze with them as they worry about her being alone. However, she is firm. No, she will stay in her home. Her health remains good, and she has many friends.

Perhaps her sister and brother-in-law from Sienna will come to join her in Roma for a time. The siblings note that their mother has no interest in their father's study or its contents. That has always been her husband's domain, and she requests that they arrange to move everything in the study to Firenze as a reminder of their father in their own homes. She will turn the study into an extra drawing room to meet with her friends, perhaps a perfect room to have intimate discussions of current culture, a kind of salon.

The Bianchi business in Roma will be run by Signor Bianchi's second-in-command, and Niccolo and Martina will take turns traveling from Firenze to oversee the operations. They are mindful of their father's instructions to trust no one but each other.

Martina makes arrangements for their departure in a week's time. The contents of their father's study and especially the painting of Lucida by Alessia Salvatori need to be packed for transport. Niccolo and Martina spend much of each day at the Bianchi headquarters, instructing the staff and ascertaining that no funds can be spent or transferred without the approval of both of them. Signor Bianchi would be proud of his offspring.

They bid farewell to their mother, promising to return in three months to check on her and the business. She assures them that she will be fine, and perhaps in the spring, she will journey to Firenze to see her grandchildren.

Boisterous greetings meet Niccolo and Martina when they arrive at the villa. Lucida, Alessia, Pietro, and the children gather round, insisting that Martina stay for a celebration that evening. The footmen begin unloading the carriages with the luggage, furniture, and painting from Signor Bianchi's study. Niccolo directs the men to take the painting directly into his study. They can sort through the furniture later.

Lucida and Niccolo are delighted to be reunited, and he takes her by the hand and leads her into his study, closing the door for some privacy. They enjoy a long and loving embrace, relieved to be at peace with one another. Niccolo removes the packing material from the painting, placing it in the light of the window so that he can admire it. Lucida is so moved that she is unable to speak, tears trailing down her cheeks.

The star of the show for the celebration dinner is *coniglio brasato* (braised rabbit). It is accompanied by a multitude of vegetables and panna cotta with berries to finish. Pietro has provided wine from his favorite *buchette del vino*. The Stratassis and the Bianchis eat heartily, laughing freely, everyone enjoying the evening and the reuniting.

Pietro and Niccolo decide to go for a stroll when the children are sent off to bed, leaving the women alone.

Martina addresses Alessia, "My dear, I did not know that you are such a talented artist. The painting that Niccolo inherited from our father is stunning and to think that our Lucida is the subject is such a surprise. You have such a talent."

Alessia glances nervously at Lucida, trying to decide how to respond and deny that the model is Lucida.

"Alessia, it is all right. Niccolo has confided in Martina. She is aware of the story of the paintings," Lucida reassures her friend.

Martina turns to Alessia. "I am an art patron, and I would love to see your work. Shall we wander over to your studio and have a look?"

Alessia demurs, "The light is poor in the evening. We don't have enough candles to illuminate the work properly. Why don't you and Lucida visit in the morning once the children are settled and we can view all of the new work in proper light?"

They agree to a studio visit the following day and embrace as they wish each other *buonanotte*.

Dawn arouses Alessia. It is very early, but she is yearning for some time to herself to contemplate. She slips from her covers, careful not to disturb Pietro. Pulling a wool shawl around her shoulders, she steps delicately out the door and makes her way to her studio. She rests on the divan that holds Lucida's poses and indulges herself, watching the light of day emerge. Settling in, she is hypnotized by the beauty of the dawn light. Soon she has dozed off.

In the dream, she is back at the Tempietto with Lucida. Again, they are dancing freely. It is dawn, and they are entranced by the golden hues caressing the city below. They are startled by a figure approaching them. It is a woman in a crimson robe, a crown with a mantle reaching to her hem. She is carrying a large coin with a pentacle engraved on it.

As she approaches, she begins to speak. "I am the Queen of Pentacles. I bring you support in your earthly desires, and I warn you of manipulation by someone close to you."

A bird lands on the windowsill, merrily greeting the morning with his song. Alessia startles herself awake, struggling to recall her dream. The studio is filling with light, and she moves to contemplate the paintings she has completed. The portraits of Lucida are strong. She thinks perhaps even better than the first series. She so desires to be recognized for her work, but she is not sure how to approach making herself known. With a deep sign of resignation, she walks back to her villa, entering through the kitchen, and greets the cook who sweetly gives her a cup of coffee and warm milk. She decides to return to her bedchamber and wish her husband *buongiorno*.

Once the children are settled with Ariston and the Bianchi children for their lessons, Alessia goes back to her studio to await Lucida and Martina. She is surprised that the two women are already at the door of the studio, waiting for her.

"*Buona giornata, buona giornata,*" they greet her warmly.

Alessia unlocks the door and invites them to enter. The light has flooded the room, highlighting the finished paintings lined against the wall. Lucida cannot help but catch her breath, even though she has seen them many times. Martina studies the work, standing for long minutes in front of each painting. Finally, she turns and faces Alessia and Lucida.

"What do you intend to do with this work?" she inquires.

Alessia sighs, replying, "I don't know, Martina. I believe the work is strong, and I want recognition besides the work for the church, but because I am a woman, I don't know if it is possible. Look what happened in Roma, when I had to be packed off to Firenze by my father. Look what happened when our husbands discovered these new paintings. Also, we need to think of Lucida's reputation."

Martina addresses the two women as she is thinking to herself that she is certainly glad that she is a businesswoman who does not cower in the face of obstacles. She knows how to take charge of a situation.

"You may not know this, but I am an art collector and not of religious works, I can assure you. I will buy all of these paintings. Name your price, Alessia. And don't consult your husband. You can make this decision. Now what do you deem is a fair price?"

Alessia and Lucida exchange a glimpse. What an interesting proposal to be offered to Alessia. Lucida is silently rooting for her friend, sending her a message. *This is an opportunity for you, Alessia. Seize it.*

Alessia realizes that she has no qualms about making a decision without her husband's counsel. *Perhaps this opportunity is what I have been yearning for. I would be foolish not to take advantage. In fact, I rather like the idea of selling my work to a woman, and Martina is a smart businesswoman.*

Alessia names her price. Martina looks directly into the artist's eyes. "You are underestimating yourself. What would be the price if you were a male artist?"

Alessia is taken by surprise. She takes a few moments to digest Martina's question, thinking to herself, *Well, what would a man charge for these paintings?* She squares her shoulders, drawing herself to her full height, and names a new figure.

Martina and Lucida clap loudly. "Bravo, bravo, Alessia."

"Very well. I will send my framer around tomorrow morning to collect the paintings, and I will return this evening with your payment. Perhaps the three of us could have a toast to celebrate my acquisition. Agreed?" Martina pronounces.

In unison, Alessia and Lucida declare, *"Sì, sì la celebrazione!"* The women embrace, and Martina takes her leave.

During the return carriage ride to her villa, Martina congratulates herself. Alessia's paintings are stunning. *I am going to make a fortune selling her work. The Bianchi business has so many wealthy partners who will gladly pay top dollar for these paintings. I will override any objections from Niccolo and Lucida, even if they do find out about my plans.*

She imagines how popular her new art salons will become. She will begin with musical performances, and then things may get a little naughty as she introduces these seductive paintings. Martina is chuckling to herself as she arrives home, deciding to relax for the siesta before returning to Alessia's studio to present the payment and celebrate. There is an ornate box from her father that she will fill with the coins to award Alessia.

Following the siesta, Alessia and Lucida meet in the studio to await Martina's arrival. Alessia attempts to describe to her friend how wonderful it feels to be in control of the sale of her work without her father or husband managing everything, like with the church commissions or when her father enlisted Signor Ruel.

"My heart is full, Lucida."

"I am so thrilled for you, Alessia. You have waited so long for this recognition."

"Lucida, have you been to Martina's villa? Can you imagine my paintings there? Do you think she will invite me to see them when they are hung?"

"She has a lovely villa with vistas of the countryside and the river. I believe that she entertains her friends frequently, but Niccolo and I mostly see her at our home with the children. We don't socialize with her friends. I don't know any of them. I will suggest that we arrange for a viewing of the paintings. I am sure that she will agree."

Martina arrives at the studio accompanied by a servant who sets up a small table with glasses and prosecco wine for toasting. She presents Alessia with the guilted wooden box, heavy with coins. She explains that the box was a special gift from her father when he formally brought her into the Bianchi business as a full partner. She asks Alessia to accept the box as a gift, as a symbol to take charge of her art career.

Lucida puts her arm around her friend's shoulders, their eyes filling with tears as they allow the occasion to fill their hearts.

The three women accept a glass to toast the transaction, laughing and thoroughly enjoying themselves.

Martina instructs the framer to use a heavy baroque golden frame for her new paintings. She feels this adds to the seductive quality of the work. She is a forceful woman, and the framer agrees to have the framing completed and delivered to her villa promptly even though he will need to hire additional workers to accommodate her.

She sets about penning invitations to a select group of women for a special soiree. They are all married to wealthy businessmen but discreetly enjoy certain forbidden pleasures, as does Martina. They meet periodically under the guise of enjoying some music and discussions of current events and, of course, some naughty gossip and frolicking. Several of the women have talent with the piano and the mandolin and customarily begin the evening celebrations.

On the appointed evening, the paintings have been placed in Martina's ballroom, covered with drop cloths. Divans and low tables are arranged in groupings around the paintings. The guests arrive in twos and threes, greeting one another affectionately. Servants have placed stations of wine and plates of fruit and cheese near the divans. Once everyone is present, Martina claps for their attention.

"May our evening of pleasure begin." She indicates that the musicians begin. "Mi Manca L'amore Conte" ("I Miss Making Love to You") wafts through the ballroom, setting the mood for the evening. The women sway to the music as they begin to form twosomes, enjoying the wine and laughing softly.

"This evening, I have a special surprise for you. I have just purchased some amazing paintings that I am going to share with you. I would love your impressions, especially since a talented female artist is the painter."

There is a hushed anticipation as the women listen to Martina. They follow as she moves to the row of paintings and removes the drop cloths with a practiced flourish.

Murmurs arise from the group of women as they move closer to the work. "*Bella, bella, supremo, eccezionale,*" they exclaim.

"*Sì, sì*, these are extraordinary indeed. The model in the marigold chemise seduces us. It is powerful, would you not agree?" Martina addresses her friends.

Agreement is anonymous. "I take it you like my new acquisitions. Let's get on with the evening."

The women seem reluctant to move away from the paintings, but gradually, they move in twos and threes to the divans for their pleasures. Martina sees to it that everyone has wine before she takes her favorite lover by the hand and leads her to her bedchamber.

The candles are burning low, and it is time for the women to depart. They look longingly over their shoulders at the model seducing them in her marigold chemise as they take their leave for the evening.

Gossip travels rapidly among the group in the following days. Many of the women desire to approach Martina to convince her to sell them a painting, or in the case of her favorite lover, to ask for one as a lover's gift.

Martina is coy as she rebuffs their requests. "*Allora*, I cannot part with these beauties, but perhaps I can convince the artist to create another body of work. I could organize a salon to sell them to you, *sì*? Do I detect interest in this idea?"

One by one, the women encourage Martina to approach the artist about new work and assure her that they are willing collectors. Perfect art for their private boudoirs. Of course, her favorite lover expects one as a gift, and Martina will most likely oblige.

Martina thinks it is good fortune that she is expected the next evening at Niccollo's. The Salvatori family will be present as well, perfect for Martina to maneuver a private discussion with Alessia and Lucida. She and Niccolo have been planning for Martina to return to Roma to check on the business and their dear mother. This will be a perfect opportunity to arrange a meeting with Signor Ruel. She will bring two of her new paintings to entice the greedy dealer. Yes, her plan is beginning to take shape.

Alessia and Lucida have been inspired and encouraged by the sale of the last body of work. Alessia has been sketching Lucida in new poses, some in garden settings. They agree that the marigold chemise should remain a constant in the paintings. Lucida is still transported to another realm whenever she dons the chemise. Alessia's assistants have been busy preparing ten new canvases for her, and they are almost complete. Today she is studying her sketches in the gardens and contemplating the palette incorporating Lucida in the marigold chemise.

Lucida knocks softly on the studio's door and lets herself in. "Good morning, my friend. I see your mind is busy planning the new paintings. Will we be ready to begin later this week?"

"*Si, si.* Make sure you save plenty of time for me. I will need you to sit for me on most days." Alessia is happy to be working so hard and can't help but eagerly anticipating some long overdue recognition of her work.

"Martina's boy delivered a note to me this morning. She would like to slip away after dinner this evening for a private meeting with the two of us. I am sure Niccolo and Pietro will go off for a stroll after dinner as usual, leaving us behind. I wonder what she wants to discuss. I did not tell Niccolo about Martina's purchase. Did you tell Pietro? They have both been so busy and distracted lately. I think Niccolo is dispatching Martina back to Roma for a short time to check on business."

"No, I did not tell Pietro about the sale. I think that he is still angry about discovering the paintings, and he has been distant and never visits the studio any longer. He has probably taken on a mistress although I am not sure. Truthfully, I just want to concentrate on the new work without distractions."

The Bianchis' cook prepares a family favorite, pappardelle with rosemary portobello mushroom ragu, for the two families to enjoy. As usual, Pietro has supplied the wine, and Alessia has wrangled her cook into preparing *crocetta di caltanissetta* of *limone* and *arancia*.

Everyone looks forward to these shared meals on the terrace connecting the villas. Following everyone's enjoyment of the meal, Piero and Cristina treat their families with a mandolin duet. They have been practicing a romantic rendition to surprise everyone. It is very apparent that the duo has sweet feelings for one another, and their parents would not stand in the way of a marital union. Laughter and applause peals into the sky, serenading all within the ears' range.

Pietro and Niccolo rise to announce that they are going for their evening stroll. Martina, Alessia, and Lucida head to the studio, reminding the children to not stay up too late. The children are delighted to be left in peace with the remnants of the wine. Piero and Cristina pick up their mandolins and entertain the others.

Lucida helps Alessia to light candles, and the three women settle in. Martina sees that the new canvases are near completion and notes that Alessia has multiple sketches and studies for the new work.

"When do you estimate the new work will be ready for purchase, Alessia? I already have potential buyers ready to become collectors of your work. Are you planning to pose Lucida in the marigold chemise?" Martina inquires.

An excited glance is exchanged between the artist and the model. This is better news than they had hoped for.

"Who are these potential collectors?" asks Alessia.

"Oh, that is for me to manage, my dear. You just concentrate on your work. I will take care of everything. I must return to Roma for the business this week, but when I am back in Firenze in a month, we can review your progress, yes?" Martina has a commanding presence, and the two women nod in agreement.

"Lucida, why don't you change into the marigold chemise and pose on the divan? I feel energized, and it might be nice for Martina to watch me do a quick study. What do you think, Martina?" asks Alessia.

"Oh yes, please. That would be most amazing. Go change, Lucida." Martina is already thinking that she will ask to buy the study and present it to her favorite lover as an enticement for a pleasurable evening.

Lucida has positioned herself on the divan with the marigold chemise glowing in the candlelight and relaxes into the pleasant reverie as the marigold chemise performs its magic.

The women are so engrossed that they fail to note shadows pass by the studio window. Pietro and Niccolo are curious as they return from their stroll and notice the glow of the candles. The two men see Lucida posed dreamily in the marigold chemise, with Alessia sketching and Martina looking on. Something about his sister's expression bothers Niccolo, but he can't identify it. He motions Pietro to move away from the window, and they stroll back to join the children.

Niccolo confides in Pietro, "Please, let us not tell our wives what we have observed tonight. Lucida and I are just mending our marriage, and I also want to see if she will reveal to me what is happening. Will you agree?"

Pietro sighs deeply. "Yes, I will remain silent. Alessia and I are barely speaking. Neither of us has made a move to be conciliatory."

The men move to join the children and the music, and before long, Alessia, Lucida, and Martina stroll across the terrace as well. Martina has a roll of paper tucked under her arm.

"Martina, what have you brought from Alessia's studio?" Pietro inquires.

"Oh, it is just a sketch of the gardens, a study, and Alessia was kind enough to allow me to enjoy it. Perhaps I will see if Mother might like it when I visit her in Roma. I must hurry off now. It is getting late, and there is much to do before I leave for my journey. Niccolo, please be so kind as to let my coachman know that I am ready to leave." Martina gathers her bag and begins to make her way to the street as the coachman readies the carriage for his mistress.

Servants are scurrying to prepare for Martina's departure. Two of Alessia's paintings are secured along with her wardrobe trunks and business documents. The carriages with Martina, her maidservant, and the luggage will be accompanied by guards, as they may encounter some unsavory characters on the route to Roma.

Martina's favorite lover is pleased with the sketch of Lucida in the garden and extracts a promise to have a painting from the study for her own. Martina replays the evening of pleasure in her mind's eye as she readies herself for departure. She is sure that Signor Ruel will be pleased to see her, and she is eager to have a visit with her dear mother.

Once she has rested from the long journey, Martina installs herself in the Bianchi offices. Her coachman has loaded her business documents and the paintings into her private office. She dispatches him to Signor Ruel's gallery with a request for him to meet her that afternoon at the Bianchi office. The morning passes quickly with employee meetings and instructions that she and Niccolo intend for the business. She works through the siesta, reviewing documents and making notes for Niccolo.

Her assistant announces that Signor Ruel has arrived for their meeting. Despite himself, Signor Ruel is intimidated by Martina as she stands to greet him.

"*Buon pomeriggio*, signor. Thank you for coming to meet with me. I have brought something with me from Firenze that may interest you." Martina directs him to a wall near the windows and removes drop cloths from the paintings with a practiced flourish.

Signor Ruel cannot believe his eyes. Before him is the model in the marigold chemise. The same model from the work he sold at the businessmen's meeting. Martina's late father, Signor Bianchi, had purchased one. Do the Bianchis know the model and that Signor Galvani's daughter is the artist? He stares at Martina in wonder, lost for words.

"Well, speak up, man. What do you think of this work?" demands Martina.

"I know this work. It is from the studio of Orazio Galvani. I sold five of this artist's paintings at a business meeting organized by your father. These are new. How did you get them?"

"I purchased them. Five new paintings by this talented artist. I thought you might be interested in selling these two here in Roma. Do you think you might be able to find interested collectors?"

"Do you know who the artist is? What about the model? Do you know who she is?" Ruel asks slyly.

"Are you interested or not?" Martina demands. "The artist and model are in Firenze, and they ask to remain anonymous."

"*Si, si*, I will take them. I can have my assistant fetch them tomorrow."

"Very well, signor." Martina produces a document with her terms for the sale, giving herself a more generous amount of the proceeds than his. "Please sign here." She indicates the space for his signature. "If you sell these quickly, I may consider allowing you to sell more of the work. The artist has already begun working on new paintings."

Signor Ruel is cowed. He doesn't even try to negotiate better terms. "Of course, signora, of course." He signs the agreement. *Orazio was easier to deal with*, he thinks to himself. Nevertheless, he knows he will have no difficulty in finding collectors to purchase the paintings.

The employees have left for the evening, and Martina is alone in her office. She turns her chair to face the paintings. She is almost certain that Signor Ruel knows who the artist and the model in the marigold chemise are. He is a greedy little man with no principles, and he will be no doubt allow the scandal to spread, with no implication to her. She sighs with satisfaction, as she contemplates the power of the marigold chemise. Lucida is transformed as she poses in it. Her brother is a fortunate man, she thinks. Alessia and Lucida will serve her well.

Signor Ruel returns to his gallery and dismisses his assistant after informing him that he must go to the Bianchi offices in the morning and fetch two paintings. He locks his shop and climbs the stairs to his living quarters. He sees that his housekeeper has left him a soup and some bread and wine for his evening meal. He removes his boots and jacket and settles into his favorite armchair, the leather cushion worn from much use. He needs to think. One of the businessmen who lost out on the bidding for the paintings at the business meetings has been asking after the artist, inquiring if there was any more work available. Signor Stassi is an effeminate man who thrives on gossip. A little scandal could escalate the price of the paintings, wouldn't it?

When Signor Stassi arrives at the gallery, Signor Ruel greets him heartily, inviting him to the private office at the rear of the studio.

"You recall the special paintings that we sold at the businessmen's meeting, do you not? I seem to recall you inquiring about any additional work if it became available," Signor Ruel inquires.

Signor Stassi replies, "*Si, si*. Have you heard of any new work? The men mentioned that the artist and model are from Firenze. One of the businessmen's son told him that Niccolo Bianchi brought all of his friends to his father's villa to view the painting that Signor Bianchi purchased. There is gossip that his wife, Lucida Galvani, may be the model. After Signor Bianchi passed away, the younger Bianchis moved to Firenze. The rumor is that the artist is a woman, the daughter of the painter Signor Orazio of Via Margutta. Have you heard the gossip?"

Signor Ruel ignores the question, instead directing Signor Stassi's attention to the far wall. "I have a little surprise for you." With his trademark flourish, he allows the drop cloths to pool on the floor beneath the two paintings.

Before Signor Stassi are two paintings. He is astonished and thinks to himself, *Yes, this is the same model and artist with the marigold chemise taking center stage.* If anything, these paintings are more powerful than the original ones.

"Where did you procure these paintings?" demands Signor Stassi, as he thinks that he must have them at any cost. He will place them behind his desk in the room where he conducts business. The men will be so distracted that he can almost guarantee that the deals will end up in his favor.

"Interesting, I received summons from Signorina Martina Bianchi to come to the Bianchi offices. She and her brother Niccolo now reside in Firenze, but they return to Roma from time to time to oversee business. She indicated that the artist and the model reside in Firenze, but they wish to remain anonymous. She had purchased five of the artist's paintings, bringing two with her to Roma to sell. I told her that I have interested collectors. Are you interested?" Signor Ruel has regained his confidence now that he is no longer in Martina's presence.

Signor Stassi takes his time to respond the art dealer. He is well aware of the dealer's greed, and he has no intention of making this transaction easy for Signor Ruel.

"Well, I have been contemplating another purchase, so perhaps I should take some time to think about it," he suggests.

"Signor Stassi, I am giving you a first look at these incredible paintings. I will show them tomorrow at a special reception for selected collectors, and I can assure you that they will be purchased promptly," he fabricates.

Signor Stassi moves to collect his coat and depart the gallery, chuckling to himself.

"Wait, wait, signor. I know you have been hoping to collect work by this artist, and you are one of my prized customers. If you agree to purchase today, I will give you my special discount. What do you say?" Signor Ruel speaks with urgency. He can't help himself.

Signor Stassi turns and moves closer to the paintings. He takes several long minutes to view them, allowing himself to be seduced by the work. It is not the female in the painting that seduces him, as that is not his personal preference, but the quality of the work and the artist's use of paint and structure. In his mind's eye, he clearly sees the paintings in his office, seducing the men who come to do business with him.

"Very well, I will make the purchase. They are special paintings, and I have the perfect place for them in my villa. Arrange to have them delivered to my villa tomorrow. I will have my solicitor bring you payment after siesta today. Arrivederci, Signor Ruel." He exits the gallery with a spring in his step.

Signor Stassi returns to his villa and directs his secretary to deliver invitations to a select group of fellow businessmen to join him at the villa the following evening for dining and conversation and to direct his cook to prepare something special for six. The secretary and cook are used to his extravagances, and since they are well compensated, it is advantageous for all.

Sitting in his study, he attends to a few business matters and then moves to one of the seats a visitor would take and revels in the image of the two paintings strategically placed behind him in direct view of his visitor. The paintings will be delivered tomorrow, and he thinks it best that he does not reveal them to his guests but instead to wait for the opportunity for them to discover his new acquisition for themselves individually. Instead, he will sprinkle little references to the past business meeting where the paintings were sold, deftly alluding to the gossip about the artist and the model. He may even suggest that he had an encounter with the art dealer Signor Ruel, who indicated that he may be acquiring new work from the mysterious artist from Firenze. Perhaps another business meeting could be arranged for Signor Ruel to show the paintings if he does receive them. What would the men think about that?

Alessia and Lucida work steadily. The new paintings feature Lucida in the marigold chemise but in a garden setting instead of posed on a divan. The marigold chemise remains the star of the show, adding to the narrative and allusion to seduction in nature. Lucida is transported by the garment and can't help but drift into a dreamlike reverie of power and seduction. She is embarrassed when Alessia brings her back to attention, asking that she concentrate on posing.

Lucida has been contemplating confiding in Niccolo about the new paintings. Since they have reunited, she doesn't want to keep secrets from him. She wants their love to be strong and trustworthy. When she is posing in the marigold chemise, she feels more confident, so today she addresses Alessia with her thoughts.

"My friend, I am going to confide in Niccolo about these new paintings. I know that you are the artist, not me, but I am a part of the work as well. We don't have anything to be ashamed of. Your work is beautiful, powerful, and you deserve to be recognized. I don't really care what others think or gossip about. I believe that Niccolo will be pleased if I tell him. After all, he now has his father's painting for himself, and he loves it. He will pass it on to one of our children, and it will be part of our family story. If fact, I think that we should confide in Niccolo and Pietro together, the four of us."

Alessia pauses, paint brush aloft, and regards her friend. The two of them have matured since the days in her father's studio. She still recalls with a sharpness to her heart, her father's need to protect her from scandal and send her away, marrying her off for convenience. By a miracle, she and Lucida have been reunited, and their families are as if they are one. *Lucida is right*, she thinks. Why should she care what others think? She knows that her work is strong, just as good as any man's, even superior to many.

"I believe that you are correct, Lucida. Pietro will follow Niccolo's lead. He admires him. I too am tired of having secrets. Let's speak with our husbands. The sooner the better. Perhaps this evening?" Alessia turns her attention back to the painting.

The two families have gathered in the shared courtyard for the evening meal as usual. The children drift off to practice their music and work on their studies, leaving the four adults alone. Alessia looks directly at the two men, addressing them.

"Pietro, Niccolo. Lucida and I have something to discuss with you. Let's retire to my studio to have the conversation. Come, follow me."

The men exchange curious glances as they follow Alessia and Lucida across the courtyard and wait as the women enter, lighting the studio candles.

Although the light is dim, they are able to see that Alessia has multiple paintings in progress. They see that a woman in a marigold chemise is posing in various gardens. Moving closer, Niccolo sees that it is his wife posing in the same marigold chemise as in his father's painting purchased years back at the men's business meeting.

"Yes, Niccolo, that is me, posing for Alessia. Her work is stronger than ever, would you not agree?" Lucida addresses both her husband and Pietro.

Silence reigns for several long moments as each of them contemplates the paintings before them.

Alessia breaks the silence. "Martina has purchased five paintings from me, and she has requested more work. She is very encouraging and has paid me well. Pietro, I can contribute to the household purse. I feel that it is time for me to receive acknowledgment as an artist. I am tired of waiting."

Niccolo silently recalls seeing Martina and the two women through the studio window recently and feels the same unease as that evening although he says nothing.

Pietro speaks up. "Alessia, I have always admired your work. In fact, I am jealous that you are so talented. Our marriage has been strained lately, and that is not good or right. I will trust you to proceed, and I will not mind the added coin to the household purse." He moves to embrace his wife.

Niccolo holds his wife's eyes. "Lucida, my dear, I know that you want to continue to model for Alessia. You two started something as very young women back in Orazio's studio at great risk to your reputations. But now, I agree, it is time to celebrate Alessia's talent. I must note that when you don the marigold chemise, posing for the paintings, there is a certain power and strength that exudes from you… I can't find the exact words to describe it. Pietro and I will look forward to seeing these works when they are finished, and we will celebrate. Right, Pietro?"

"*Si, si*." Pietro nods in agreement.

Niccolo finds himself disturbed by the revelation that his sister has intruded in such a manner. She has always been the more ambitious of the siblings. He is used to that, but this time, he feels it is wrong. He vows to speak to her as soon as she returns from Roma.

Niccolo hurries home, bundling his cloak tighter in the sharp autumn evening. His business meeting ran longer than he expected. He realizes that he will have to make the journey back to Roma to accomplish his intended outcome in strengthening the ties between the Bianchi operations in Firenze and Roma. Unfortunately, Martina will now be leaving Roma just as he will be leaving Firenze. His opportunity to confront her about Alessia's paintings will have to be postponed.

Lucida is engaged with Cristina and Antonio when he arrives home. He is greeted warmly by his family and realizes that he will miss them while he is away.

"Dear ones, I am regretful, but I must leave for Roma at once. We have pressing business to attend to, and I won't be able to get a word to Martina to remain in Roma. We did agree to take turns having oversight in Roma when we moved." Niccolo plants kisses on the crown of his children's heads and steps into his study to prepare documents for his departure.

Lucida informs the servants that they need to prepare for Niccolo's journey as he will depart the day after tomorrow. She knocks softly on his study door and enters the room, noting how the painting dominates the space even in the candlelight. She can feel the power of the marigold chemise just from viewing it across the room. She moves to her husband's chair and settles herself in his lap. They are silent in the embrace, knowing that they will be apart in the coming days.

The journey is blessedly uneventful. He enjoys an evening with his dear mother who makes it clear to her son that she still intends to stay in Roma where her heart is despite him urging her to join the family in Firenze. She loves hearing stories of the children and finds it amusing that Cristina and Piero are sweet for one another.

After a long day of business meetings, Niccolo finds himself yearning for some easy companionship. He thinks of his friend Signor Stassi, who is always of good cheer. The Stassi Villa is an easy walk from the Bianchi offices. It is comforting to stroll the familiar streets and enjoy the happy chatter of families out for the *passeggiata*, and he allows nostalgia to waft over him.

Soon he sees that he has reached the Stassi Villa. The servant responds to his knock.

"*Benvenuto, benvenuto*, Signor Bianchi."

"I am in Roma to attend to business. Is Signor Stassi available?"

"*Si, si*. I will inform him that you are here." He directs Niccolo to the sitting area outside of Signor Stassi's study.

Signor Stassi greets Niccolo warmly. "*Mio amico*. What a wonderful surprise. I did not know you were in Roma. It is good to see you. Let us take some refreshment in my study, and you must stay for the evening meal."

Niccolo agrees readily, thinking that this is just what he was yearning for.

The two men enter the study, and Signor Stassi busies himself with pouring an Aperitivo Biancosarti for each of them. He settles himself behind his desk, inviting Niccolo to make himself comfortable across from him. The men salute with "*cento di questi giorni*" laughing in good cheer.

"What business brings you to Roma?" inquires Signor Stassi.

Niccolo is about to reply when he glances up at his friend and is greeted by two large paintings hanging behind Signor Stassi. He cannot speak, his mind attempting to grasp the images before him. There is his Lucida posing in a garden in the marigold chemise. Her pose is seductive, inviting the viewer to commune with her. *Where did Signor Stassi find these paintings?* he wonders.

Niccolo is finally able to compose himself. "My friend, where did you find these paintings? It looks to be the same artist and model that my father purchased years ago at a business meeting."

Signor Stassi astutely observes his friend's response. He had no idea that Niccolo would be seated across from him this evening with a full view of his newly acquired treasures.

"Do you recall the art dealer Signor Ruel? He approached me with the news that he had acquired two new works from the same artist. He promises that he will soon have more new work. You must agree that they are stunning."

"But who did Signor Ruel procure the paintings from?" demands Niccolo.

"You did not know that your sister, Martina, has acquired work from this artist from Firenze?" Signor Stassi replies. "I believe that she intends to buy all of this artist's works and sell it through Signor Ruel and perhaps other dealers in Firenze as well. Your sister is quite the businesswoman, isn't she? The model is stunning. The marigold garment seems to be made for her by the angels. What a lucky man you are, Niccolo, to be married to this beauty."

Niccolo feels anger and indignation surface from his belly in a heat wave. He does not care for the idea of other men ogling his Lucida, even though he has agreed to support Alessia's work as an artist. And Martina, he is furious with her. What is she doing? She is exploiting both Alessia and Lucida.

He stands abruptly and fairly shouts at Signor Stassi, "*Buonanotte*, signor. I will not be able to dine with you this evening." He makes his way hastily to the door, exploding on to the street. Making his way back to his mother's villa with long angry strides, he mutters over and over to himself, "How could she, how could she?"

Signor Stassi chuckles to himself. He understands why Niccolo is upset and regrets the early termination of their evening, but he can see how it will all work out in his favor. *That Martina is a wily one*, he thinks. Niccolo is certainly no match for her. *Oh well*, he thinks. Niccolo's anger is really not his problem, and the man will no doubt calm down in time. He feels hungry and goes to arrange for his dinner to be served. The businessmen will be joining him tomorrow evening, and he wants to be certain that his plan to entice them with the temptation of new paintings is well-thought-out. Maybe it is better that Niccolo is not joining him tonight. He will have more space to contemplate the nuances of his conversation.

Alessia and Lucida have had a productive session in the studio and decide to take their midday meal on the plaza between the villas. They are relaxing and chatting about the mornings work while waiting for the servant to bring their meal. Piero and Cristina approach their mothers, hand in hand and both grinning from ear to ear.

"*Madri*, may we join you?" inquires Piero.

"*Si, si*," both women respond in unison.

Cristina takes the lead. "*La mamma*, Piero and I are going to marry. We are telling you of our plans first, without our fathers, because we have made the decision, and no one is going to deter us. When Father returns from Roma, we will gather everyone and make our announcement."

The young couple scan their mothers' faces for any sign of response to their news. They hold hands tightly and lock eyes in complete devotion. Small birds flitting in the shrubbery break the silence.

Finally, Lucida speaks, "Piero, I will enjoy having you as my son-in-law. I am delighted by your news."

Alessia finds that her eyes are spilling over, and she moves to Cristina for an embrace.

"However, Piero and Cristina, you both must honor your fathers. When Niccolo returns, we will gather as we often do, and the two of you will ask for your fathers' blessings. Alessia and I will not acknowledge that you told us your news first. Agreed, Alessia?" Lucida is firm.

Privately, she is proud of the two, but she is also traditional and feels that Piero should approach Niccolo to ask for Cristina's hand in marriage.

Alessia directs her attention to her son. "Piero, you must follow the tradition. Your father will insist on it. You don't want to have the beginning of your future marriage marred by a quarrel with him."

The young couple assure their mothers that they will abide by the traditions. They are so excited and happy that it doesn't matter. They move off to the far end of the garden for some privacy, love surrounding them in an envelope for two.

"Lucida, I never imagined in my wildest dreams that our families would be bound together in marriage. Now we will be intertwined for eternity, and with grandchildren, the line of connection will be even stronger." Alessia struggles to keep from being overwhelmed with emotion.

"Yes, my friend, the gods have conspired to bring us comfort and cemented our friendship. I don't foresee any objections from Pietro and Niccolo," agreed Lucida.

Martina bustles into Alessia's studio unannounced. The new group of paintings are completed, and Alessia is consulting with her carpenter on building new canvas. Startled, she greets Martina with an edge, as she is annoyed at the unexpected and presumptuous entrance.

"I have arranged for my man to transport the new paintings to the framers today and have brought your payment as well." The satchel of coins land with an impressive thud on Alessia's desk. "You better get to work on more paintings. I assure you, they are in demand."

Now Alessia is quite annoyed. Yes, she did agree that Martina could purchase the finished paintings, but no further agreement was made. She finds a stream of dislike emerging from her heart and treats Martina to a stony silence as she returns to her consultation with her carpenter.

"My man will be here shortly and will help you prepare the paintings for transport." Martina ignores the stony silence and marches out the studio's door.

Alone in the studio after the carpenter leaves, Alessia stretches herself on the divan that Lucida has spent hours modeling for her in the marigold chemise. She studies the new work soon to be taken from her studio. The thought arises that perhaps her work will pivot in a new direction. She senses that Martina is taking advantage of her, and she doesn't like the idea of not knowing who is buying her paintings. Where will they end up? Perhaps the marigold chemise series with Lucida has reached a conclusion. The longer she contemplates, the more certain she is that she will not allow Martina to dominate her or have control over the sales of her work. She will have a heartful conversation with Lucida, knowing that her dear friend will support her even if Martina is her sister-in-law.

Signor Ruel instructs his assistant to prepare the new shipment of paintings for viewing in the back room of his gallery. Martina Bianchi has indeed kept her word, and the new paintings featuring the model in the marigold chemise arrived as promised. He shoos the boy in annoyance as he is eager to contemplate the new work in private. Orazio's daughter has displayed her considerable talent with even more force than the past work, he decides. Yes, the presentation with Signor Stassi and his colleagues will be quite successful indeed.

The following morning, Signor Stassi is fetched by Signor Ruel's assistant to come immediately to the gallery. Signor Ruel greets him magnanimously and changes the shop's sign to *chiuso* so that they will not be disturbed. He ushers Signor Stassi into the back room of the gallery and presents the new paintings with a flourish.

"Oh, *si, si*, my man," Signor Ruel declares as he imagines the relish with which the paintings will be purchased.

The two men decide that the best venue for presenting the work would be at the businessmen's meeting the following week. Signor Ruel proposes that they instigate a bidding system, such as they did before, as that will bring them the best price. They depart with a handshake in agreement. Signor Stassi will be in charge of introducing the work following the dinner.

On the appointed evening of the businessmen's meeting and dinner, the servants are rushing around setting tables as Signor Ruel and his assistants store the paintings safely in a side room away from prying eyes. They decide to wait at the edge of the dining room to prevent anyone from accidently discovering the work.

Soon the men begin to arrive. Conversation is jolly as they share gossip and news of business and politics. Niccolo relishes greeting his friends and associates, as he has missed them, being in Firenze for much of the time. He makes a point of avoiding Signor Stassi after their uncomfortable encounter.

This evening, the chef has prepared a boar along with fried calamari served with lemon slices. Also, there are savory herb and vegetable tortes. For sweets, there are marzipan tarts and candied fruits.

As the men are finishing their meal and enjoying the last of the wine, Signor Stassi taps his wineglass to signal silence for his announcement.

"*Gentiluomini*, for our entertainment this evening, I am pleased to present new paintings from the esteemed anonymous artist from

Firenze. You recall what an exciting evening we enjoyed when we had a glorious bidding war over the last group of paintings. Signor Ruel, please bring the new paintings out. At the front of room is perfect for viewing."

The room is abuzz with anticipation as Signor Ruel and his assistant bring out the paintings covered in their drop cloths and line them up. With his signature flourish, Signor Ruel allows the cloths to pool at the foot of each piece. As with the original work, these paintings feature the seductive model in the marigold chemise. They are set in garden scenes instead of a studio, making them all the more enticing.

Niccolo's mind is spinning. How did Signor Ruel come in possession of these paintings? He sees his Lucida posing seductively in the marigold chemise, there in full view of the men ogling his wife. He glances across the room at Signor Stassi, who briefly catches his eye, giving him a pleasant nod. He is seething with anger as he listens to the proceedings. He notices that several of the men are glancing his way knowingly and then whispering to one another. Signor Ruel is taking bids on each of the paintings one by one. In a short while, the paintings are all sold, and Signor Ruel is making arrangements for payment and delivery.

The men prepare to leave the meeting, and the servants begin to clear the tables and clean the room. Niccolo exits the building and waits at the side of the entrance for Signor Stassi.

"Signor, we must have a word." Niccolo steps in front of Stassi, blocking his way.

"As you wish, Signor Bianchi. Let us adjourn to the café across the street. Follow me," replies Signor Stassi.

The two men find a table in the far corner of the café and order a *digestivo of amari*. Niccolo finds himself becoming increasingly upset and struggles to maintain his composure.

"How did Signor Ruel procure those paintings? Are you working with him? I cannot abide ruining the reputation of my dear wife. Do any of the men know the model in the paintings is my Lucida? And if so, how do they know?" Niccolo demands.

"*Alora, alora*, Niccolo. Did you not know that your sister, Martina, has been supplying Signor Ruel with paintings? You know

Signor Ruel is greedy and wily. I would not be surprised if he has gossiped about Lucida modeling for the paintings. The word may be out as titillating gossip, I'm afraid. You have to admit that it serves to drive up the price of the paintings. Martina and Signor Ruel stand to make a tidy profit off the work of Orazio Salvatori's daughter," instructs Signor Stassi.

"No, I did not know that Martina is working with Signor Ruel. Why would she do that and take advantage of her sister-in-law? Has she no shame?" Niccolo is appalled.

"You don't know your sister very well, do you, Niccolo? You know she is enjoying lovers of the female persuasion, don't you? It is common knowledge that she hosts evenings of entertainment and pleasure. I am sure that the paintings of Lucida, so seductive in the marigold chemise, are of great interest to her. She is quite the businesswoman, so why not make some money as well as have enjoyment of the paintings? You must agree that Orazio Salvatori's daughter is a great talent. If she were a man, she would be famous." Signor Stassi is enjoying himself.

Niccolo slams his glass on the table, his chair crashing on the floor as he stands, and storms out of the café, muttering obscenities to himself.

The following morning finds Niccolo in the Bianchi offices preparing for the meetings of the day. He approaches the room where five men are waiting his arrival to discuss a loan for a new venture. The door is ajar, and he catches snippets of the conversation and laughter the group is enjoying. He hears the name of his wife and words such as seduction, temptation, corruption, and not reputable. He clears his throat loudly to announce his arrival and the conversation ceases abruptly.

"*Gentiluomini, buona giornata.* Shall we proceed with our negotiations?" Niccolo has no intention of discussing the paintings, but now he is certain that the gossip is spreading. He will have much to say when he returns to Firenze to confront his sister.

Meanwhile, Pietro Stratassi summons his son Piero to his study. He greets his son warmly and directs him to the chair across his massive desk. Piero is unprepared for what his father will propose, as his father often summons him to the study for a good-natured chat.

Pietro leans forward, resting his elbows on his desk and temples his fingertips as he addresses his son. "My boy, your uncle has approached me with an interesting proposition. He has a childhood friend who has moved to America and is starting a business importing fine fabrics. He predicts that the business will thrive, but he doesn't have enough good men to work for him. You remember that his sons were killed in a horrible carriage accident, and his daughters are still too young and not interested in working. He would like to make a proposal to you to join him in America, and in exchange, he will grant you a portion of the business after one year of working for him. I think that you should consider it. You are still young, and it could be a great opportunity for you. If it doesn't work out after one year, you can always return to Firenze and work for me."

Piero is stunned. He doesn't know what to think. He likes the idea of an adventure, but what about Cristina and their engagement? Should he confide in his father before Niccolo returns?

"Father, this is a surprise. This is not something I would ever have dreamed of. I will speak to uncle's friend to get more details. The idea of an adventure is exciting to me. However, I must share a secret with you. You must keep it a secret until after Niccolo returns from Roma. I have proposed marriage to Cristina, and she has accepted. I want to be proper and ask Niccolo for her hand in marriage, but you must know that the two of us have made up our minds to get married regardless of what anyone thinks." Piero is firm in his delivery.

Pietro's wide face breaks into a huge smile and a chuckle. "Bravo, bravo! This is a good match. I am sure Niccolo will be pleased as well. Your mother and Lucida will be eager to join our families. Well, of course, why not marry and bring Cristina along to America? You two could have an adventure, and if it you are not happy in the new land, you can return home and begin the life you expected. Do you think Cristina will resist?"

"Father, I do not know how Cristina will react to this news and a new possibility for our future. I will not go if she refuses to come with me. I do not want to live without her. There will never be anyone else for me. I will discuss this with her, and if she is agreeable, I will go directly to uncle and direct him to arrange for me to meet his friend." Piero finds that he is becoming excited by the idea of traveling to America and hopes that his bride-to-be will be agreeable to this unexpected news.

Piero gallops across the terrace to the Bianchi villa. He stops in front of the window to Cristina's bedchamber and shouts, "Cristina, Cristina! Come out to meet with me. Hurry, it is very important."

Cristina has been perusing her wardrobe. She will be making a list of items to complete her trousseau and wants to consult with her mother. She isn't worried about obtaining her father's permission to marry Piero as she is sure he will agree. But if not, they have agreed to marry regardless. Briefly, she wonders if her mother ever felt rebellious. Her reverie is interrupted by Piero's shouting, and she rushes to her window to see what the commotion is about. There is Piero, hopping up and down in a little jig, calling up to her to hurry down to meet him. She grabs a shawl to wrap around her shoulders and hurries down the stairs and out the door to meet her betrothed.

Piero clasps her hand and leads her out of the villa grounds and to the Lungarno Benvenuto Cellini along the Arno River. They have a favorite alcove that they often go to for some privacy and to enjoy the view of the river and the bustle of commerce at a distance. Upon reaching the alcove, Pietro pulls her close for a sweet kiss.

"My love, I have some important news. We have a big decision to consider for our future. This morning, my father summoned me to his office. My uncle approached him with a proposal for me. Uncle has a friend who is building a business in America. They are importing fine fabrics. He has requested that I join him in America and will offer me a portion of the business after one year of work. It would be a big adventure, an exciting turn of events. What do you think? You know I will not go without you, so I think that we should decide together. Is this what we want for our future? Father points out that if it does not work out, we can always return." Piero holds

Cristina's hands in his and waits patiently for her reply, giving her time to consider his words.

Cristina is not certain what to think. Here she is contemplating mundane decisions about her trousseau just moments ago, and now she is presented with something she never dreamed about, and Piero expects her to make a decision.

After several long moments, Cristina replies, "Piero, go with your father and uncle to meet with his friend. Question him about the details of his business. Determine what the remuneration will be and if he is willing to sign a contract stating that he will offer you a portion of the business after one year. The details must all be in writing. Then if after the meeting, you are assured that he is an honorable man and he is willing to have everything in writing and reviewed by your father's solicitor, I will agree to accompany you if you want to pursue this adventure for our future."

Piero is a bit surprised by Cristina's answer. He didn't expect her to be so precise. But then, he thinks, her father has been in business and the grandfather before, so, of course, she has heard them discuss business all her life. As he reflects, he realizes that he has made a good choice in asking Cristina to be his wife.

"Very well. You are my wise one, Cristina. I will ask Father to arrange for his solicitor to join us for the meeting." He embraces her gratefully and leads her back to the villa.

The day has arrived for Niccolo to begin his journey back to Firenze. His business has been concluded, and he is satisfied that the Bianchi firm is doing well. His mother is sad that her life is now without her husband, but she keeps busy with her friendships and volunteer duties for the church. She remains firm that she does not want to join her children in Firenze. Roma is her home. He hopes that the gossip spreading about Lucida and the paintings does not reach her. She would be livid if she found out that Martina is working with the art dealer Signor Ruel.

The carriage bumps along over the rut-riddled roads. Thankfully, he shares the carriage alone with his manservant who is trained to be silent unless addressed. He needs this time to brew upon his upcoming confrontation with Martina. Finally, his anger exhausts him, and he drifts off to sleep, his chin bouncing rhythmically off his chest.

The dream engulfs him. His Lucida is in a small temple on the top of a hill. She is dancing in the moonlight in the marigold chemise. He sees that a pair of angels carries Alessia, her paint brushes clutched in her right hand, and gently sets her on the ground in front of Lucida. The two women perform a joyful dance together, the marigold chemise billowing with Lucida's gestures. He is alarmed to see a dark cloud forming above the temple. The wind suddenly becomes harsh, and a heavy rain ensues. He sees that the women are shivering now as they cling to one another for warmth. Expressions of fear form on their faces as a black chariot crashes into the temple, threatening to topple it. A woman dressed entirely in black robes descends from the chariot and approaches the two women. She brandishes a large horse whip and proceeds to beat on Lucida and Alessia as they join hands and flee out of the temple and race down the hill. The woman turns, and in his dream, Niccolo sees that the woman is Martina. Her expression is pure evil and chills him to the bone. The carriage stops abruptly as they reach the destination for the evening. It jars Niccolo from his sleep, but the dream has formed a layer within.

Niccolo's carriage arrives at his villa in Firenze. Finally. It is good to be home. He cannot wait to embrace his wife and children. Pooches bark in chorus to announce his arrival, and Niccolo descends from his carriage and into the arms and greetings of Lucida, Cristina, and Antonio. Everyone is speaking at once, asking questions and welcoming him home.

Lucida has arranged for an evening with the Stratassi family. She and Alessia want Piero to ask for Cristina's hand in marriage tonight as they can no longer contain themselves to keep their secret. Everyone begins to gather in the Bianchi drawing room awaiting the dinner announcement. Piero asks Niccolo if he may have a word with him in Niccolo's study.

"Of course, Piero, of course. Let us adjourn to my study," invites Niccolo.

Piero throws Cristina a knowing glance and follows his future father-in-law into the study. Piero has never been in Niccolo's study, and he is invited to be seated across from Niccolo. He notices a large painting as he seats himself. He tries not to stare as he sees that the painting is of a woman in a marigold chemise seated on a bed and looking to invite the viewer to join her. He feels embarrassed and forces himself to address Niccolo.

He begins formally. "Signor Bianchi, I am honored and humbled to make an important inquiry. As you know, your daughter Cristina and I have known each other for some time now, and we have grown fond of each other. We have formed a solid friendship that has grown into love. I am respectfully asking for Cristina's hand in marriage."

Niccolo releases a hearty laugh. This is by far the best news he has heard in days. He knows that Piero is a good young man, and, of course, everyone is aware that he and Cristina have been sweet for each other for years. He also knows that Piero can work for his father and that Cristina will be treated well and provided for appropriately.

Niccolo rises and gives Piero a warm embrace. "*Si, si*, my son. You and Cristina have my blessing. Let us go share with the others. We will celebrate this evening."

"*Fare un annuncio!*" shouts Niccolo, clapping his hands sharply. "Piero has an announcement for us."

Piero moves to Cristina's side and tenderly embraces her. "Yes, we have news to share. Cristina and I have Niccolo's blessing to wed. We will be joining our two families, which is only proper."

The young couple are beaming. A pair of doves celebrates the moment from the persimmon tree. Their song is sweet.

"Bravo, bravo!" cries ring out from the family. Lucida and Alessia embrace, tears of joy trickling down their cheeks.

The cook indicates that the evening meal is ready to be served. Joyful murmurs accompany the group as they make their way to the table. Tonight, they are dining on *macceroni* and a salad of tomato and basil along with a hearty bread and fruits and cheese to finish.

As usual, Pietro has supplied the wine. He generally indulges, which only exaggerates his fondness of hearing his own voice.

He stands and proposes a toast to the Piero and Cristina. "*Congratullazioni, congratullazioni i miei figli*. May your union be happy and fruitful. You will soon be off on your new adventure to America. May it be prosperous."

Puzzled glances are exchanged.

"America? What does that mean?" Niccolo speaks up.

"Pietro, what do you mean America? Have you had too much wine?"

"Yes, yes. What did you mean?" Lucida, Alessia, Lucia, and Antonio are chiming in.

Piero and Cristina treat Pietro to an angry look. How could Pietro be so careless? There has been no formal decision made, and the meeting with his uncle's friend has not yet taken place.

Pietro pours himself another glass of wine and takes his seat rather sheepishly. Piero takes charge.

"Everyone, my father is being premature. My uncle has a friend who has proposed a possible business venture in America. I do not have all of the details, but I will be meeting with him soon. Cristina and I have discussed the possibility and agreed that we will make the decision together based on the outcome of the meeting. It would mean moving to America for at least a year. We promise to keep you informed."

Cristina nods in agreement indicating that she confirms Piero's words.

Lucida finds that she wants to speak to her daughter in private. This is so much news in one evening, and Niccolo has just returned home. She sees that everyone has finished enjoying the meal, and normally, they may enjoy some music together, but she decides that she will cut the evening short.

"Everyone, my dears, I propose that we retire for the evening. Niccolo has just returned from his journey, and we all need time to enjoy the happy news of Piero and Cristina's coming marriage. I find that I am a bit tired from all of the excitement. Please excuse us. We will have plenty of time to talk tomorrow. *Buonanotte*."

Parting embraces and kisses ensue. The Stratassi family strolls back to their villa, leaving the Bianchi family to themselves.

Lucida takes Cristina's hand. "This is a very special moment. I must impart a mother's wisdom to her daughter. We will rejoin you shortly," she informs her family.

The mother and daughter move to Lucida's bedchamber. Lucida directs her daughter to a chair by the window, and Cristina watches curiously as Lucida goes to her wardrobe and rummages among the contents. She locates the item she is seeking and approaches her daughter with a muslin parcel tied with a golden ribbon.

"Open it, my dear," Lucida requests as she places the parcel on her daughter's lap. "I want you to cherish this gift. It is very special to me, but now it is your turn to own it until you pass it to the next generation."

Cristina carefully releases the ribbon, and the muslin falls to the sides. She lifts the garment up in front of her, admiring the marigold chemise.

"Oh, Mother, it is lovely. I will cherish it always. But where did you get the chemise? Why is it so special to you?" Cristina rises, holding the marigold chemise in front of her as she stands in front of the wardrobe mirror, turning to admire her image.

Lucida puts her arm around her daughter's waist as the two of them are reflected in the wardrobe mirror. They are the same size, and their features are almost identical. Lucida's heart is full as she admires her daughter.

"I was just your age when I first came upon the chemise. My dear friend Alessia was working with her father in his studio. He is the well-known painter Signor Orazio. Alessia wanted to start working on paintings of her own instead of just assisting her father with his church commissions. However, she had to be discreet because she is a woman. She implored me to model for her, and I couldn't resist her plea for help.

"The marigold chemise was a garment that one of Signor Orazio's clients gave him. Alessia suggested that I model in it for her series of paintings. She felt that the marigold color would be powerful in her compositions. I must tell you that when I first modeled for

Alessia in the marigold chemise, it took hold of me. I cannot fully explain it, but it was a powerful force. I felt very alive and almost invincible when I was wearing it.

"Alessia initially completed five stunning paintings of me in the marigold chemise. They are powerful and seductive. It was an exciting time. I would sneak out of my villa and make my way to the studio to work with her and then sneak back home. I confess that I so loved the marigold chemise that at one point, I actually stole it from Alessia. Eventually, she gave it to me. Signor Orazio arranged for an art dealer, Signor Ruel, to sell the paintings. They were sold to businessmen, one being your grandfather. Signor Orazio was fearful of a scandal, and he arranged for Alessia to marry Pietro and sent her off to Firenze. There are more paintings now as Alessia and I have continued to work together. But we have decided I will no longer pose for her in the marigold chemise. The time has come for Alessia to take a different direction.

"I want you to have the marigold chemise. It is powerful, and you will see that when you are wearing it, the garment will bring you strength and confidence. Please treasure it and pass it along when you are older. Perhaps you will be blessed with a daughter to be the next keeper of the marigold chemise. The next time we have the house to ourselves, we will go into your father's study, and you will see the painting of me in the marigold chemise. This is the painting that your grandfather purchased from Signor Ruel." Lucida sighs as she concludes her explanation.

Signor Stratassi, Piero, Uncle, and their solicitor are greeted heartily by his friend, the businessman. Introductions are made, and the men begin to settle themselves in Signor Reda's office. There are swatches of fabric everywhere, piled high. Signor Reda's assistant scurries to make room on the chairs for the men.

Signor Reda directs his attention to Piero. "Young man, your uncle tells me that you are an ambitious and hardworking lad and that you may be ready for a new adventure. I also understand that you are now betrothed to Signor Bianchi's daughter. Congratulations. The Bianchis are a fine family. What do you know about our business, our fine fabric?"

Piero is taking measure of Signor Reda. He recalls his conversation with Cristina. He had made some inquiries about the Reda's business. He knows that the mill is in Valle Mosso and that their specialty is exceptionally fine wool.

"Sir, I understand that you specialize in very fine wool fabric. Your fabric is very sought after. Why are you starting an operation in America? It is a new country. There must be risks in managing a business so far from home. I know little about fine fabric, but I have worked with my father in his business."

"My father always taught be to be bold, to take risks that other men fear to. I have just returned from America. My top assistants accompanied me. We found that New York City is growing and bustling. There are reasonable arrangements for office and production spaces to be made. My accountant has worked the numbers for us, and he feels it is a viable opportunity and will be a good investment for the future. We signed a lease agreement for a large space to receive our fabrics. I plan to manufacture garments on the site and sell them to merchandisers. The venture is just beginning, and I need someone on the site to manage it along with several assistants. I need a hardworking, honest man to bring this venture to full fruition," Signor clearly states his intention.

"What are you thinking of for terms of compensation for this hardworking person?" inquires Piero.

"I will offer a salary large enough to cover living expenses for a man and his family. Of course, transportation to America would be paid by the company. For an incentive, if the man has worked hard and we can see progress made in the business, I will offer a percentage of profits and percentage ownership of the enterprise after one year. If the work is not mutually agreeable, the man can then leave and return home if he desires. He would have to cover the cost of that journey himself," Signor Reda explains.

Piero and Signor Reda maintain steady eye contact. Pietro and Uncle sit quietly, studying the two men. They exchange a quick glance and subtly affirmative nod. They are proud of Piero and can see that he is blossoming as a young man. It is his son's decision to make, and for once, Pietro vows that he will not bombard his son with lectures and advice. Alessia would be proud of him, he decides.

"Your offer is intriguing and fair, Signor Reda. I am honored to be considered for the position. I am not an expert on fabrics, but I am willing to learn and to work hard for you. I would like to consult with my family and my betrothed. I will give you an answer tomorrow, if that is acceptable to you, sir," Piero declares as he nods, indicating the solicitor should speak.

The solicitor informs Signor Reda that the contract must be in writing.

"*Si, si.* Come to my office tomorrow, and bring your betrothed and her father, Signor Bianchi. I have not seen him for a long time, and I am always interested in speaking to potential investors in my company. I will have a contract ready for signatures."

Piero, Pietro, Uncle, and the solicitor depart Signor Reda's office. Uncle and the solicitor take their leave, and the father and son stroll back to their villa, taking advantage of the warm spring sunshine.

"My son, it looks like you will be off to America with your bride. It seems that I was not premature in my announcement after all." Pietro chuckles.

"I must admit that I have made up my mind to take this opportunity and do my best to be successful. However, I won't leave Cristina behind. She is smart and brave, and I am fairly certain she will agree. I very much hope so. She will be pleased that Signor Reda invited her and her father to meet with us. That will give her more confidence to proceed," Piero confides in his father.

Part III

The newlywed couple are deposited on the dock in Genoa, their luggage forming a small fortress around them. They can't stop grinning at each other in a wave of excitement and anticipation. Although they are sad to leave their families behind, they are confident in their decision to embark on this adventure to America. The port is packed with men and women and a few children. It is loud and unruly, a real stewpot. An official begins to shout names from a list, directing passengers to line up on the dock. When Piero and Cristina hear him shout "Stratassi, Piero," they direct the young boy assisting them to help gather their luggage and move toward the line.

Cristina holds her carpet bag close, a protective arm around the red and gold tapestry. She has carefully wrapped the marigold chemise in an extra layer of muslin to protect it on the journey. She vows to guard it carefully. Right now, she regards it as her most precious possession. The day following the meeting with her mother and receiving the marigold chemise as a special gift, the two women made a discreet visit to her father's study to view the painting. There she had stood next to her mother in awe as she felt the presence of seduction in her mother's pose in the marigold chemise. She had no words for what she experienced but had held her mother's hand in silence. Later that evening when she was alone in her bedchamber, she slipped the chemise over her head, letting it fall along the curves of her young body. She stood in front of her mirror for a long time, staring at her image and feeling the powerful sensations the marigold chemise transferred to her soul. Carefully she removed the garment and folded it, reverently wrapping it back in the muslin. She hid it in the back of her wardrobe and snuggled under her covers for a deep sleep.

Once the young couple are settled in their cabin on the ship, they bundle up and head to the deck to experience the departure from the port. They squeeze their way to the front of the railing, Piero enfolding Cristina in his arms as the ship horn sounds and the journey begins. They watch until they can no longer see land. The ship will be stopping in Naples to board more passengers and then sail across the vast Atlantic to the port of New York City. They hope that the seas will not be stormy, as they have heard stories of some very unpleasant crossings. At least Signor Reda has arranged for them to have a closed berth to themselves, unlike many who will be in steerage.

When they approach the port of Naples, they again crowd on to the deck to watch the boarding of more passengers. They are surprised that there are hundreds of people making their way up the gangplank, mostly men, but also some families are boarding the ship.

So far, the seas have been fairly calm as the ship journeys south along the Italian coast. Now they begin the ocean crossing. Piero and Cristina lie awake holding each other close in the dark as they feel the ship riding the waves, port to starboard, starboard to port, and occasional slamming down on the waterline. They will be grateful when they reach New York and feel their feet securely on the land.

One morning, they are awakened by shouts and cheers from the passengers. "Land, ho! Land, ho!" Cristina and Piero hastily dress and rush to the deck. The port of New York City slowly comes into view, the early morning light turning from rose gold to clear and reflecting off the buildings.

Debarking the ship is a slow process. Passengers in first class berths are the first to depart, followed by those in private berths, and finally those in steerage. Porters struggle with luggage down the gangplank and into a large holding area where passengers will later claim their luggage.

Finally, Piero and Cristina complete the medical exam and are allowed to proceed to claim their luggage. Cristina leans on her husband. She is feeling a bit light-headed. Piero supports her with a comforting arm around her waist. He is wondering how he will be able to flag down a carriage and some assistance with their luggage. He isn't sure he should trust the motley crew of barkers bellowing with offers of assistance for a price. He fumbles in his coat pocket for the paper with the address of the lodging Signor Reda has arranged for them. He is about to engage in one of the barkers to assist them when a large man with a sign "Stratassi" in bold letters appears to his left.

He approaches the man and introduces himself. "At your service, Signor Stratassi. Signor Reda has arranged for me to take you to your lodgings. Madame." He bows, addressing Cristina. "I am called Stefano," he informs them.

Stefano hoists their luggage on a large cart, and they follow him to a waiting carriage. Piero and Cristina settle into the carriage and are swept along the streets, fascinated by the flurry of activity and the energy of the people, loud and bustling.

Signor Reda has secured rooms for the young couple at the rear of a large town house on West Twentieth Street. Stefano halts the carriage and assists Cristina to the ground. She is happy to be off the ship and feels stronger now, eager to see her new home. Stefano rings the door, and the matron who manages the building greets them. She shows them to their rooms. There is a large sitting area, a bedroom, and a small bath. There is a window overlooking a very small garden. Otherwise, the rooms are rather dark although clean. She explains that she provides meals and is available to answer their questions. She tells them that she will go over the house rules later after they are settled.

They bid Stefano a thankful goodbye. He promises to collect them in the morning after breakfast to transport them to the workspace and offices of Signor Reda's company.

Piero enfolds Cristina in a warm embrace. "We have arrived, my love." Cristina rests her head on Piero's shoulder as she wonders how she will occupy herself in these small dark rooms with Piero working and she with no friends or family to keep her company. *Well, first I will need to unpack our belongings and find a special place for Mother's marigold chemise*, she muses.

The matron raps lightly on their door and announces that the evening meal will be served in the dining room in one hour.

Cristina is led to the dining room by Piero. Three men are seated at the heavy mahogany table, chatting among themselves. They break from their talk and stare at the newcomers. Piero realizes that he is going to have to learn English quickly if he is to navigate in this new world. He stumbles with the few words he has learned from shipmates on the voyage and manages to convey that he and his wife have just arrived from Italy. The men are not impressed; it is clear by their dismissive expressions. The landlady enters the room and places a large dish of ham and potatoes baked in milk. *Apparently, one was to serve oneself,* decides Cristina. She sighs as the men make clear that as a lady, she should serve herself first. Gingerly she spoons a small portion onto the plate in front of her. She valiantly attempts to mask the disgust she is feeling at this hideous food and presentation. She is already homesick for the beautiful meals of her childhood. The men devour their portions and take their leave, with only a quick nod as they exit.

Back in their room, Cristina wants to complain about the experience. However, she refrains. This is Piero's big adventure, and she must put on a brave face and do her best to make a new life for herself with Piero. She thinks of her mother, of the marigold chemise, and of her mother-in-law, Alessia, and her paintings. *No,* she tells herself. *I am from a strong family, and I will carry on the strength of my heritage.* She gives herself over to Piero's advances and their sweet love. Sleep is deep and comforting.

Stefano arrives in the morning as promised. Cristina has implored Piero to include her in this first meeting at Signor Reda's workspace. She is fascinated by the horse drawn omnibuses hustling their passengers to their destinations. She notes that the atmosphere is harsher than in Firenze, and she can't help but think that the city is dingier and even ugly when compared to her home city.

Signor Reda greets the young couple and expresses surprise that Cristina has accompanied Piero. She counters his insinuation.

"Signor, my father, Signor Bianchi, as you know, is a fine businessman. I spent my childhood dinners listening to my grandfather, my aunt, and my father speaking about the Bianchi business. I am most interested in the workings of a business, and I want to support my dear Piero."

Privately, Signor Reda is impressed. He muses to himself that perhaps he can get the work of two people for the price of one.

"That is most interesting, my dear. *Si, si,* please join us today as I show Piero the workspace and introduce him to his workers. First, to your right, next to my office, is the office we have set up for Piero.

It is large enough to add a desk for Signora if she would like." Signor Reda bends over Cristina's hand for a respectful kiss.

They proceed to tour the workspace. On the ground floor is a vast space that will be filled with sewing machines at one end. At present, there are just five workstations set up. The other end is divided in half. One half contains bolts of fabric and sewing supplies. The other half is set up with steamers, irons, and tables along with garment racks and boxes for packing. The second floor is office space for Signor Reda, Piero, and a bookkeeper. Cristina's mind is already racing ahead as she notes that there is plenty of space for the business to grow. She feels excitement growing. She has already determined that she will not be spending her days in the drab living quarters they left this morning. *Piero better not object, or he will be an unhappy husband,* she tells herself.

The days and weeks turn to months as Piero, Cristina, and Signor Reda work long hours. Fine Italian fabric arrives at regular intervals. Bolts of merino wool, cashmere, linen, and silk line the shelves. They have hired patternmakers who translate Italian suit designs suitable for stylish men. The first floor of the Ruda workspace is a beehive of activity. The hum of the machines is steady from morning to night. They plan on branching out to produce more items, sweaters, shirts, ties, and so on.

While Signor Reda is occupied with finding wholesale buyers for the garments, Piero is managing the workers and keeping production on schedule. He finds that he is a good fit for the position and treats his charges with respect.

Meanwhile, Cristina finds that she is drawn to the bolts of silk, Milano silk and charmeuse in a rainbow of colors. She finds that her thoughts move to her mother's marigold chemise and a plan begins to surface. Unobtrusively at her desk, when Signor Reda and Piero are busy at work, she begins to sketch. She sketches versions of a chemise and various undergarments. Discreetly she snips swatches from the bolts of fabric and begins to imagine the garments taking shape. At the end of her workday, she stuffs the sketches and swatches into her satchel. Often, she leaves the workspace in the afternoon before Piero returns in the evening. These hours of solitude in their rooms are the magic of her days. She retrieves the marigold chemise from its hiding place and studies it along with her sketches and swatches.

The dream visits her every few nights. She sees two women dancing in the Tempietto. One is wearing the marigold chemise and the other has paint brushes clutched in her right hand. They are happy, laughing. Suddenly the sky turns dark, and a storm threatens. Thunder and lightning in the dream startle her awake.

There are just a few months remaining before the year of Piero's commitment with Signor Reda is complete. Cristina is keenly aware that Piero has not initiated a discussion with her about his intentions beyond the year deadline. It feels as if there is a gulf between them, and she knows that she will have to be the one to bridge it.

Her monthly visit did not arrive this month, and as the days pass, she notices that she feels tired, and just the thought of attending the meals the landlady prepares makes her nauseous. She decides that she will wait to see if the next month brings her womanly visit. If not, she will ask the landlady if she can recommend a physician.

It is raining with a vengeance on the day she is to visit the physician. Fortunately, Stefano remains at their disposal, so she arranges for him to transport her. The physician is kindly and happily provides her with the joyful news. She can expect her child in seven months' time. She appears in good health, but he advises that she make sure she rests and has adequate nutrition. Does she want him to speak with her husband? Cristina declines but longs for her mother to share the news with her and to feel comfort in her advice.

When Stefano deposits her at the Ruda workspace, she makes her way to the second floor, hoping to have a little solitude at her desk to digest her news. As she approaches Signor Reda's office, she sees that the door is slightly ajar, and that Piero and Signor Reda are engaged in conversation. With her back to the wall beside the door, she stops. Their voices drift to her waiting ears. With her hands cradling her belly, she catches the drift of their conversation. Signor Reda is praising Piero's performance but is suggesting that he work for another six months before Signor Reda is prepared to relinquish a portion of the company to Piero. She hears Piero's protest but is surprised that he is not more forceful in his objection. Not wanting to be caught eavesdropping, she retraces her steps to see if Stefano is still waiting in the carriage. Thankfully, there he is, talking to another driver. He assists her into the carriage and transports her back to their rooms.

Piero returns to their rooms and is surprised to see that Cristina is sleeping soundly. Not wanting to disturb her, he joins the other boarders in the dining room for the evening meal. He informs the landlady that his wife is resting and inquires if she may provide some bread and a bit of fruit for Cristina.

When he quietly enters their quarters, he sees that Cristina has awakened, and she is removing papers and scraps of fabric from her satchel. Piero has surprised her, and she greets her husband with a guilty look. Piero sits on the bed next to her and kisses her reddening cheek.

"My love, what is this?" he says, indicating her piles of paper and fabric.

"Oh, Piero. I have had an inspiration. What if we branch out the business and produce lingerie? For women. I have been sketching designs, and we have some lovely fabric that we are not using. Ladies always want fine undergarments," she explains.

A deep sigh escapes Piero's lips as he shakes his head. The conversation with Signor Reda has left him deflated. He is hoping that he would be able to bring happy news to his dear wife and that the promotion to part owner of the business would allow them to find nicer living quarters, perhaps to buy a town house of their own.

"Cristina, I am so sorry. I do not bring you good news this evening. Signor Reda called me into his office today. He praised my work but wants to delay a final decision for six more months. I was so hoping that we would have more money. I thought that we would be able to move to better accommodations, maybe even purchase our own town house. We want to have room for a family." Piero looks defeated.

Silently Cristina rejoices. This is actually good news, she thinks. She realizes that what she wants more than anything is to return to Italy, to her family. Perhaps Signor Reda has given her an opportunity.

"Piero, you know what my father and my aunt would say? Signor Reda has not kept his commitment to you. I believe that he is stringing you along, and he may never offer you a portion of his business. You agreed to help him grow his business for one year, and you have managed the production very well. He couldn't have been free to procure more customers without you holding down the daily operations. He has and will continue to take advantage of you. That is my opinion, my love."

Piero takes his wife in his arms, gently rocking her back and forth. After a time, Cristina decides that she should share her news.

"Dear, I also have some news. Today has been a big day for us. In seven months' time, we will be welcoming our first child into the world. I visited a physician this afternoon, and he confirmed that I am expecting. He says that I am in good health and that I should rest and receive good nutrition." Tears flow from Cristina's eyes, and she needs to blow her nose before she can continue. "Piero, I want to return home. I want to have our baby in Firenze with my family and your family around. I do not want to make New York my home. I have tried, but it does not make me happy to be here. I'm sorry."

Piero finds that he has conflicting feelings. He is overjoyed by the news of the pregnancy. But he feels as if he has failed in his dealings with Signor Reda, and he doesn't want to admit that he is being taken advantage of. What will his father and his father-in-law think if he returns home without a part ownership of the business? He loves Cristina beyond measure. What to do?

"I understand, my love. I really do. But I am tired. Let us rest and think about our options and have a long talk tomorrow. If it is not raining, let us stroll in the park and decide what we will do about our future. I love you, Cristina." Piero holds her close.

Sunlight streams in the windows of the boarding house, welcoming the day with promise. The birds are flitting about entertaining the landlady's scrawny cat. Piero awakens before Cristina and steps outside for a smoke. He observes Stefano's carriage approaching from the end of the street. Making a swift decision, he signals Stefano that he wants to speak.

"Stefano, Cristina is not feeling well. I must accompany her to the physician. Please inform Signor Reda that I will not be in today and will see him tomorrow. Thank you."

"As you wish, Piero. Shall I return to transport your wife?" the driver inquires.

Thinking quickly, Piero lies. "Oh no, that will not be necessary. The physician has arranged to send his carriage for us."

Stefano belts a hearty "Ha!" and his team moves forward in unison as he flicks the reins.

Piero extinguishes his smoke and steps back into their rooms. He kisses Cristina awake and gently brings her to greet the morning. "My dear, the morning is beautiful. The sunlight is brilliant. I have a surprise. We are not going to Signor Reda's workspace today. This day is for you and me. We will meander through the park. We will laugh and talk. We will plot our future. What do you think?" The deflated Piero of yesterday has transformed into his old boyish self.

Cristina throws herself into his arms, laughing with delight. She quickly dresses, and after partaking of bread and tea, the two lovers join hands and proceed to the Bowling Green Park. It is an oasis in the busy city and not far from the Staten Island Ferry and Battery Park. They decide to walk until their feet are completely fatigued. They complete a loop and find themselves back at Bowling Green. They claim a bench under a magnificent plane tree that allows for dappled sunlight to surround them.

"I have been thinking about our conversation last night," Piero begins. "I, too, miss our families and Italy. When I think of raising our child here, I don't think it is the best thing for us. To be honest, I don't feel as if I belong here. I just don't want to disappoint my father and your father as well. They will see me as a failure."

Cristina's business mind begins to percolate. "I have an idea, Piero. What if we return with a business plan? Think about my sketches for women's lingerie. With my father and aunt and their connections and money to invest, we could start a new lingerie company. We could offer the most delicious garments that no woman could resist. I can already see us expanding into Milano and Roma from Firenze. You have learned much about the production side of the business, and I think that I have a flair for design. I could even tap mother and Alessia for inspiration."

Piero feels himself being caught up in Cristina's enthusiasm. He feels a new optimism. The thought of raising their family in the midst of their families is right. He knows it is right.

Signor Reda greets Piero the following morning. "Piero, is Cristina all right? Stefano informed me that she is not feeling well."

"The physician diagnosed the problem, signor. Cristina is with a child. We are delighted." Piero is beaming new father-to-be pride.

"Congratulations. Now you can settle in to serve your additional six months with me," Signor Reda declares.

Piero finds that he is insulted by Signor Reda's presumption. *What a jackass*, he thinks. With a force that surprises him, Piero replies to his boss, "Sir, I must inform you that Cristina and I will be departing for home immediately. I am going this afternoon to arrange for our passage back to Italy. We want to raise our child with our families, and I do not want to delay travel any longer for Cristina's sake. She deserves to have her mother and my mother as well with her at this time. You broke your word to me by adding another six months to our agreement without even consulting me. My father-in-law, Signor Bianchi, would be angry, and I am sure he would counsel me to end this business agreement. Good day."

Signor Reda sputters his shock at Piero's words. He can't believe that good-natured Piero has become so stern. He watches in disbelief as Piero gathers his things from his office and descends the stairs to the workroom.

The workers pay no attention, as they are used to him supervising the floor. He marches to the wall where the bolts of fabric are stacked. He chooses five bolts of the best silk that Signor Reda has imported from Italy and loads them on a cart. Stefano is waiting by the side of the building. He is surprised but says nothing as he helps Piero load the bolts into his cart. When they arrive at the boarding house, Piero unloads the bolts of silk and turns to Stefano.

"Stefano, you are a good man. Cristina and I are returning to Italy, so this is goodbye. Good luck to you, my man."

Stefano sighs. He will miss the young couple, even though he is only their driver. "*Buon viaggio,*" he declares as he gives Piero a hearty pat on the back. He climbs back up to his driver's seat and flicks the reins with his signature "Ha!" and he is gone.

By nightfall, Piero has purchased two passages from New York City to Genoa on the *SS Ancona*. The ship had just docked and emptied a full load of immigrants with a return sailing scheduled in a few days. He greets Cristina with their documents for passage, and they dance around their rooms with Cristina wrapped in a layer of marigold silk.

Wisteria in full bloom tumbles over the trellis in the Bianchi garden. Lucida is relishing a quiet moment as she waits for Alessia to appear for their morning chat. Both women cherish this little ritual to gossip, confide, and comfort each other.

"Lucida, Lucida!" shouts Alessia as she sprints across the terrace, panting to catch her breath. She is waving an envelope wildly in her right hand. She pulls Lucida to her feet and embraces her with exuberance.

"It is a letter from Piero. They are returning home, and Cristina is pregnant!"

"Oh my, oh my," stammers Lucida. She is attempting to let the news sink in. "Let me see the letter."

She reads Piero's words and begins to weep with joy. She has not realized how deeply she missed them. "When will they arrive?"

The two friends try to calculate when the ship will arrive in Genoa. They have heard that the Atlantic sailing can last anywhere from six to fourteen weeks, depending on the weather. The letter must have arrived on the last sailing. Perhaps they will be home in another few months.

"We must gather everyone together this evening to share the news as soon as Pietro and Niccolo arrive home. I am so pleased." Alessia embraces Lucida again before she returns to her studio for an afternoon of work.

Since he arrived home from Roma, Niccolo has been in a serious internal stew. The excitement of the marriage of Piero and Cristina and their departure for America distracted him for a brief time, but his anger at Martina came barreling forth into his every waking thought. He has decided not to confide in Lucida and Alessia for now. He needs some time to decide how he will confront his sister.

One fine evening, he decides to take a stroll to clear his head and relax after a long day's work. Since he sees Martina regularly at the Bianchi office, he has done his best to avoid her. When they encounter one another, he takes on the air of the busy, rushed businessman. So far, he has managed to keep his distance. As he is strolling, lost in his thoughts, he comes to attention and realizes that he is on Martina's street. On impulse, he decides that he will visit her and confront her with his discovery. *Yes*, he agrees to himself, *tonight is the night.*

Niccolo rolls his shoulders, pulls in his abdomen, and lengthens his torso to maximum height. He straightens his garments and approaches Martina's door. The heavy knocker, a lion's head with a ring caught in its mouth, scowls at him with fierce eyes. Boldly, he announces his presence with three firm raps of the ring. Presently, Martina's butler responds to his knock. His expression belies his surprise at Niccolo's presence.

"I am here to see my sister," Niccolo announces to the butler.

"I am afraid Signora Martina is not available at this time, signor," replies the butler.

"I am afraid that I must see her regardless," Niccolo responds, as he moves to step inside the door.

The butler does his best to dissuade Niccolo, but Niccolo pushes him aside and proceeds into Martina's villa.

Niccolo detects music and laughter from the direction of his sister's ballroom. Moving swiftly, he approaches the room. He stops at the wide entrance in shock. Before him is an astonishing vision. There are women lounging on divans, drinking wine and partaking of nibbles in various stages of disheveled dress. Peals of hilarious laughter and music are the background to intimate whispers. It is difficult for Niccolo to take it all in. His eyes circle the room, and there on one wall is a series of paintings featuring his Lucida in the marigold chemise. His blood boils.

The women are so engrossed in their pleasures that no one has noticed his presence. He detects the presence of the butler approaching.

"Where is Martina?" he demands. "I must see her at once. It is an emergency," he lies.

"She may be in her private chambers," the butler replies as he makes haste to hide, contemplating Martina's wrath if she discovers he has allowed her brother to enter her villa during one of her special soirees.

Niccolo is so angry that he is shaking as he climbs the staircase, clearing two steps with each stride. At the top of the stairs, he turns right and proceeds to the end of the hall. The door to Martina's private chamber is closed. No matter, he enters without knocking. As he steps into the chamber, he halts abruptly. There on her bed, Martina is nude and tangled with her lover, her female lover, who is also nude. They are so engrossed in each other that they do not detect Niccolo's presence. Near the bed, he now sees a large painting propped against the wall. Lucida is posing in the marigold chemise provocatively posed in a lush garden.

"Martina! What are you doing with this painting in your bedchamber? And what are you doing with the woman in your bed?" Niccolo is shaking as he shouts at his sister.

Now the two are fully aware of his presence. They scramble to retrieve bedcovers to conceal their nudity. There is a weighty silence in the bedchamber.

"Niccolo, remove yourself from my bedchamber and my villa immediately. You have no right to invade my privacy. *Partire!*" Martina shouts. She is flushed, wrapped in bedcovers and moving herself in front of her lover as if to protect her.

"I will not depart until you provide me with an explanation. Why do you have these paintings? What is your intent? What are all of these women doing in your villa?" Niccolo's voice registers louder and louder.

"At least allow me to dress. Stand outside the door, and I will join you shortly." Martina is defiant, but she sees that her brother is so angry that he will not leave her villa peacefully. She is not embarrassed or apologetic in the least.

Niccolo shoots a murderous glance at his sister, turning abruptly, slamming the door on his way out.

Martina dresses hurriedly, indicating to her lover that she should remain in the bed and await her return. She sees that Niccolo is overcome with anger and disbelief as she leads him to her library down the hall. It is quiet and private for the conversation they need to have.

Over an hour later, the siblings are still caught in a stalemate. Martina remains defiant and unapologetic. Niccolo feels betrayed by his sister's unilateral use of Alessia's paintings with no consideration for Lucida's reputation. He is not sure how he feels about Martina's fondness for other women. He is still in shock about that aspect of Martina's life.

Niccolo finally takes his leave of Martina's villa, noticing on his way out that her soiree is beginning to break up. The women are donning their cloaks, and the butler is signaling to their drivers that the women are ready to depart.

As he makes his way home, Niccolo determines that he will need to inform Lucida, Alessia, and Pietro of Martina's intent to use Alessia's paintings for her own purposes without gaining the artist's or model's permission.

The following evening, the two couples gather in Alessia's studio. Pietro supplies the wine, as he surmised from Niccolo's invitation to meet in Alessia's studio that the conversation may not be entirely pleasant.

Struggling to remain calm, Niccolo relays the events of the previous evening at Martina's villa. Additionally, he adds his experience in Roma with his friend Signor Stassi and the sale of Alessia's paintings at the businessmen's gathering. His audience is strangely silent. Alessia and Lucida appear very still, hardly breathing. Niccolo glances inquiringly at Pietro and then to the two women.

"What do you think we should do?" he asks.

Alessia responds first. She stands and begins to pace back and forth across the room, muttering to herself. She halts in front of Lucida.

"That conniving woman. I hate her. We will find a way to get my paintings back. I will not have her own my paintings. I refuse." She glances at her companions for their reactions.

"Yes, Alessia. We will do whatever it takes to retrieve those paintings. Also, the ones that are in Roma. Although that may be more difficult. Niccolo, perhaps your friend Signor Stassi could be of assistance," Lucida offers.

The four friends talk well into the night, consuming several bottles of wine and completely forgetting about the evening meal. Pietro formed the most viable plan for dealing with Martina. He surprises the others with his cunningness. He happens to know a chemist by way of many entertaining evenings in his gentleman's club. The chemist reveled in relaying tales of an unsavory nature as he enjoyed his drink. Piero recalls one such story where he assisted one of his friends in dealing with his wife and her lover by way of poisoning. The unfortunate deaths were attributed to food poisoning and his poor wife's reputation was ruined. There was little sympathy for her in death nor for her lover who left his long-suffering wife a poor widow. He recalls the merriment among the men as the chemist was an excellent entertainer.

Pietro agrees to visit the chemist and discretely inquires about his willingness to assist in a matter of great urgency. The plan unfolds as such. Piero knows of a certain signora who supplies young women for the entertainment of gentlemen. He is quite sure that the signora would be able to persuade one of these young women to attract the attention of Martina. For a price, the young woman would be instructed to share a refreshment with Martina, slyly slipping a dose of cantarella into Martina's glass. Poor Martina. She will be caught up in a game and doomed by her own desires. Of course, Niccolo, being her only sibling, would be in charge of his sister's estate that would include Alessia's paintings. Alessia is unsurprised and keeps her thoughts about Pietro's knowledge of the poison cantarella and his relationship with the signora to herself.

When Lucida and Niccolo are back home in their bedchamber, they whisper about the plan. They have their doubts but not enough to stop Pietro from proceeding. Sleep is fitful for them that evening.

Pietro is very busy the next few days. Procuring a packet of cantarella from the chemist is easy. The chemist produces a small packet, making a great show of labeling it as a treatment for headache, *medicina per il mal de testa*. Since Pietro is a frequent visitor to the signora's quarters, she is not surprised when he arrives and asks to consult with her. "Does the signora have any young women in her employ who may be interested in seducing a powerful businesswoman?"

Signora is intrigued by his request. "*Si, si,* I believe that one of my girls may be up to the task. Her name is Adonna. She is quite beautiful and fancies herself to be an excellent seductress. She is also greedy and is very willing to follow instructions in order to make the most money possible. What you are asking will take a bit of time, and the fee will be double to what I normally ask. You understand?"

"*Si, si,* signora. The fee will not be a problem. Would the young lady be available to speak to us now?" Pietro inquires.

A short while later, the signora appears with Adonna. Pietro is taken aback. He has to give the signora credit. She knows her girls. He can't see how Martina will be able to resist this one.

Pietro arranges for Adonna to meet him the following morning at a café near the Bianchi office. He will be introducing Adonna as his niece who has moved from the country to the city to seek employment in a good household. Niccolo will introduce her to Martina, as Martina is always looking for young women to employ as maids. She prefers them to be attractive. He ushers Adonna into Niccolo's office, introducing her as his niece. Niccolo has to admire Pietro's handiwork. He has little doubt that Martina will take the bait. They chat among themselves, leaving Niccolo's office door invitingly open.

Shortly, Martina passes by the office. She slows as she hears voices emerging from Niccolo's office. Curious, she peeks her head in the door.

Recognizing Pietro, she addresses him. "Signor Stratassi, what are you doing here? And who is your friend?" Her gaze lingers over Adonna.

"Signora Bianchi, it is my pleasure to see you today. I was just telling Niccolo about my niece. Her parents have sent her to the city to secure employment in a good household. Be pleased to meet my niece, Adonna. She is young but a good worker." Piero gestures for Adonna to stand as courtesy to Martina.

"Signora, it is an honor to meet you today." Adonna presents herself as demure, not meeting Martina's eyes.

"How good of your uncle to assist you in finding employment in the city. Sadly, one of my maids has informed me that she must return to her family, as her mother has taken ill. She will be departing this week, so your interest in a position is timely. Would you care to come to my villa for a proper interview tomorrow?"

Adonna glances nervously at Pietro as if seeking his approval. *Oh my*, Pietro and Niccolo think to themselves. *This one is perfect for the job*. Pietro nods his approval to Adonna.

"*Si, si*, signora. I would be grateful for the opportunity for an interview. At what hour shall I make my appearance?" Adonna keeps her head slightly bowed and her hands clasped tightly in front of her body.

"Nine tomorrow morning will be perfect. Niccolo, give her the address," she orders.

Martina gives Adonna once last glance, ignoring the men as she exits Niccolo's office.

Niccolo stands and shuts his office door. He keeps his voice low as he thanks Pietro and Adonna for their visit. Pietro will provide

Adonna with additional instructions once he has escorted her back to the signora's.

Pietro and Adonna pretend not to notice Martina observing their departure from the end of the hallway.

Martina returns to her office and closes the door. She smiles widely as she savors the meeting of a young innocent, she presumes, girl from the country. Of course, she lied about needing a new maid. *One must snatch opportunity when it presents itself,* she tells herself. She decides she will leave work early today. She is sick of Niccolo's angry, righteous attitude. She composes a note to her favorite lover to meet her at her villa this evening for dining and conversational pleasure. Instructing her secretary to have their messenger boy deliver the note, she calls for her carriage to transport her home.

On their nightly stroll that evening, Pietro and Niccolo go over their plan to deal with Adonna. They have arranged for payment to be made to the signora for the use of Adonna's services and are in agreement that she is well worth the high fee.

Signor Reda is unable to persuade Piero to remain in his position. Despite being offered an additional stipend, Piero stands firm. He notes that Signor Reda did not offer to turn over a share of the business as promised, so he feels even more justified in making his decision to return home.

With their passage secured and in possession of several bolts of the finest silk from Signor Reda's stock, they make arrangements for transporting their belongings to the ship. Cristina is anxious for the journey to begin. She prays each evening before bed for a safe journey and happy reunion with their families.

Fortune is with the passengers on this journey. They are blessed with relatively fair weather as they cross the mighty Atlantic and encounter no serious storms. Cristina's condition is now apparent, her child growing safely in the protection of her womb. She finds that she tires easily and is more sensitive to odors. She divides her time between getting fresh air on the deck and resting in their quarters.

Piero is attentive to his wife and always accompanies her when she takes the fresh air. He joins in conversation with other men on the ship when Cristina is resting. They speak of politics and compare their experiences in America. Some are eager to return to America to seek their fortunes, and others, like Piero and Cristina, find themselves homesick and are ready to renew their lives in their home country.

Finally, the ship is in view of land. Everyone crowds on deck in anticipation. They can't wait to feel solid ground beneath their feet. Piero and Cristina will spend a day or two in Genoa while securing carriage passage back to Firenze. Cristina cradles her belly and silently whispers to her child, "You will be home soon."

Antonio and Lucia are working on their school assignments. Ariston has been increasingly insistent that the two work harder at their studies as this will be their final year under his tutelage. They are disturbed by the dogs sounding alarm. Stepping to the nursery windows, they see a carriage enter the villa gates. They have been anticipating the arrival of their siblings Piero and Cristina.

"Here they are!" they exclaim, performing a little jig together. They race down the stairs and out to the carriage, yelling at the top of their lungs, "They are home, they are home!"

Everyone streams out of the villas. Embraces, tears of joy, and ecstatic shouts abound.

Lucida has prepared Cristina's room to accommodate the couple, and Alessia has arranged for storage of their extra belongings in Piero's old room. The two mothers, soon to be grandmothers, are acting like mother hens, fussing over their offspring. Cristina is exhausted by the journey and allows her mother to settle her comfortably in her bed. She falls sound asleep quickly, so happy to be home. Piero finds that he is charged with energy and steps across the terrace to visit his parents and sister.

They speak late into the evening. Pietro assures his son that he has made the correct decision.

"Signor Reda broke his word. Never be in business with someone you cannot trust," Pietro advises.

Piero begins to relay Cristina's idea for a business designing and
producing women's lingerie. The more he speaks of it, his enthusiasm grows. Alessia is particularly interested in the plan and indicates
that she will assist in any way she can. Lucia listens attentively and
reminds them that she will be finished with her studies soon and that
she would be available to assist as well. Piero can't wait to relay their
enthusiasm to Cristina. The seeds have been planted, and they will
nurture Cristina's idea into fruition.

The marigold chemise visits Cristina in her dream the evening
of their homecoming. She visits the Tempietto as an angel floating in
the marigold chemise and peering in through the columns. She sees
that the Tempietto is filled with women. They are dancing slowly,
each in their private trance and wearing a chemise. Some are marigold in color and others are marine, *roso*, and a pale green, the color
of spring rain. Her tears of joy wake her from the dream. She lies still,
attempting to recapture the image. Slowly she awakens fully and sees
that Piero is not in bed with her. The villa is silent. She must have
slept late. It feels so wonderful to be home. Cradling her belly, she
unpacks her mother's marigold chemise from the safety of the muslin
and drapes in across her body. She finds that it brings her peace and
confidence.

Adonna's step is lively as she makes her way to Martina's villa
for the interview. Once she approaches the villa, she reins herself
in and envelopes her body in the character of the shy country girl
hoping for a position. Her knock is tentative as she allows the ring
in the lion's mouth to make contact with the doorplate. There is no
response, so she knocks again with a bit more force. Martina's butler
appears. He ushers her inside and asks her to wait in the library while
he announces her presence to his mistress.

When Martina appears, she notes that the young girl has seated
herself tentatively on the edge of a chair, looking nervous and unsure

of herself. Martina seats herself behind her desk and invites Adonna to be seated on a small chair across from her so that they are facing.

"Well, my dear, I see that you have arrived on time for our interview. Remind me of your name," Martina commands.

Adonna barely raises her head, keeping it bowed and only glancing up at Martina through her lashes. "I am called Adonna," she replies softly.

"Relax, Adonna. I am not going to bite you. Speak up."

"*Si*, signora," Adonna speaks a bit louder.

"Let me tell you what your duties will be. You will assist me in my toilette, washing, dressing, hairstyling, preparing for my day. You will manage my wardrobe and accessories, making sure everything is ready when I want and need it. You will coordinate with the laundress and housekeeper to keep my clothing and bedding fresh and in good repair. The position includes your room and board. You will have your own room in the attic with the other servants, and the cook will apprise you of mealtimes. Your pay will be distributed to you at the end of each week by the butler who manages the purse for running my household. I expect you to begin at the beginning of next week." Martina is crisp in her delivery.

Adonna allows several minutes to pass before she responds. "I will do my best to fulfill the duties of the position. Thank you for giving me the chance to be at your service, signora." She portrays just the right amount of shy gratitude.

As the days pass in Martina's employ, Adonna calculates how she will complete the terms of her contract. She reports back to her signora each afternoon. She tells the butler that she enjoys a walk in the fresh air as she misses the country. He is a kind man and encourages her to take a break in the afternoons.

Signora and Adonna agree that it is prudent for Adonna to ingratiate herself to Martina, even if it takes a little while longer than Pietro and Niccolo prefer. Keeping her inspiration to herself, Adonna decides that if she administers the cantarella to Martina in very small doses, Martina will become weaker and require Adonna to be more available. She can always procure additional cantarella. She is not the only one who has access to a friendly pharmacist who will gladly supply her with whatever she requests in exchange for her gratifying form of payment.

Martina is enjoying the company of her new maid Adonna. She requests her service frequently and is slowly conniving to have Adonna be more at ease in her presence. She generally enjoys a glass of Amaro before retiring in the evening. Adonna is instructed to bring her the small goblet in her bed after she has assisted Martina prepare for bed, brushing her hair to free it of any tangles from the day. A very small pinch of cantarella falls from the tiny spoon in Adonna's pocket into the bottom of the goblet followed by a pour of Amoro. Adonna arranges it on a silver tray along with a little blossom or petal from the garden and presents it to her mistress with a shy smile.

This evening, Martina pats the bed by her side, indicating that Adonna should join her. Adonna nervously hands the goblet to Martina and gingerly sits on the bed next to her mistress.

"Mistress, that is a beautiful painting you have. I can't help but admire it. It is so powerful. Who is the artist?" Adonna inquires.

"Yes, Adonna, it is a special painting, isn't it? I have more of the artist's work in the ballroom. I will be having a special gathering next week of women who appreciate the arts. Perhaps you would like to join us. Why don't you come closer and share my Amoro? It is delicious and so relaxing in the evening," Martina offers as she places her hand on Adonna's knee.

"Oh, mistress, I couldn't. It would not be proper." Adonna moves to stand away from the bed.

"Well, perhaps tomorrow evening then. Why don't you bring two goblets on your tray? You work so hard for me. You deserve a little treat, don't you think?" Martina catches Adonna's eye with a seductive smile.

"*Buonanotte*, mistress." Adonna bows and retreats to the door. She makes her way to her little room in the servant's attic and secures her door. She smiles and chuckles to herself as she drifts off to a restful sleep.

Martina also smiles and chuckles to herself as she finished the last drop of Amora and drifts off to a restful sleep.

The following evening, Adonna assists Martina to ready for bed, brushing her hair as usual. Martina reminds Adonna to bring two goblets of Amoro so that she can relax with her mistress.

"*Si, si*, signora," Adonna responds. As she makes her way to the liquor cabinet near the dining room, she decides to abandon her plan to administer the cantarella in small doses and complete the job tonight. She finds that she is repulsed by Martina and her domineering manner. She isn't inclined to play at being seduced. She prefers the regular assignments from her signora. By the time she places the goblets on the tray, along with a blossom, she has made up her mind. She empties the packet of cantarella into one of the goblets and places the blossom at the foot of the goblet to mark Martina's Amoro. She pours another serving for herself and makes her way back to Martina's bedchamber.

"Ah, my dear. Join me for a relaxing drink." She indicates a spot next to her as she sits against the plumped pillows.

Adonna does not meet Martina's eyes and instead places the tray on the table next to the bed. She serves Martina the cantarella-laced Amora and moves a chair close to the bed, taking her goblet from the tray.

"Oh, come now, my dear. Don't be shy. We can chat and enjoy our drink." Martina's voice projects a command.

"Mistress, that would not be proper. I can enjoy a chat and drink from here." Adonna lowers her eyes, glancing at Martina from beneath her lashes.

"Very well," Martina hisses. "Perhaps you are not enjoying your new position." In a huff, Martina quickly empties her goblet, grabbing Adonna's goblet from her hand and emptying that one as well.

"You are dismissed," she practically shouts at Adonna.

Adonna bows and collects the goblets and tray, swiftly exiting Martina's bedchamber. She makes her way to the kitchen and washes the goblets and tray thoroughly, being mindful to not leave any traces of the cantarella or fingerprints on the goblets. She returns them to the liquor cabinet, placing the two goblets in the back row of the crystal. The villa is quiet as she makes her way to her little attic room.

Unable to drift quickly to sleep, she wonders which of the maids will discover Martina in the morning.

Adonna is enjoying coffee and bread in the kitchen with the other servants when a maid comes rushing in, white as a ghost. There are stains on her apron from the breakfast tray crashing from her hands as she came upon her mistress sprawled on the bed, her head hanging at a precarious angle off the side. The butler appears at the kitchen door, and she indicates he should follow her. Of course, the whole group tags along. Martina's door is open, and the breakfast tray and broken dishes litter the bedside.

Martina's heavy dark locks are in disarray, and her head hangs at an odd angle. The bedcovers are tangled, indicating that she had struggled. Her mouth is gapping open, little drops of dried blood at the corners of her lips. She is pale and very, very still. It is clear that she is not breathing, but the butler moves closer to determine if he can detect any sign of life.

"Adonna, run and get the medico, hurry!" he commands. "And the rest of you...*uscire, uscire!*"

They all scurry, leaving the butler to ponder the fate of his mistress. He is not fond of her, but he is the type of man who takes his duties seriously and performs them well.

Niccolo is finishing his morning coffee when there is a commotion at the door. A young boy follows the maid into the breakfast room. He is panting and his cheeks are rosy from running.

"Signor, the medico has sent me from your sister's villa. He insists that you come at once."

"What has happened, Ragazzo?" Niccolo demands.

"Hurry, hurry, you will see. Follow me," the boy responds as he turns to exit.

Niccolo grabs his coat and rushes to keep up with the messenger boy. At Martina's villa, they rush in, and Niccolo hears a commotion coming from Martina's bedchamber. He pauses at the door, taking in the chaotic scene. There are broken dishes littering the carpet. The medico is standing over Martina who lies lifeless on her bed. He notices Adonna along with the other maids huddled in the corner of the room. He dares not to glance at her.

Taking command, Niccolo orders the maids out of the room and closes the door. He approaches the medico who addresses him.

"Signor Bianchi, I am sorry, your sister has perished in her sleep. A maid found her this morning, and the maid who attended her last evening says that she was fine when she left her for the evening. I saw her a few weeks ago, and she was fine. She has always been healthy and strong."

"What do think is the cause of her death?" inquires Niccolo.

"She may have had a heart attack. It sometimes happens with healthy people. I am not quite certain," replies the medico. "Do you want me to arrange for the body to be prepared for burial?"

"*Si, si, grazie.* I will arrange for our priest to set the memorial service for her."

Adonna returns to the kitchen with the other maids. They are all talking at once, trying to make sense of what happened. She repeats to the butler that when she left her mistress's room last evening, her mistress seemed tired and ready to sleep, but there was nothing unusual about the evening. She decides that she will stay the night as usual at the villa, but the next day, when she returns from her afternoon walk, she will tell the butler that she is going to return home to help her parents with her younger siblings. She doesn't think the butler will be upset, as Martina is no longer in need of a maid.

When she slips out that afternoon for her walk to check in with her signora, she sees that Niccolo and Pietro are entering the signora's villa. They do not see her. She decides to enter from the servant's entrance, and as she rounds the corner, she notices that on this warm day, the windows of the signora's reception room are ajar to let in the cooling breeze. She slips behind the plantings beneath the windows and slows her breath in order to detect the conversation.

Signora is thanking the two gentlemen for the payment for service rendered. She is requesting that Adonna return to the signora now that her contract has been filled. She has plenty of work waiting for her girl. Adonna cannot quite hear the response from the two men but hears the door shut as they leave. She remains in her hiding place until she is certain they have left and then makes her way to the front entrance of the villa to meet with signora.

Signora greets Adonna with a broad smile, making her face powder cake in the creases of her face and invites the girl to be seated.

"Well done, my dear. I knew you were the right girl for the job. I need you back straight away. We are busy, and men have been requesting you."

"I will inform the butler tomorrow that I am returning home to help my parents. I want to inquire about my payment for this contract. You promised me that it would be a larger amount due to the special circumstances," Adonna addresses her employer.

"All in good time, my dear. You will receive your payment at month's end as usual. You know that is when I do my household accounts and add up the board fees for you girls. Don't be greedy. Where else would you find employment these days?" Signora's smile fades as she returns to her usual nasty self.

Adonna forces her face into a neutral expression. "*Sì*, signora." She leaves the room quickly and turns on to the street. All the way to Martina's villa, she fumes. She knows that signora will cheat her as usual and would never protect her if it was ever found that Adonna had poisoned Martina.

By the time she arrives back at the villa, Niccolo and the butler are supervising the removal of the body, and the maids are starting to clean up the mess and restore Martina's bedchamber to order. That evening, Adonna waits until the household is silent with slumber. With great care, she tiptoes down the attic stairs and makes her way to Martina's bedchamber. She slips in the door. The moonlight is shining through the window where the maids had neglected to draw the drapes tightly. She lights a candle and stands in front of the painting of the girl in the marigold chemise. She studies the painting for a long time and becomes drowsy. She extinguishes the candle with a soft puff and crawls into Martina's bed.

In her dream, she finds herself in a Tempietto on a hill. She is wearing a marigold chemise as she dances in the moonlight. She feels alive and free and more hopeful than she has ever felt before.

Dawn brings the song of birds, and sunshine streams through Martina's windows. With a start, Adonna wakes up and realizes that she is in Martina's bedchamber. Before she departs the room, her bodice is stuffed with as much of Martina's jewelry as she can fit in her corset.

That evening, Niccolo and Lucida meet Pietro and Alessia in Alessia's studio, away from the ears of the household staff and their children. They are silent as Alessia lights a few candles. Each one is thinking that they have plotted to murder a woman. There will be no confessions to the priest. They need to learn to live with the sin they have committed.

Finally, Niccolo speaks. "It is done. The medico attributes my sister's death to a heart attack. I believe that we can trust Adonna to be discrete. She will not want to draw attention to herself, becoming a notorious murderer. Given her low class, she would surely receive a death sentence."

"I agree," Pietro responds. He notices that the two women seem very tense.

"And now we can retrieve my paintings," Alessia declares. "Niccolo, when will you be dealing with her villa and her belongings?"

"We must act swiftly. I will arrange to have the paintings moved to your studio tomorrow. Martina's butler will choose discrete movers. They will wrap the paintings to protect them from prying eyes. I have been thinking. Since Martina's villa is now my property, perhaps Piero and Cristina can live there. With the baby coming, they will be happy to have a home of their own. What do you think of that idea?" Niccolo realizes that this plan had just occurred to him. But the more he thinks about it, the better he likes the idea. He and Pietro can help the young couple out with the expense of maintaining the villa until Piero can manage. He will keep the butler on and work with him to trim the household staff. After all, Cristina and Piero do not have the extravagant tastes of his dearly departed sister.

Early the next morning, Niccolo arrives at Martina's villa. He directs the butler to have the paintings wrapped and delivered to Alessia's studio. As they are speaking, he notices Adonna gathering her cloak and heading for the door. They do not acknowledge one another. The butler confides in Niccolo that Adonna had quit her position to return home to assist her parents. The butler sighs.

"That young girl was a favorite of your sister," he states, giving Niccolo a knowing glance. "Well, since we will be reducing staff, it is just as well."

"*Si, si,*" mutters Niccolo. He wonders to himself why he doesn't feel more guilt in his heart.

The Bianchis are a well-known business family, so, of course, the funeral is extravagant. A reception is held in Martina's villa. Most notable in attendance are many women arriving to express their condolences. Several of them sidle up to Niccolo to inquire about Martina's paintings. He deftly brushes them off, pretending not to know what they are talking about. At one point, he notices that Adonna is part of a group of maids gathered in a corner whispering. He wonders briefly why she has appeared. Lucida and Alessia remain close to each other throughout the proceedings. Pietro mingles and flirts with the women.

Piero and Cristina find a quiet corner to sit together. Cristina's belly is enormous by now, and she finds it fatiguing to stand for any length of time. They survey the grandeur of Martina's villa and try to imagine themselves living here. Cristina confesses to her husband that she doesn't like the feel of the villa. She isn't sure why, but it does not give her a good or peaceful feeling. She has been thinking a lot about their future and their business. Now she decides to share her musings with her husband.

"My dear, what I would really love is to return to Roma and live with my grandmother if she will have us. She must be a little lonely and having a young child would enliven her home. I have a feeling that we might have more success with our business in Roma. My father has many business connections and still needs to travel there to attend to the Bianchi business. What do you think?"

Piero regards his wife. He finds himself thinking how many times he has felt thankful that he married her. He ponders Cristina's proposal and thinks that she may be correct. They could leave for Roma soon after the birth of their firstborn, as soon as Cristina feels that she is able to travel. They could ask Niccolo to begin smoothing the way for business connections, and the next few months could be spent finalizing their business plans. He pulls Cristina close, kissing her ear and murmuring words of love and devotion.

"Yes, let's send word to your grandmother. I have no doubt she will agree. Let's share our plan with our families tonight."

Part IV

Signora Bianchi cradles her new great-granddaughter, Maria Stratassi. At three months, Maria loves to smile and coo, studying faces intently. Cristina and Piero have settled in with her grandmother nicely. She is grateful that they are with her as she wonders how many months she has left on this earth. She finds that she is going to church to light candles and pray on most days now. It brings her comfort.

Orazio Salvatori has fallen ill, and Alessia's mother has sent for her. She wants her daughter and husband to make peace with one another before Orazio is gone. Lucida decides to travel to Roma with her dear friend Alessia as she, too, would love to see her family. She finds herself longing for her old days in Roma, and, of course, she can't resist the opportunity to see Cristina and Maria.

The two friends spend the carriage journey from Florence to Roma reminiscing, and before they know it, they are plotting to move their families back to Roma. Especially given the circumstances of Martina's demise, they wonder if it may be for the best. Pietro and Niccolo will most likely have objections due to business concerns, but the women are confident that they can persuade the men.

Alessia arrives at her childhood home with little time to spare. Orazio is fading quickly. He is weak and unable to leave his bed. When he sees Alessia, tears flow, and he embraces his daughter from his bed, his arms weak and shaky. Oh, how he has missed his dear daughter. He pleads for her forgiveness for sending her off to Firenze. Alessia sobs and sobs. There will be no time to share everything with her father. Or for him to see her new paintings. She knows he would be proud of her. Her mother enters the bedchamber with the medico in tow. The mother and daughter wait outside while Orazio is being examined. Soon the medico steps through the door and softly instructs Signora Salvatori to send for the priest. Alessia returns to her father's side and holds his hand as they await the priest.

Lucida has decided to surprise her family. She makes her way along Via Giulia, her heart full of emotion as she stands in front of her door. Rapping with anticipation, she steps back and waits for the maid to answer. She doesn't recognize the young woman who opens the door.

"I am here to see Signor and Signora Galvani. Please tell them that Lucida Bianchi is here to call."

The maid indicates that she should enter and leaves to inform her mistress that they have a visitor. The reunion is joyful as everyone is home for the dinner hour. The family encircles Lucida, everyone talking at once, laughing and flinging so many questions back and forth.

Orazio's funeral is well attended. Artists, friends, neighbors, and family crowd into the family courtyard following the service. Signor Ruel, from a spot near the table of refreshments, observes the daughter Alessia as she and her mother attend to their guests. Word of Martina's demise has not yet reached him. He wonders if Martina is still in Roma at the Bianchi offices or if she has returned to Firenze. He makes a note to himself to send out feelers for any gossip.

Later that evening, when the solicitor goes over Orazio's will with his widow and daughter, they are relieved that Signora Salvatori will be provided for. Orazio has left his studio to his daughter with instructions to sell his remaining work with proceeds to go to his wife.

When Alessia climbs the stairs to the studio the following morning, she is overcome with emotion. The aroma of oil paint greets her like a dear friend. She is grateful for the solitude as she takes inventory of the paintings and notes that her corner of the studio remains untouched with prepared canvas ready for her return. Her paints, charcoals, brushes, and palette knives are cleaned and lined up neatly on the table next to her easel. She notes how large the studio is. Larger than she remembered. Exploring further, she sees that Orazio has expanded the space, purchasing the adjoining room to add to the property. *Well,* she thinks to herself, *I will be moving back to Roma and work in this studio. Pietro can decide if he and Lucia will be joining me.*

The day is pleasant, so she decides to stroll to the Bianchis to visit with Piero and Cristina and especially to hold her granddaughter. She finds that she is deeply happy to share a grandchild with Lucida.

The maid leads Alessia to the courtyard where Signora Bianchi, holding Maria, Lucida, Piero, and Cristina are enjoying the fresh air and chatting happily. She is greeted warmly and asks if Signora Bianchi would mind if she took a turn with Maria. Once Alessia is settled with the baby, Lucida inquires after Signora Salvatori and asks how Alessia is doing. Alessia relays the news of Orazio's will and tells the others about her visit to the studio that morning. Unintentionally, she spills her heart.

"I feel compelled to return to my father's studio. It is where I belong." She meets the eyes of her son Piero. The mother and son exchange a silent understanding.

"I believe that you should follow your heart, Mother. Father loves Firenze and his family is there, but he may agree to make a change for you." Piero glances around at the others.

"Cristina and Piero, how are the business plans coming?" Alessia changes the subject.

"We are almost finished with the first draft of our business plan and have already reached out to Niccolo's business contacts with some promising responses. We haven't had any luck finding a workspace. Everything we have seen is not large enough or is too expensive," relays Cristina.

"Cristina and Piero, I have just had a flash of inspiration. Come back to the studio with me this afternoon. My father expanded the space while I have been away. I don't need all of the studio to complete my work now. Father always had assistants to help him with his large multiple works, but I will only have one assistant. It is a pleasant space. See what you think."

Cristina and Piero exchange glances before Piero responds. "Mother, that is an interesting thought. Thank you for inviting us to view the studio. Let us take a stroll to Via Margutta after the siesta. Maria loves going on walks."

The little group enjoys the stroll, greeting other families as everyone enjoys the later afternoon *passeggiata*. The shopkeepers call out, inviting customers to peruse their wares. The nameplate beside the door has been recently polished. Orazio Salvatori, Il Pittore receives a light caress from his daughter as she places the key in the lock.

Piero and Cristina survey the space while Alessia holds her granddaughter, Maria's little head resting on her shoulder. They are envisioning a workspace for their business with tables near the windows for their workers, fabric storage along the wall away from the light, and a space for them to meet with clients near the front of the large room. A small cubby used to store painting supplies could be turned into a changing room for models. They see that Alessia is correct. Her workspace partitioned off by the far windows doesn't take much of the room and could easily be more clearly divided from the business space. It doesn't take long for the two to accept Alessia's offer to use the space for their business. In Alessia's mind's eye, she already sees two new nameplates beside the studio entrance on Via Margutta: Alessia Salvatori, Il Pittore and another with Piero's and Cristina's names and the name of their business when they decide on a good name. Their business nameplate will be her gift to them. They hurry back to the Bianchi villa to share the good news with great-grandmother Bianchi.

Niccolo and Pietro share a long evening meal at their favorite *ristorante*, consuming a great deal of beautiful wine and share their final evening stroll together. Niccolo finds that he is eager to return to Roma and reside in his childhood home. His mother is beginning to be troubled by poor health and will take comfort in having him close. The Roma Bianchi offices are thriving. He can trust his second-in-command to manage the business in Firenze with occasional visits from Niccolo. He is going to miss Pietro. The two have become close over the years and have fond memories of family gatherings between the families.

Pietro finds that he cannot leave his family and business dealings so rooted in Firenze. He is angry at Alessia for choosing her painting and her father's studio over their marriage but is not really surprised. She didn't have much choice to move to Firenze and marry him years ago. He knows that they never bonded completely, and, of course, he has had his dalliances. He will miss Niccolo more. The two friends embrace at the end of the evening. Pietro wishes Niccolo a safe journey, and Niccolo vows to stay with Pietro when he returns to Florence to check on the Bianchi business.

Pietro notices that there is light in Lucia's window. She must be still awake at this late hour. He climbs the stairs, a little wobbly from the evening's wine and knocks softly on his daughter's door.

"Father, it is late. Are you all right?" Lucia looks concerned.

"*Si, si.* Niccolo and I just returned from our farewell dinner. I will miss him. I am sorry that your mother has chosen to return to Roma. I will miss her as well. We will remain married, you know. Thank you for remaining here with me, my dear."

Lucia embraces her father. "Don't worry, Papa. I will stay with you, and when I am married, my husband and our children will be here. Maybe I will take over mother's studio. I have a secret. Antonio hasn't told his parents yet, but he has decided to stay. We have been talking together a lot. I think I may love him, but you must promise not to tell anyone."

Pietro doesn't have the heart to tell Lucia that it is no secret to anyone else that Lucia and Antonio are sweet on each other.

Lucia bids her father good night, extinguishes her candle, and burrows under her bedcovers. She replays the fantasy in her mind's eye. Alessia's studio is now Lucia's. She prefers to paint elaborate still life compositions, and she sees her paintings in the galleries. So what if she has to sell them under a man's name? Her wedding to Antonio is perfect. They will take over the Bianchi villa, and she will have many beautiful children. She will look after her father. She doesn't care if he has dalliances. Who is she to judge? She doesn't judge her mother either. Lucia drifts off to sleep with a happy smile on her sweet face.

The tradesman has just completed installing the nameplate to the right of the door on Via Margutta. Alessia can't wait for Piero and Cristina to arrive this morning. *Calendula, Biancheria Intima per la Donna* (Marigold, Lingerie for Women).

After Lucida and Alessia confided the story of the marigold chemise to the couple and Cristina was using the chemise as inspiration for her new designs, they agreed to the name their business after the marigold chemise.

Lucida accompanies Piero and Cristina to the studio this morning. The nurse tags along with Maria to help Lucida take her to the Borghese this morning for an airing. The workman is just replacing his tools in his satchel when they arrive. He is pleased at their exclamations of "*molto buona, molto buona*" upon viewing the nameplate. Piero and Cristina are touched by the gift. The studio has proved to be perfect for their enterprise. Their first collection is coming together nicely. The samples are almost ready for showing to potential buyers.

The first appointments are set for next week. Buyers will come to take orders for their wealthy clients. If these first showings go well, they will expand to additional buyers in Firenze and Milano. They want to keep their brand exclusive, so they will limit production for each season. Cristina has taken a risk in her designs. They are more modern and free than the usual stiff corsets women have been wearing. She has a feeling that women will adore them.

For this first collection, she is featuring a wireless brassiere. It is a faint violet chiffon and adorned with shiny storm blue patches of silk charmeuse. There is underwear cut in robin's egg blue cotton, which is given a navy crochet trim. Finally, there are silk chemise in choices of three colors: marigold, pale coral, and creamy white. She is pleased with her choices. Her seamstress will arrive tomorrow morning to complete the final details on the garments and help her press them for display. Piero has helped her fashion frames to display the garments, as if they were a still life painting. She will gauge the buyers' interest before they invest in live models to showcase the garments. She finds that she has her father's instinct for business, and she is determined to make a profit and not take on unnecessary debt.

Piero and Cristina are enjoying the last of the evening meal. Maria has been tucked into bed and her grandmother has bid them good evening. They are thrilled with the results of the week's appointments. The buyers placed large orders and will bring measurements from their clients. No one objected to the cost of these bespoke intimate garments. Piero has been able to procure their fine fabrics at a fair price. They will need to hire additional help. An additional seamstress will be needed. Cristina is pleased that the business is taking shape, but she confides to Piero that she is a bit worried that they won't be able to keep up the pace of new collections and managing more employees. What about competition? What if someone tries to copy her designs and make them cheaper?

Piero tries to reassure his wife. "My dear, we need to take things as they present themselves. It is okay to grow the business at a reasonable pace. Let's not get ahead of ourselves. I forgot to tell you. I saw Ariston the other day. He was with his son who is looking for work. I was wondering if we should hire him to assist us. There are many tasks we could use a strong young man for. Ariston also mentioned he may have a contact who knows reliable seamstresses."

"You are right, Piero. Yes, let's hire Ariston's son. It would be good to have an extra pair of hands, and we will definitely need more seamstress help." Cristina is beginning to relax.

Luca, Ariston's son, is proving to be a hard worker who catches on quickly. An additional seamstress has been engaged, and the studio on Via Margutta is pleasantly humming with industrious activity.

This afternoon, a young woman comes to the studio inquiring after Luca. When he sees her, Luca's face lights up, his cheeks blushing. He introduces the young woman.

"Please meet my friend Adonna. She has recently moved from Firenze and is staying with her aunt. She is looking for work in a fine household."

Adonna lowers her eyes and shyly greets Cristina and Piero. "It is my honor to meet you." She stands close to Luca, looking up to him with adoration.

She can't believe how easy these people are to fool and how quickly it was to track Niccolo Bianchi here to Roma. She only had to perform a few "favors" to elicit information, and it was a stroke of good fortune that she was introduced to Ariston and Luca. Her "aunt" runs a discreet bordello and readily hired her when she arrived from Roma. One of her first clients was a Signor Reda, who proved to be loose with his tongue following a bit of drink.

Glancing around the studio, she finds herself wondering if she should position herself to be a model for Cristina. After all, she is Niccolo's daughter, and it would suit her desire to be privy to their business. The idea of appearing in fine lingerie definitely appeals to her. It won't take her long to gain the family's trust. She can't wait to see Niccolo's expression when he sees that she is now residing in Roma.

Luca is clearly smitten, and Adonna finds it amusing to toy with his affections. They take long walks in the Borghese, stealing a few kisses in the shadows of the landscaping. He would do anything for her, and it isn't long before he makes it known to Cristina that his friend Adonna would be happy to model the lingerie if they need a model for their next collection. Cristina asks him to bring Adonna to the studio one day, and she will speak to her. She is working on the new designs for the next collection, and perhaps it would be good to have a live model for fitting and draping.

Adonna is adept at modeling the beautiful garments as she works with Cristina and the seamstresses to demonstrate how the garments sit on the body. Cristina notes how the young woman curiously changes her persona from the shy, demure girl to a seductive young woman. There is something about this young girl that doesn't quite ring true. She observes how the girl manipulates Luca. At any rate, she has enough to worry about without adding concern for Luca to her list. She tells herself to dismiss these thoughts and returns to her sketchbook to work on new ideas. Their second collection needs to be ready for showing in just a month's time, and they have double the appointments from the initial showing, many of them are repeat clients.

Niccolo and Lucida have arranged for their tenants to leave their villa, and they have happily moved back into the villa where they began their marriage. All of Alessia's paintings of Lucida in the marigold chemise have arrived from Martina's villa. They have decided to display the paintings in their private chambers and invite Alessia to help them arrange the work.

Niccolo has decided that he will make it his business to buy all of the work that was sold at the business meeting through Signor Reda. It is better to have the paintings remain safely in the family.

He enters Signor Reda's gallery and pretends to study the work lining the gallery walls. Most of the paintings are bucolic landscapes. He waits for the other customers to leave and approaches Signor Reda. At first, Signor Reda appears to not recognize Niccolo.

"*Allora*, Signor Bianchi, I did not recognize you at first," Signor Reda lies. "Please, welcome to my gallery. May I assist you or answer any questions about the work?"

"I have interest in some particular paintings, and I may have an interesting proposition for you." Niccolo detests Signor Reda but does his best to be charming to the man. "Do you recall some work by an anonymous artist? The paintings are of a young woman in a marigold chemise. I believe they were sold at a businessmen's meeting. My late father purchased one and I inherited it. I have recently moved back to Roma in order to attend to my business dealings, and I am interested in adding my private collection."

"Ah, signor, yes, I do recall those stunning paintings. I am trying to find out if the artist has new work to sell. My contact in Firenze has not returned my messages. I will let you know if I am able to locate any new work." Privately, Signor Reda cannot believe that the intimidating Martina is the sister of Niccolo. "By the way, has your sister, Martina, returned to Roma as well?"

With great self-control, Niccolo replies, "You have not heard. My dear sister has sadly departed this earth. She had a heart attack in her villa. It was a shock to us."

Signor Reda is now the one who is shocked. That explains why Martina has not been in contact with him. She still owes him money.

"I am sorry, Signor Bianchi. I am sure you miss her very much." Signor Reda's wheels are turning rapidly, trying to make sense of this new development.

"*Si, si,* my sister is missed. She managed a large part of our business in Firenze. However, it is not new works by this artist that I am seeking. I want to acquire the paintings that you sold. They would complete my father's collection. Really, it is in his honor," Niccolo informs the gallery owner.

"The paintings are already in the other gentlemen's collections. I doubt they would be willing to part with them," replies Signor Reda, his fat face contorted with an insincere smile. His wily mind is swirling with thoughts of making this opportunity pay dividends for him.

"Perhaps I could arrange a private showing for the gentlemen to appreciate their works. If you include your father's painting, you could make a case for having the paintings together in honor of your father. I would, of course, take a commission on the sales if the gentlemen are willing. Who knows if any of these businessmen might be in need of some extra money at the moment?"

"Very well, signor. Please arrange a private showing as soon as possible. I am eager to complete the purchase." Niccolo has no trust for Signor Reda, but he has to agree that the man's idea might just bear fruit.

Cristina and Piero decide to honor the staff for all their hard work. The collection sales went very well, better than expected. They decide to have a reception party at their home and invite Niccolo and

Lucida as well. The elder Signora Bianchi is excited to have a celebratory gathering. She misses the entertainment she and Signor Bianchi did in their younger years and volunteers to organize the food and drink for the event.

The household staff bustle with the preparations. They will be serving prosecco with fritters of vegetables to accompany and small sweet cakes to finish.

The appointed time arrives. Cristina and Piero welcome their staff warmly. Everyone is chatting about the new collection and congratulating each other on a job well done. They are all excited to be part of this new enterprise. Adonna stays close to Luca. She takes on her shy, demure demeanor.

Niccolo and Lucida arrive last. Piero introduces them to the staff, proudly outlining the jobs that each of them perform for the company. When it is Adonna's turn to be introduced, she performs a small curtsy, muttering that she is pleased to meet Signor and Signora Bianchi and keeps her eyes downcast. Niccolo's heart skips a beat as he recognizes Adonna. The girl chooses that moment to raise her eyes and hold eye contact with Niccolo for a long moment. They are interrupted by Piero loudly proposing a toast to the success of *Calendula, Biancheria Intima per la Donna.* "Bravo! Bravo!" they all join in amid cheers and laughter.

The evening ends on a high note. The staff feels appreciated and proud. The elder Signora Bianchi is beaming with joy at having her household filled with celebration.

Adonna maneuvers herself into position next to Niccolo as the guests depart. When they are out of earshot, she quickly whispers, "Meet me at the entrance to the Borghese near Via Pinciana tomorrow at the beginning of siesta." She swiftly moves forward to Luca's side, slipping her hand to take his elbow, and beams a smile at the boy.

Cristina observes Adonna's performance. She is puzzled and curious, making a note to herself to keep her eye on the girl.

The following morning, Niccolo arrives early at his office. He informs his assistant that he is not to be disturbed today, as he wants to review contracts and needs to concentrate without interruption. *What is on Adonna's mind?* he wonders. He is fairly certain that she cannot be trusted, and it is a mystery to him how she managed to make her way to Roma and find employment in his daughter's business. He contemplates his options. He did not like the way she gazed at him last evening. He detects the sinister in her eyes and is not fooled by her performance of being the innocent young girl. Adonna knows too much about Martina and the cantarella poisoning. She is aware that he and Pietro purchased her services. He berates himself for his foolishness. Why was he so trusting of Pietro and the madame? Why did he not foresee blackmail as a possibility? How could he be so stupid? What is the solution to this problem? He closes his eyes, breathes deeply, and begins to formulate a course of action.

Gathering his cloak, he informs his assistant that he is taking an early luncheon with one of his business colleagues. Making swift strides, Niccolo makes his way to the section of the city known as Monti. There he locates the office of a man he has used in the past for detective services when researching the backgrounds of business associates that are a bit unsavory. Although he is not proud of it, his father had taught him that his business negotiations could benefit at times from arranging for a man to be caught unawares in a compromising position.

Giovanni responds to his knock and happily greets him with a hardy embrace. "What a surprise to see you, signor. How is business?" he inquires.

"Business is wonderful, my man. There is just a small problem at the moment, and I believe that you may be just the man to assist me."

"*Si, si,* signor. I am always at your service. Tell me about the problem."

Niccolo explains that there is a young woman, a prostitute, that may be attempting to blackmail him. He is supposed to be meeting her this afternoon at the entrance to the Borghese near Via Pinciana. He would like Giovanni to follow him. It would then be prudent for Giovanni to follow the young woman. Could Giovanni determine when she might be vulnerable and alone? Perhaps there could be an unfortunate accident?

Giovanni is swift to calculate Niccolo's problem. He knows just the man who is an expert in arranging unfortunate circumstances for his clients. He agrees to follow Niccolo to the meeting with the young woman and to trail her. The two men shake hands and agree upon a suitable renumeration for the job.

Niccolo settles himself into his favorite restaurant at his usual seat near the back. He relaxes as he congratulates himself on finding a solution to his problem so swiftly. The waiter takes his order, and he enjoys his meal before making his way to the entrance to the Borghese near Via Pinciana at the beginning of the siesta.

Upon exiting the restaurant, he takes a moment to glance up and down the street. It is quiet at the beginning of the siesta. The clanging of dishes being cleaned following the midday meal and murmurs of conversations float through the windows. There, a few meters down the street, Giovanni leans against a stone wall, partially hidden by a planter containing a large mulberry tree. He looks relaxed, enjoying a smoke. *Good*, thinks Niccolo. *Giovanni is ready.*

Soon Niccolo is at the Borghese entrance. In the distance, he sees Adonna settled on a bench. She has a book in her lap and appears to be engrossed in its pages. He approaches the bench, and she ignores his presence. Finally, she glances at him through her lashes and indicates that he should join her on the bench.

Slowly she turns toward Niccolo and addresses him in a low seductive voice. "Signor, you have a lovely daughter. Cristina and Piero treat me like family. Their business is thriving. I am sure you are proud. I wonder how they would take the news that their fathers arranged to have their aunt Martina poisoned. I am also sure *la polizia* would be quite interested in prominent businessmen and their illegal activities. The gossip would surely sell many newspapers. The stigma would no doubt hurt Cristina and Piero's business. What do you think?"

Niccolo finds that his anger at Adonna is surging through his body. He takes several moments to compose himself before replying. "What do you want, Adonna? You are the one who committed murder, and given your profession, I doubt the court would be sympathetic to you. Most likely, you would be climbing the scaffold to the gallows with a crowd cheering below."

"I don't believe that you will take that chance, signor. I want to be set up in my own villa. A beautiful villa with enough room for a dozen young girls that I can supervise. In return, I will move back to Firenze and vow never to see you, your family, or to breathe a word of your crime to anyone. I will give you one week to begin making the arrangements. I am sure Pietro can be of assistance. If you do not agree with my request, I will be writing a letter to the most notorious of the broadsheets with titillating gossip. It will be the ruin of you and your family. Meet me here at the same time a week from today with your decision." Adonna stands and quickly walks down the path, exiting the Borghese.

Niccolo remains on the bench, allowing his rage to fully return. He watches as Giovanni slips from the cover of a grove of rose bushes and follows Adonna at a discreet distance. After a time, he finds that he is tired and decides to return home for the remainder of the siesta.

At home, he climbs the stairway to the bedchamber he shares with Lucida. The paintings line the walls. He still is awed by the view of his dear wife posing in the marigold chemise, so lovely in her youth. He lays down beside the sleeping Lucida, praying that she will never discover the darkness of his deeds.

Luca bounds up the stairs to the workshop. He is gasping for breath, and his innocent face is red and contorted with anguish.

"Cristina, Piero, something terrible has happened. I went to pick up Adonna at her aunt's villa, and her aunt informed me that there has been an accident. A carriage got out of control, and the horses trampled poor Adonna before she was able to get free of their path. She was killed instantly. Her aunt was furious, and she yelled at me to never come by the villa again." Poor Luca is now sobbing.

Cristina moves to comfort Luca, trying to get him to calm down. She thinks Piero should take Luca home to his father Ariston and rest for a few days; he is so distraught. Piero agrees and departs with Luca under his wing.

Signor Ruel is sorely disappointed. When he made his weekly visit to madame's villa, she informed him that it was impossible for him to have his regular client. The poor girl was killed in an accident involving a runaway carriage. The horses trampled her to death before she could escape. He had enjoyed the cunning little thing. He decides to forego his pleasure this week and hopes that madame will have a suitable replacement for him soon.

He returns home and writes out a message for his boy to deliver to Signor Bianchi in the morning. He has managed to arrange for the businessmen who own the paintings with the woman in the marigold chemise to gather for a special meeting in the back of his gallery next week. He includes the date and time for Niccolo to arrive. The amount of his commission sings a happy song in Signor Ruel's greedy soul.

Niccolo arrives at his office the following morning and sees that there is a note from Signor Ruel on his desk. His assistant informs him that the boy had arrived early with the note as well as some gossip. Apparently, a young girl named Adonna was killed in a carriage accident. The carriage was out of control and the horses trampled her. He said everyone was talking about the accident, saying that the carriage was going too fast on the narrow street, making it almost impossible for one to escape.

Niccolo expresses his shock at the accident and thanks his assistant for delivering the note. They review the business for the day, and the assistant leaves Niccolo to attend to business.

The bottom left-hand drawer of Niccolo's desk has a secure lock. He unlocks it and stares down at the pile of coins. Carefully he extracts the amount that he and Giovanni agreed upon for the job and places it in a velvet bag. It will weigh down his leather valise as he makes a lunchtime visit to Giovanni. He marvels at how efficiently his problem has been solved. *May Adonna rest in peace*, he muses.

The day that Signor Ruel has set for the viewing of the paintings has arrived. He and his shop boy are setting up the room. He had to cajole the gentlemen into agreeing to this viewing. He wonders if they will be willing to sell the paintings to Niccolo. There have been so many requests for new work from the mysterious anonymous painter, and now that Martina is no longer in the picture, he is not sure how he will squirm his way out of this dilemma.

He steps back to gaze upon the five paintings, reminiscing about the evening when they were all sold in a frenzy of bidding. His boy rushes to his side informing him that the gentlemen are beginning to arrive. He moves to the front of the shop and welcomes the men into the back room. His boy takes their cloaks and offers them refreshment. Chairs and a small table are set in a semicircle before the paintings in such a manner that everyone has a nice view of the beautiful young woman in the marigold chemise.

Niccolo is the last to arrive. The boy ushers him into the room where Signor Ruel is holding court. His heart stops for a moment as he views the group of paintings all together. The painting his father had purchased is on the far right at the end of the row.

"Greetings, gentlemen," Niccolo announces as he approaches the men for a welcoming embrace. "Thank you for responding to Signor Ruel's request and allowing your paintings to be here for this viewing. I will get right to the heart of the matter. As you all know, my dear father has passed away and I have moved back to Roma to carry on the Bianchi business. My father purchased the painting on the far right, as you will recall. I have inherited the stunning painting. As I grieve my father's passing, I have been thinking that in his honor, I would like to unite the five paintings as a tribute to him. I would like to propose a purchase. It would be a great honor if you would consider my request. I am willing to pay you double the amount you paid for your painting. This would give you a generous return on your investment, and the paintings will be reunited."

Murmurs arise from the group as Signor Ruel observes carefully. The boy discreetly refills goblets as the gentlemen consult one another. Finally, one of the men stands and approaches Niccolo. He extends his hand and indicates that he is willing to make a profit on the painting. Niccolo knows that this gentleman has pressing business debts, but he is not sure about the others.

"Bravo, signor, bravo." Niccolo pats the gentleman on the back, as he smiles encouragingly to the remaining three men.

There is more discussion among the men, and finally, one by one, they approach Niccolo to affirm that they have agreed to sell. There is a hardy round of applause to conclude the evening. Signor Ruel is ready with his ledger, calculating the amounts each of the gentlemen will receive. They sign the bills of sale and are told that their funds will be delivered to their villas the following day. Signor Ruel is pleased.

Lucida invites Alessia to witness the arrival of the original paintings at their villa. The movers heft the large pieces to the room where they will be displayed along with Martina's collection. The arrivals are set in a row across from Martina's in the oval room. Niccolo and Alessia remove the protective wrappings as Lucida observes the revealing of the canvases.

Alessia and Lucida stand as one, with arms locked around one another's waists. Their heads touch as they remain very still. They are both in a reverie, back in Orazio's studio surrounded by the aroma of oil paint and turpentine. The power of those hours creating the paintings seeps back into their pores, bringing with it contentment and happiness. They both turn to Niccolo, pulling him into their embrace.

"*Grazie, grazie, grazie*, Niccolo for reuniting the work," they exclaim in unison.

The two friends retire to the terrace to reminisce. The early autumn air is gathering a bit of chill. The moon is almost a complete orb, providing a romantic glow to the evening. They wrap themselves in quilts and enjoy a Sambuca together.

Alessia misses Pietro and speaks of going back to Firenze when Niccolo returns later this month for business. She hopes that Pietro will visit her in Roma. She does not hold much hope for that in her heart. She tells Lucida that she believes that her true home is in Roma and in Orazio's studio. She is working on a new series of portraits, mothers and daughters in their daily surroundings. She wonders how much longer she will be able to paint. Her eyesight has begun to fail her.

Lucida is sad for her friend. She has seen the new series of paintings and believes that they are strong. It seems that her friend may not achieve the recognition for her work that she deserves. It isn't fair. She shares with Alessia that she notices that Niccolo becomes short of breath frequently and is often fatigued. She doesn't share that often, especially at night, her heart beats wildly and it is difficult to catch her breath. She reminds herself to go to Santa Maria in Trastevere tomorrow and light candles for her friend and Niccolo and for herself as well.

Niccolo has wished the women a *buonanotte* and retires to his study for the evening. He has been wondering what will become of the Bianchi business. He will travel back to Firenze later this month to meet with his senior partner who has expressed an interest in eventually taking over the business, but he would prefer that the business remain in the family. He will bring Antonio along. Antonio misses Firenze, and it would please his father if he agrees to pursue the family business. Niccolo has included his son in the business for several years now, and he shows promise. Martina would have been the ideal mentor for him. She was so astute and strong in business matters. He hopes that Antonio would never know the cause of Martina's demise.

Calendula, Biancheria Intima per la Donna on Via Margutta has been an astonishing success. Cristina and Piero now have locations in all of the major cities of Europe. The brand is exclusive, and despite the expansion, they have to be very nimble to keep up with demand. Cristina continues to design and manage the creative aspect of the business while Piero is in charge of the operations. Luca has grown into a valuable employee, as he has earned the trust and respect of Cristina and Piero. He has fallen in love with one of Cristina's models, Rosa. They marry and their son, Ariston, named after his grandfather, delights everyone with his happy nature and antics.

Maria has inherited a gift for design from her mother. They love working together on new creations for their line. One afternoon, they are alone in the studio. Maria takes a break from her sketching, and with her chin resting in the palm of her hand, she quietly observes her mother. Her face is drawn and sad, her shoulders slumped.

"Mother, what is wrong? You appear distressed," Maria gently inquires.

Cristina glances up at her daughter and sighs. "I didn't want to bring you distress, but I find that am becoming more fatigued every day. I am sinking into despair despite trying to fight it. The physician thinks that I am just aging. He says there is nothing he can do for me. I went to speak to the priest about it, but he just told me to perform more Hail Mary rosaries."

Tears form and slip down Cristina's cheeks.

"Mother, it is getting late. Let's stop work for the day, and I will bring you home. We will relax in the courtyard with a glass of wine and enjoy a nice evening meal with Father. Come now."

Maria takes charge, closing the shop and taking her mother firmly by the arm. They make their way down to Via Margutta, greeting their neighbors politely, and stroll toward the original Bianchi villa.

Later that evening, Cristina invites Maria into her bedchamber for a visit. They review some of the plans for the new collection. Cristina rises and moves to her wardrobe. She turns to Maria with an ornate wooden box and opens the lid. Inside is a bundle wrapped in muslin. She unfolds the fabric, revealing the marigold chemise. Reverently, she lays the chemise in Maria's arms.

"My dear, it is time for me to pass the chemise on to you. I have told you the story of Alessia and Lucida and the power of the marigold chemise. You are now the keeper of the treasured garment. It has inspired our business, and I trust that it will continue to inspire you." Cristina's hands are shaking slightly as she returns the marigold chemise, carefully wrapped in the muslin to its box for safekeeping.

"Mother, I am honored. I will treasure the marigold chemise and always return to it for inspiration and strength." Maria embraces her mother and finds that she is overcome with emotion. She is worried about her mother and knows that the time for the business to be passed to her is coming soon.

Maria closes the door to her bedchamber softly and turns the key to lock the door. She does not want to be disturbed tonight. Carefully she removes the marigold chemise from the box and lays it on her bed. She undresses, allowing her garments to pool at her feet. Carefully she slips the marigold chemise over her head and stands in front of her mirror. As she gazes into her reflection, she feels sensations reverberate throughout her body. They are pleasant sensations, leaving her with a feeling of peace and confidence. After a time, she slips the marigold chemise over her head and returns it to the box, carefully wrapped in the muslin. As in the tradition of Lucida and Cristina, Maria stores the wooden box in the back of her wardrobe for safekeeping.

Slumber comes quickly and deeply as Maria burrows under the covers. The dream is vivid. She finds herself floating over and around the Tempietto. She is wearing the marigold chemise, and the silk is soft and sensuous as it flutters against her skin. As she peers through the columns of the Tempietto, she sees figures lying in a circle, their feet toward the center. Curious, she moves closer into the Tempietto until she is hovering above the figures. Observing, she sees that the figures are lying on the top of coffins. Each one is covered in a gauze fabric. Now she can make out the faces of the figures. She sees Niccolo, Lucida, Alessia, and her parents, Cristina and Piero. The wind is picking up speed, and she hears the sound of thunder coming closer. A bolt of lightning strikes to her right, and as she turns to look, she sees Martina dressed in a voluminous black gown, her face twisted in anger. Martina pulls a sword from the fold of her skirt and advances toward Maria. She is about to overtake her when Maria awakens, her bedsheets drenched in sweat.

Signor Ruel has proposed that he would like to visit the Bianchi villa now that all of Alessia's paintings are together again. Perhaps they could have a celebration. Before she left Florence, Adonna had given Signor Ruel a special case of wine that she had stolen from Martina. He was not aware that she had stolen the wine as she told him Martina gave her a gift in return for certain favors. There had been extra cantarella to dispose of, so Adonna had decided to infuse an additional case of wine. Better to remove the evidence from Martina's villa. Signor Ruel was, of course, flattered that the courtesan would give him a gift.

Niccolo advised the women that the only reason he agreed to Signor Ruel's request was that he had agreed to arrange the selling of the paintings. On the appointed evening, Niccolo greets Signor Ruel and escorts him to the room where Lucida and Alessia wait with the paintings.

"*Buonasera*, signoras. How kind of you to have me here to celebrate the uniting of the paintings. I have brought some special wine. It was a gift from Signora Martina when I assisted her in acquiring some art. Landscapes, I believe. Let us toast the reunion of the special paintings." Signor Ruel is oblivious to the shocked expressions of his audience.

The servant standing by has already uncorked the wine and is pouring everyone a glass.

"*Saluti, saluti!*" declares Signor Ruel as he raises his glass.

Niccolo, Lucida, and Alessia murmur pleasantries as they sip the wine. Niccolo takes charge and informs Signor Ruel that they are expected at a colleague's villa for dining, so they need to bid farewell. He thanks Signor Ruel for the wine and signals to the servant to show the gentleman to the door.

"The carriage has arrived," announces the servant.

At the close of the evening, they deposit Alessia at her villa. She remarks that she has had a bad headache all evening. They wish her well, and before the carriage has arrived at their villa, both Niccolo and Lucida are feeling ill. They decide they should go directly to bed and rest.

Niccolo, Lucida, and Alessia are discovered the following morning by their servants. Their families are shocked and grieved. Preparations for mourning are put into motion. Signor Ruel's boy discovers his master's body slumped on the floor of his gallery.

Following the passing of Niccolo and Lucida, it takes months to sort their affairs. Antonio moves into his parents' villa with his new wife and steps into the role of leading the Bianchi enterprises in Roma and Florence. All of Alessia's paintings have been moved to the Bianchi villa. Piero and Lucia will divide and sort them later. Cristina and Piero pour most of their inherited funds into their business. They remain living in the Bianchi villa as per Signora Bianchi's wishes. Maria will inherit everything. The responsibility of it all weighs on her, but she is determined to make her parents, grandparents, and great-grandmother proud.

The marigold is likewise associated with the sun—being vibrant yellow and gold in color. The flowers are open when the sun is out. The marigold is also called the "herb of the sun," representing passion and even creativity. It is also said that marigolds symbolize cruelty, grief, and jealousy.

Part V

Maria is inspired to modernize the business. She launches new lines under her name, *Maria*. She misses her parents but is certain they would approve of the changes she is implementing. They taught her to trust her instincts. This evening in the St. Regis Rome Hotel, the debut of her latest collection is taking place. Attendance is by invitation only to their most loyal clients, with a few of the newly rich and famous sprinkled in for spice.

Standing on the runway, Maria welcomes her guests to the show. She is wearing a marigold slip dress in honor of her grandmother, accessorized with a stunning necklace she has designed using jewels from Lucida's and Cristina's collections. She honors them in her speech, providing a brief history of the company. The guests are invited to enjoy the latest addition to the company's offerings, a swimwear collection.

The models begin to strut down the runway. Maria's brand is classic, sensuous, and elegant. The swimwear is classic in style with details such as wide braided straps and fastenings. The suits are tailored for a flattering fit. One- and two-piece suits are displayed in noir, ceil, poppy, and terra-cotta. Flowing robes over bras and panties follow the swimwear. Maria likes to end her shows with her collection of chemises. The garments are varied in style and length. Geranium, blanc, magenta, noir, blush, and pearl swish down the runway. She always reserves the marigold chemise as the finale of the show.

The models return to the runway for their closing walk.

"Bravo! Bravo!" the guests shout, applauding wildly.

Maria and her staff form a line, joining hands and bowing their gratitude. She thanks her guests and invites them to enjoy a drink and nibble. Waiters begin winding through the crowd with trays of champagne and canapes.

Mingling with the crowd, Maria receives compliments on the collection with promises to visit her showroom to place orders. She relaxes and enjoys the evening, happy that the collection is well received. Across the room, she catches the eye of a gentleman she doesn't recognize. He flashes her a smile and then resumes his conversation with his companion. The evening is beginning to wind down. Guests are retrieving their wraps when the gentleman approaches her.

"May I introduce myself? I was brought to your show this evening by a business associate. I must say that I am very impressed with your collection. I am Lorenzo Alberti. Would you care to dine with me this evening? I would love to hear more about your business and more about you."

"It is lovely to make your acquaintance, signor. But I am afraid that I have plans for dining this evening. I like to celebrate with my staff after our shows." Maria is intrigued but has been caught off guard by the invitation.

"Of course, I understand," replies Signor Alberti. "But please allow me to arrange another time for us to dine together. I will deliver a message to your showroom tomorrow. *Buonanotte.*"

He turns and departs the room. Maria notes that his companion awaits him by the doorway.

Maria, Rosa, Luca, and Ariston Jr. are in a meeting in the newly remodeled studio on Via Margutta. They are analyzing spreadsheets for the distribution of their garments. The buzzer sounds, indicating that someone is at the door. Rosa sees through the security camera that it is a messenger with some packages and letters. She retrieves the parcels and quickly sorts through the envelopes. One is hand addressed to Maria.

Maria slits the envelope with the antique letter opener left behind by Orazio. She feels like the spirits of the painter and his daughter will always permeate the studio. She is grateful to have their history surround her as she works. The handwritten note falls through the slit in the envelope.

Dear Signora Bianchi,

I will send my car for you this evening at seven. The driver will be waiting for you at the west end of Via Margutta. I look forward to an evening together.

Regards,

Signor Alberti

Ariston and Rosa look up from their spreadsheets expectantly. Maria shares the note with them and notes their attempt to suppress amusement.

"What are you going to do? Are you meeting him?" asks Rosa.

Maria sighs. "Well, why not? As you both know, it has been a long time since I have had a date. He is quite handsome and charming as well. What do I have to lose?"

During siesta, Maria rushes home to peruse her wardrobe. She selects tight black jeans, a silver belt, white fitted blouse, and a geranium leather jacket. Black stiletto boots complete her look along with a woven black bag. She slips a few silver bangles over her right wrist and throws a geranium lipstick in her bag as she calls a taxi to take her back to the studio.

The afternoon passes quickly with pouring over spreadsheets and making phone calls. Before she knows it, it is 7:00 and time to meet the car. Everyone else has already left the studio, so she locks up and sets the alarm. Maria greets her neighbors as she makes her way to the end of Via Margutta. Her smile is genuine and happy as she navigates the street in her stilettos. She realizes that she feels sexy, not a feeling she has had for some time. As she approaches, a driver emerges from a black Alfa Romeo.

"Signora Bianchi?" he inquires.

"*Si, si,*" she acknowledges.

He opens the passenger side rear door and assists her into the leather seat. The driver navigates the Roman traffic expertly. She notes as they cross the Ponte Garibaldi that he turns on to Via Dandolo and heads up the hill toward Villa Doria Pamphili. He stops in front of a stone town house and exits the driver's seat to assist her exit. He approaches the door and rings the bell. A moment later, a manservant opens the heavy wooden entry door. He appraises the young woman before him and, with a nod, greets her. "*Buonasera*, signora. Please follow me."

Maria follows him into a small courtyard and through a glass door into an entry hall. He leads her into a sitting room and indicates that she should make herself comfortable.

"Signor Alberti will be joining you momentarily," he pronounces.

Maria begins to take in her surroundings when Lorenzo appears. Her heart catches a bit. His crisp blue shirt is open at the collar, and his grey slacks just brushes the top of his loafers. He looks robustly healthy, clean-shaven, and impeccable. Just the way she likes a man.

"I am so pleased that you decided to take me up on the offer of an evening together. I have taken the liberty of having my cook prepare us a meal. We can dine on the rooftop terrace. Shall we begin with an aperitif?" Lorenzo moves to take Maria's hand and leads her through the hallway to the steps leading to the terrace.

The terrace is private. The perimeter is lush with plantings and a trellis overflowing with wisteria. They settle on a small sofa. The cook appears with two negronis and some mixed nuts. Lorenzo inquires if Maria would prefer a different beverage. She tells him that a negroni is her favorite aperitif. How did he know?

Maria and Lorenzo dine on leeks vinaigrette with burrata cheese and mustard breadcrumbs, followed by herb-roasted branzino with potatoes, tomatoes, and olives. A crisp Albarino pairs perfectly with the fish. The finishing sweet is chocolate and blackberry. They compliment the cook when he brings espresso and grappa and inquires if they desire anything further.

Lorenzo informs the chef that he is free to depart for the evening. The couple continues to engage in increasingly intimate conversation. Maria realizes that she feels more relaxed than she has in years. Normally, she would bristle at a man taking over and making decisions, but she has to admit that it feels okay to let someone else take charge for a change. She hasn't realized how stressful it has been to be the sole decision maker for the business with her parents gone.

The candles lighting the terrace are beginning to expire. Lorenzo takes Maria's hand and gently leads her down the stairs and into the hallway. He pauses at one of the doors before ushering Maria into his bedchamber. His maid has left lamps softly lit and the covers turned down. Maria notes that the room is spacious and decorated to feel substantial but not overly masculine.

Maria is awakened by Lorenzo drawing open the draperies. He sets a tray with tea on the bedside table. He leans over to kiss her softly.

"I must leave for a business meeting. The driver is waiting and will take you home when you are ready. There is everything you need in the bathroom."

Maria is silent as she watches him depart. She pours herself a cup of tea and settles back against the pillows. In that moment, she decides that she will allow herself to enjoy this journey, wherever it takes her.

Rosa and Luca are busy with a fresh shipment of fabric samples when Maria arrives at the studio. She dives right into work, catching herself humming happily as she sorts the samples. Ariston Jr. arrives with the news that their production sight is humming. He thinks that they will be able to make scheduled delivery on their orders as expected.

Weeks pass with no word from Lorenzo. Maria does not allow herself to acknowledge that she is disappointed. She throws herself into her business, and when she is alone at night, she purposely distracts herself from reveries of her evening with him. She stays up late reading or watching television. She schedules dinners with friends and business associates.

It is a Friday. The balmy early summer day is lovely. She sits at her desk, staring out the window, and thinks to herself that it would be a perfect weekend to dash off to a fine hotel on the coast with a lover. *Oh well*, she sighs to herself. She will have to find another way to amuse herself this weekend.

Rosa interrupts her daydream.

"Maria, here is your mail." She places a stack of envelopes on the desk and watches for Maria's response. On top of the stack is a square envelope addressed by hand to Maria.

Maria stares at the envelope for several minutes before reaching out and opening it. Rosa can't help herself. She looks over her boss's shoulder and reads along.

Dear Maria,

"My car will be waiting for you in the same place, at the west end of Via Margutta, at five this afternoon. I am taking a risk that you are free for the weekend. I sincerely hope so. My thoughts have been filled with memories of our evening together.

Yours,
Lorenzo

"Are you finished reading, Rosa?" Maria teases her employee. She glances at her watch and informs Rosa that she needs to go home to gather a few items for the weekend.

"I will return in time for our wrap-up meeting. Please let Luca and Ariston Jr. know. Thank you."

She chats with the taxi driver as he speeds through the streets and arranges for him to return in an hour to take her back to work. By the time she is back out on the street to get in the taxi, her bed-chamber is a swirl of discarded garments. She had such indecision about what to pack for the weekend. Finally, the chosen items are precisely packed in her favorite overnight satchel. She allows herself to feel excitement in anticipation of the weekend ahead.

The Casa Angelina is cut into a cliffside on the Amalfi coastline. It is meant to be a romantic retreat, refined Italian elegance and tranquility. Maria has heard of the hotel. Several of her friends have stayed here with their lovers. She sighs contentedly as Lorenzo directs the bellboy to transport their bags to the lobby. She had a chance to study Lorenzo on the drive from Rome. He seems completely at ease with himself, she notes. Again, she reminds herself that she will follow this encounter and enjoy it, wherever it may take her.

Their suite on the top floor of the hotel offers stunning views of the sea. Maria is inspired by the clean white interiors, the Mediterranean blue, and the umber and olive of the cliffs. She will incorporate the palette into her next collection.

The weekend passes in a haze of bliss. Maria and Lorenzo seem to be made for each other. They enjoy the beach, hire a sailboat for a sunset cruise, and spend long mornings, afternoons, and evenings tangled in the bed linens. Sunday afternoon, they begin the journey back to Rome. They chat easily during the drive. Lorenzo drops her off at her villa, kissing her farewell. She does not ask him to come in.

Maria takes a long bath, and before she wraps herself in her robe, she goes to her wardrobe and removes the box that contains the marigold chemise. She slips it over her head and greets herself in the mirror.

"Mother, grandmother, and Alessia, I believe that I have found love. I wish you were here so that I could tell you every detail. Please be happy for me. I feel like you are with me when the marigold chemise is enfolding me in your love and wisdom. Thank you." Maria feels like she has communicated with them. She feels content. Carefully, she returns the marigold chemise, wrapped in the muslin, to the box and returns the chemise to its place in the wardrobe.

On Monday morning, before she heads to the studio, she crosses the Ponte Sisto and makes her way to Santa Maria in Trastevere. She had come here to pray with her grandmother many times. Today, she lights a candle and prays for this new love to be real and to bring her contentment and joy.

The days pass quickly. With Maria, they are working on production of the swimsuit collection as well as the fresh colors for bras, panties, robes, and chemises. Maria is also beginning to sketch for the next collection. Her palette is inspired by the heavenly weekend with Lorenzo.

The couple spends several nights a week together at Lorenzo's home. Sometimes they go out to dine, and other times his cook prepares dinner for them. Maria sinks into a blissful state. She can hardly believe that she has found her true love at last. One evening, as they are finishing their dinner on the patio of one of the trattorias in Trastevere, Lorenzo informs Maria that he must return to Milano the following day. He tells her that his business in Roma is concluded and that he is needed at the Milano headquarters. He is not sure when he will be back in Roma. He must depart very early the following morning, so he will drop her off at her villa.

Maria is silent. She doesn't know what to think. Why has she allowed herself to proceed with her head in the clouds? Yes, she had told herself that she would follow this relationship where it would lead her, but the abruptness of Lorenzo's departure alarms her. Her heart feels unsettled.

"Oh, yes, of course. It is getting late, and I have an important meeting early tomorrow. We should call it a night." Maria will not relinquish her pride for this man or any other man.

When they arrive at her villa, Maria is frosty with her departure. She exits the car and swiftly moves to her door, calling out a *buonanotte* with her back to Lorenzo, not bothering to wait for his response.

She draws herself a warm bath, pours herself a generous goblet of wine, and settles into the warm jasmine-scented water. Tears flood down her cheeks. After a time, she towels off, and pulling a chemise over her head, she settles into her bed. The warm water and the wine have made her dozy.

In the dream, she is on a small sailboat. She sees Lorenzo on the balcony of the hotel where they had stayed. He is gazing out at the dark Mediterranean, the moon reflecting off the water. Her boat is right in front of him, illuminated by the moon. She removes her white chemise and waves it wildly, calling out to him. There is no response. He is completely unaware of her presence.

Bright sunlight forces Maria to open her eyes. She had neglected to draw the drapes, and the morning light is quite strong. It is going to be a very warm day in Roma. The dream has left her feeling sad and very alone. She misses her parents.

She decides that she needs to take a day to herself. She never allows herself to stay home from the studio, even when she is ill. She calls Rosa and tells her that she is not feeling well and will be taking the day to rest.

She has no appetite but forces herself to dress and take a table at her favorite café. The proprietor has placed a few tables and chairs to the side of the building. She settles into the table farthest from the street. The waiter brings her a cappuccino and warm cornetto. Maria has chosen her largest darkest sunglasses for the outing. Hopefully, she will not encounter anyone she knows. She needs solitude today to clamp down on her heart.

After finishing her breakfast, she strolls over the Ponte Sisto and makes her way through Trastevere and up the hill toward the Villa Doria Pamphili. It feels good to stretch her legs. On the way, she passes the Tempietto. This morning, no one is visiting the temple, just little birds flitting through the columns. Maria enters the temple and sits at the base of one of the columns. She removes her sketch pad from her bag and settles into sketching ideas for the new collection. She begins to feel relaxed, and slowing her breath, she can feel the presence of her mother, grandmother, and Alessia surround her. Before she realizes it, she has made a little drawing of the four of them, joining hands and dancing in their chemises. She will keep this sketch by her bedside to draw strength from. After a time, she continues to the Villa Doria Pamphili, taking a brisk walk through the grounds and nodding to the joggers, the young mothers pushing carriages, and the older men beginning to gather for a game of boccie.

Maria enjoys people watching in the square of Santa Maria in Trastevere as she slowly finishes a salad on the terrace of the main restaurant in the square. She decides to spend a moment praying and lighting a candle in the church before she returns home. *I will not allow myself to be distracted by this love affair,* she pledges to herself as she prays for strength.

There is no word from Lorenzo. Maria keeps her attention focused on the business. Their customer base is growing, and they have orders from around the world. She and her staff can barely keep up with the work. She will have to hire more employees, especially to oversee production.

It is late summer when she begins to feel nauseated in the mornings and fatigued in the afternoons. Maybe she is dehydrated from the summer heat, she thinks and vows to drink more water. After a few weeks, the nausea has not subsided. She is drinking plenty of water. Slowly it dawns on Maria that she has not had her *mensus* for several months.

Her physician is kind as he delivers the news that she is indeed pregnant. He congratulates her enthusiastically and does not inquire about the father of the baby. Maria leaves his office and walks home in a trance. Her mind is blank. She is unable to process the news that she has just been given.

The plane trees along the Tiber River are beginning to dry from the late summer heat. Maria decides to take the long route from the studio along the riverside to her physician's office near the Santo Spirito hospital for her maternity exam. She has been slowly coming to terms with her situation and has determined that if she hires a nanny, she should be able to manage raising the child on her own. Maria has not confided in anyone. She won't be able to keep her secret much longer. The stigma of being a single mother may be difficult. Her priest will not approve for sure. *Well, that is too bad*, Maria thinks to herself. At this point she has no plans to consult Lorenzo or notify him that he has fathered her child. She finds that her heart has hardened a little more with each passing week.

The nurse welcomes Maria warmly and shows her to the examining room.

"Doctor has scheduled an ultrasound for this visit," she informs Maria. "We will see how things are progressing. How are you feeling? Is the nausea subsiding?" the nurse inquires as she checks Maria's vitals.

"The nausea is much better. I am a little more tired than usual, but otherwise, I am feeling fine," Maria responds.

The technician preps Maria for the procedure. When she is ready to proceed, her physician enters the room and greets her. They exchange pleasantries. Maria watches the monitor as the transducer moves across her belly. She begins to feel excitement as she observes the images. The technician points out the tiny form.

"There, see the little shape?" she asks. "Oh, wait a moment. There is another one. There are two." She looks to the physician to confirm. He moves closer to the monitor.

"My, oh my, Maria. She is correct. You are having twins. Do you want to know their sex, or do you want to wait? We can be more certain in a few months' time when we do a second ultrasound."

Well, this is a surprise, thinks Maria. "I think I will wait until the next time to know the sex of the babies. I need a little time to get used to this news."

Maria is thankful for the long walk back to the studio. She wishes her parents were still with her. They would be able to advise her. Perhaps it is better that there will be two children. They will be able to keep each other company when she has to put long hours into the business. She thinks of some of her friends who have children. When she rallies the courage to share, she can elicit advice on nannies and child-rearing. She will have to consider so many things. Their education, their religious training, and their character development all needs to be considered. Thankfully, her villa is spacious with more than enough room for a family. Despite herself, she begins to imagine the nursery. Yes, she will start her babies out together in the same room. They can have separate rooms when they are older.

Maria's friends and Rosa, Luca, and Ariston have rallied to provide support. They have encouraged her and assured her that they will be available to help with the babies. Her best friend Sophia has volunteered to be with Maria at the birth. Sophia has three young children, so Maria considers her an expert. They have long discussions about Maria's situation and endlessly evaluate the pros and cons of informing Lorenzo that he is about to become the father of twins. Sophia thinks that she should inform him, advising Maria that the children have a right to know who their father is, and, of course, they will be increasingly curious as they grow older. Although Maria sees her friend's point, she remains adamant that she will not make any contact with Lorenzo. Her heart is now stone when it refers to him.

Sophia is with Maria when the time comes for her to deliver. The labor is long and arduous, but at last, the baby boy and girl arrive safely. Even at birth, the twins resemble Lorenzo. Tears flood Maria's tired eyes, and Sophia holds her hand and comforts her while the nurses clean and swaddle the newborns. She will call the girl Laura and the boy James. Sophia accompanies Maria and the twins to her villa and helps them get settled. Celia, the nanny Maria has hired, is a dear woman. She is very experienced and has agreed to live at the villa with Maria. Between Celia and her household staff, Maria feels that she can manage the twins and her business.

One evening, when Celia has settled the twins into their cribs for the evening and has retired to the adjoining room, Maria slips into the nursery. Laura and James are three months old now. They are healthy and thriving. No one could doubt the resemblance to their father. Celia is warmly maternal, which Maria is grateful for. She has been able to continue with her business dealings without feeling any guilt or remorse. She wonders why she feels a bit removed from her babies. Sophia thinks it is because she does not have their father to share in the delight and love of seeing the babies grow. Maria is not sure.

Maria and her staff are immersed in planning the presentation of their newest collection. The event will be at the Hotel Principe di Savoia in Milano. They are introducing an intimate collection in soft French stretch lace. The palette is expanded to include hickory, forest, heron, peony, and acai, along with marigold. They have been working hard to form partnerships with production vendors to make the brand sustainable. The past year has been focused on reducing waste and incorporating excess materials into future seasons. They have produced new brochures for clients and buyers to educate them on the direction of their brand.

They have been in Milano for a week, busy preparing for the event. It is fast-paced and nerve-racking, but it always seems to come together in time for the show. Maria is overseeing the final touches to the runway when she notices a group of businessmen and women observing the activity. One of the women approaches Maria. She introduces herself as Signora Alberti. She tells Maria that she has heard of her brand and has seen her lingerie in a boutique here in Milan. "Would it be possible for her to attend the show? I would love to purchase some garments for an upcoming special vacation with my husband, Lorenzo Alberti."

Maria is the consummate professional. "It is a pleasure to make your acquaintance, Signora Alberti. Yes, it would be fine if you attend the show. The buyers for the boutiques will be in attendance. They can make arrangements for your order. Here is a ticket for the show, and my business card to show the buyers." Maria reaches into her bag and hands the ticket and card to the signora. She smiles. "Please excuse me, I need to consult with the workers." She moves swiftly toward the runway and the workers. After a few words, she walks to the lobby elevators and pushes the button to take her to her room.

She can't afford to take time to indulge her emotions. She pours herself a large glass of mineral water and takes a moment to compose herself. So Lorenzo is married. Thinking back to the first time she met him, she now recalls that the companion he was speaking with is his wife. She is sure it is the same woman. How could she be so stupid? She debates with herself if she should inquire about Signora Alberti among the boutique owners. They are a group that loves to gossip. *No,* she decides. *I will stay focused on ensuring this show is a success and return home to my babies.* In that moment, she realizes how much she misses them and loves them.

Maria addresses her audience wearing her signature marigold slip dress and jewelry. As usual, she honors her parents and provides a little history of the marigold chemise. She spends a few moments talking about the company's plans for a more sustainable business for the future. As she turns to exit the runway and signals her staff to begin the runway show, she sees Signor and Signora Alberti seated in the third row. They do not detect her glance.

At the conclusion of the show, the models and staff, along with Maria, return to the runway amid cheers of "Bravo, bravo" and loud applause. She invites the audience to enjoy champagne and nibbles and moves backstage with her staff. Everyone is in a jovial mood as they congratulate each other on a job well done. She mingles with her guests and is pleased to hear that buyers and boutique owners are placing large orders. As the crowd is beginning to dissipate and she and the staff are ready to depart for their celebration dinner, one of the waiters approaches Maria. He hands her an envelope.

"One of the guests asked me to give this to you." He moves away quickly to assist his team members in clearing glasses from the room.

Maria slips the envelope into her bag. She knows who this is from and definitely wants to wait to open it in private. The team leaves for home tomorrow afternoon. There is so much to be done to wind up the show and organize their contacts for orders. She will ignore the envelope until she is in the privacy of her bedchamber.

Maria's team has been working so hard. When they arrive back in the studio in the late afternoon, she tells them that they can all take tomorrow, Friday, off and enjoy a long weekend. She decides that she is going to give her nanny a long weekend as well. In that moment, she pledges that she will be more present with her children and spend more time with them. After all, they only have one parent.

That evening, when she has finished tucking the twins in for the night and sent the nanny away, she is finally alone. The maid has laid a fire in the study adjoining her bedroom. She goes to her desk and reaches into her bag for the envelope. Without examining its contents, she sets it on the flames and watches it extinguish.

Laura and James are growing rapidly. Maria is unnerved that they clearly look like Lorenzo and more so with each passing year. They are very simpatico with one another. Sometimes it seems as if they have the same mind. They are precocious. They challenge Maria and Celia to keep them engaged and learning with new experiences.

Maria takes them to work with her several mornings a week. She has set up a corner for them to draw and play with scraps of material. The staff sometimes gives them small tasks to perform. Soon they will begin school. Maria has already arranged for them to attend St. Stephens School when they turn fourteen. She has decided against sending them to a boarding school. She wants them to remain close.

Now that the twins are in school, they are very curious about families. The other children talk about their fathers. Sometimes they see fathers collect their children from school and some of them help with organizing sports for the children. They begin to hound Maria for information about their father. Although Celia and Sophia advise her against it, Maria has decided to lie to them. She concocts a story about their father dying before they were born. He was killed in a plane crash while on business in Africa. He did not know that Maria was pregnant, and because they were not married, she was not able to obtain details or contact his family. For now, they don't push her for more information. She is not proud of herself but is determined that Lorenzo will not learn of his children.

When the twins turn fifteen, they beg Maria to take them to Milano for a holiday when the business presents the newest collection. They also want to go to Firenze and to the coast to spend time by the sea. Their friends have all been to those places, and, of course, they want to go as well. They enlist Celia and Sophia to convince their mother to grant their request. Finally, Maria relents. Sophia has strongly pointed out that Maria can't keep the twins from expanding their world. She needs to allow them some independence. Laura and James are elated. The three of them spend their evenings planning. They map out a holiday, taking two weeks. Maria allows them to choose the itinerary and the hotel they will stay at on the coast. Despite herself, Maria is becoming excited about taking her children on a holiday and questions why she has waited so long to give them this opportunity. She has devoted so much energy to the business and to keeping her twins safe, that she has forgotten how to enjoy herself. Laura and James are very good at organizing the holiday. She is surprised at how adult they seem. *Celia and Sophia are correct*, she thinks. It is past time to give the twins more freedom to spread their wings.

At the collection's show, Maria's staff puts Laura and James to work. Maria is proud that the twins are capable, and the staff and models love having them around. At the celebration dinner, Rosa compliments them with a special toast. She can picture the two of them carrying on the business when their mother is no longer able to manage.

The visit to Florence is satisfying for Maria and the twins. They spend hours and hours in the Uffizi and declare it the favorite part of the visit. One afternoon, when their feet are too tired to walk another step, Maria hires a taxi to take them to the twin villas where Lucida, Niccolo, Alessia, and Pietro had lived. Maria had visited the villas just once as a child and was intrigued by Alessia's studio. It is empty now, gathering cobwebs. A maid lets them into the courtyard. Antonio is the only one remaining. He is sitting in the courtyard in a wheelchair, with a robe covering his lap. The maid informs them that his wife passed and that he had a stroke shortly after her death. Their children are planning to sell the villas, as they have all moved to Buenos Aires in Argentina. The maid, a caregiver, and a handyman keep Antonio comfortable and the villas in good repair. They are all saddened by this news and return to their hotel to rest. Tomorrow they move on to the coast.

The twins have chosen the Hotel Aurora in the hamlet of Sperlonga. They settle into a suite with three bedrooms overlooking the hotel's private beach. Maria settles into a chaise on their balcony and enjoys the sea breeze, relaxing and sipping a mineral water. She feels content.

James and Laura set off to explore the beach and the village. They buy gelato and sit on the seawall to people watch and decide that the day is perfect for a swim. There is a group of other teens enjoying the beach. Perhaps they will make some new friends. After finishing their gelato, they head back to the hotel to change into their swimsuits. They notice that their mother has dozed off in the chaise, so they quietly change and slip out to the beach.

Soon they are swimming, splashing and laughing along with the group of other teens. The group invites them to relax on the beach with their friends. They sprawl on towels. Several of the boys are playing with frisbees and the girls are rubbing sunscreen on each other. They fall into easy conversation about school and families. The group are from Milano. Laura and James are the only ones from Roma.

The group begins to break up when they tell Laura and James that they have to return to the villa where they are staying to get ready for the birthday celebration for one of their fathers this evening. It is going to be a big party. The man has many friends and business associates. There will be drinks, food, and dancing. They invite James and Laura to the party. "Bring your mother too," they say. "Everyone is welcome." One of the girls writes down the address and hands it to Laura.

"Please come tonight. It will be so much fun," she urges them.

James and Laura decide that they are definitely going to the party. They doubt that their mother will agree to come along, but they will encourage her to join them. They agree that their mother needs to enjoy herself more. All she does is work.

Maria is unpacking when the twins return to their hotel room. They are in their swimsuits. They are beaming with good cheer.

"I see that you have been swimming. How is the sea?" she asks.

"Mother, we had so much fun. We met some new friends. They have invited us to a party this evening. There will be dancing, food, and drinks. It is a birthday party. You are invited as well." Laura's face is flushed with excitement.

"Oh, we shouldn't go. We don't know these people. I was thinking that the three of us could enjoy a nice dinner at one of the restaurants overlooking the sea this evening," Maria replies.

"No, Mother. We are going. We are old enough to make new friends and meet new people. The girl said that it will be a large party, and she definitely made it clear that we are welcome. Laura and I hope that you will join us, but if not, we will be going anyway. You need to enjoy yourself. This is supposed to be a vacation for all of us. You agreed on that." James is firm.

Maria is frustrated. She was hoping for a vacation for just the three of them. She doesn't feel like socializing. She recalls her conversations with Sophia and Celia regarding allowing the twins to have more independence and new experiences. She knows that she has sheltered them too much. She sighs and joins them in the sitting area of their suite.

"My dears, you are right. It is good for you to meet new friends and have new experiences. Let's plan to go to the party this evening. We can have our dinner overlooking the sea tomorrow evening. I will change our reservation." Maria goes to retrieve her phone.

James and Laura look at each other and burst out laughing.

"We are partying tonight!" James grins at his sister.

It is a beautiful evening. The stars are brilliant, and the moonlight dances off the sea. Their taxi is waiting for them as they depart the hotel lobby. Laura gives the driver the address her new friend had given her. He nods and directs the taxi up the winding road that hugs the cliff. He turns into the drive of a large villa. Music is drifting from the open doors and windows. Maria and the twins exit the taxi and move toward the open door. A butler greets and welcomes them, inviting them to join the party. They hesitate a moment at the doorway. They can see that the rooms are packed with party guests chatting away as waiters circulate with trays of drinks and nibbles.

Maria sees that the twins are a bit intimidated. She takes a deep breath, signaling them to follow and moves toward the crowd. Following their mother, the twins scan the crowd for the friends they met that afternoon. They watch as Maria breaks into a group and introduces herself, turning to introduce her children. She laughs as she tells them that they are on holiday from Roma and that her twins had met some friends swimming that afternoon. She inquires as to where the teenage guests might be gathering.

"Oh, they will be on the back terrace," instructs one of the women. "Follow me, I will take you to them." She indicates that James and Laura should follow her.

The twins trail behind the woman as she briskly weaves her way through the crowd, periodically calling out a greeting to someone she knows. Soon they approach a large courtyard filled with young people. Trees surrounding the terrace are filled with twinkling lights. There are tables with candles placed around the edge of courtyard. The atmosphere is festive. Groups of teens cluster, laughing and joking. Laura spots their friends from the beach.

"Oh, there they are, James. Over in that far corner. Thank you, signora, for helping us find our friends." She smiles at the woman who tells them to enjoy themselves as she makes her way back into the crowd.

Laura and James are greeted warmly by their new friends. They are introduced around to others, and they begin to relax and enjoy themselves. A self-assured tall woman enters the courtyard and signals quiet to the young people.

"*Buonasera*, girls and boys. Please move to the ballroom. We are going to sing *buon compleanno* to Signor Alberni. My dear husband will love it." She moves to take the hands of one of James and Laura's new friends and pulls him from the group. "Son, let us lead your friends to the ballroom."

The group follows Signora Alberni and her son into the packed ballroom. Signor Alberni is holding court with a group of businessmen and women. Signora Alberni and her son interrupt the group and lead the signor to a stage at the far end of the ballroom. They join him, gazing down at the many guests who have come to enjoy the celebration.

Signora Alberni addresses the guests. "Many thanks to everyone for joining us this evening to celebrate Signor Alberni's sixtieth birthday. We hope that you will enjoy the food, drink, and dancing. Please join us in singing *buon compleanno* now." She begins, and the guests belt out the tune, ending with shouts of bravo, bravo.

Maria drops her champagne glass. It shatters on the stone floor and the liquid splatters down her dress. A waiter rushes over to clean the broken glass and gives her a napkin to blot her dress. She is receiving curious glances from the guests around her, but she is in a trance of shock and cannot move. She just stares at the stage. There is Lorenzo, in his element, kissing his wife and son and bowing in thanks to their guests.

Finally, she is able to shake herself out of her trance. She desperately scans the crowd for James and Laura. She must get them out of here at once. She starts moving around the room, trying to navigate the crowd as they move to the adjoining room where tables of ten are set up for guests to enjoy a celebratory meal. They will be serving Lorenzo's favorite birthday meal: a starter of spinach soup with tortellini, followed by caprese salad with mozzarella, tomatoes, and basil, and for the main course, veal piccata with lemon, wine, and capers. Dessert will be tiramisu classico cake. Waiters are busy seating guests and taking orders for beverages.

She spots her twins across the room. They are with a group of other teens making their way out to the courtyard tables where they will be served dinner. Maria rushes over to the group and calls out to James and Laura.

"James, Laura, I need to speak with you. Hurry, it is important."

The twins are alarmed. Their mother looks very distraught. They move to join her.

"Mother, what is the matter?" asks Laura.

"We must leave at once," Maria says, as she pulls them toward her.

"Why must we leave? You are acting strange, Mother." James pulls his arm away from his mother, staring at her in alarm.

"You must obey me. Follow me now." Maria is uncharacteristically harsh.

The twins lock eyes. Their mother never speaks to them in that manner. Something must have happened. They follow her reluctantly toward the entrance. They are both thinking the same thought. *We will get to the bottom of this, whatever it is.*

Maria can see the door. They are almost there. She will ask the butler to ring for a taxi to take them back to the hotel. She is going to have to invent a plausible story as to why they will be cutting their vacation short. Perhaps she can devise an emergency with the business. She will think of something.

They are about to leave the drawing room when Signor Alberni appears. He plants himself directly in their path. He is gazing intently at Maria and then at the twins. His face is blank as he sees before him a boy and a girl that have his exact features. The eyes, the nose, the shape of the mouth and jaw are his.

He addresses Maria, "Maria, it has been a long time since we have seen each other. You are looking well. And who are these handsome twins you are escorting out of my party? Why the rush to leave?

Are you not enjoying yourselves, young people?" Lorenzo asks James and Laura.

"Mother is making us leave. We want to stay. We have made some new friends and were having a great time. How do you know our mother?" James responds.

"Of course, you two should go back to the courtyard and enjoy the evening with your new friends. Your mother and I are old friends. Go along now. I will deal with your mother," Lorenzo directs them.

The twins take advantage of this turn of events and quickly turn their backs on Maria and go to rejoin their friends. Maria is livid as she watches her twins disobey her.

Lorenzo takes Maria's arm and steers her to a small room off the entry. He closes the door and stands in front of it, blocking any attempt she might make to escape.

"My dear Maria, is there something you should tell me? How old are those beautiful children? I see that they have an uncanny resemblance to their father, don't you think?" Lorenzo inquires as he moves closer to Maria.

Maria despises herself for accepting his embrace and cannot contain the weeping that floods her emotions. Lorenzo manages to lock the door, and the lovers are soon on the floor in a frenzy of passion. When they are finished, Lorenzo dresses hurriedly and announces that he must return to his birthday celebration. He turns back just before he leaves.

"You know you can't keep the twins from learning who their father is, don't you?"

Maria locks the door behind him and begins to straighten her clothing and hair. She finds that she is depleted. She remains seated on the floor of the small room staring off into the distance, her mind blank.

The butler and a few young assistants are manning the entry to the villa. She approaches them and requests a taxi to return her to her hotel. She locates a pen and her business card in her bag and writes a quick note to her twins. The butler agrees to deliver the note.

James and Laura,

I am not feeling well and have taken a taxi
back to the hotel. Enjoy yourselves and ask the
butler to call a taxi when you are ready to leave.

Love,
Mother

Well, they wanted more independence, Maria addresses herself as
she climbs into the taxi and braces herself for the wild ride down the
hillside.

James and Laura are having the time of their lives. This is the
first big party that they have attended. Their new friends are so much
fun and so welcoming. The group dances and jokes, falling into fits
of hilarity.

Lorenzo wanders to the entrance to the courtyard where the
young people are partying. He watches his son and daughter across
the room, noting that they both use similar gestures and expressions
as his son Stephano does. It is uncanny.

He gestures to one of the waiters. Discreetly, he slips a one hundred Euro note in the waiter's jacket pocket. Leaning close to the
young man, he whispers his instructions, "Do you see the twins at
the table by the vine, a boy and a girl?"

The waiter affirms, "*Si, si.*"

"Go and collect their glasses. Tell them you are taking orders
and will bring them a fresh drink. Take care to wear your white serving gloves and place the glasses in a plastic bag from the kitchen.
Place the bag into a kitchen basket and bring it to me. Go now, make
haste. Gracias."

The waiter moves to complete the task. He is used to strange
requests from businessmen and women at the events he works. As
long as he is compensated and it is not dangerous, he doesn't mind.

In a few moments, the waiter finds Lorenzo and presents him with a basket. Lorenzo takes the basket from the waiter with a curt nod, dismissing him. He approaches the butler and asks that the butler place the basket in the trunk of his automobile. Another one hundred Euro note makes its way into a jacket pocket.

Stephano accompanies James and Laura to the entrance of the villa, sending them off in a taxi. As Stephano moves back inside, he muses about how much he enjoys their company. They seem so easy with him, almost as if they are family. They make plans to meet at the beach tomorrow. The party is breaking up. Stephano sees his parents wishing the guests a good evening and goes to join them.

After the last guests depart and the waiters are cleaning up, the three of them sit in the cool evening air and speak about the party. They all agree that it was a success, and Signor Alberni squeezes his wife's hand in thanks.

Maria is asleep when the twins climb out of their taxi and tiptoe quietly into their hotel room. She spent several rushed hours on the phone, canceling the remaining week at the hotel and arranging for a car to arrive in the morning and take them back to Roma.

The Mediterranean sun awakens Maria. She stretches and pads to the balcony, allowing herself a few moments of peace before she wakes James and Laura. She is not looking forward to their objections and questioning. The previous evening was a nightmare. She just wants to get back home and forget about it. The twins will soon be resuming school and the drama of the last night of their vacation will fade away. She orders breakfast to be delivered to their room. At least there will be a beautiful breakfast for them to enjoy before they depart.

The twins refuse to speak to their mother and completely ignore her on the long drive back home. When they arrive home, they carry their luggage to their rooms in silence. Maria takes a relaxing bath and changes into a lounging robe. She carries her laptop to the courtyard to check on her correspondence. Tonight, she will prepare the twins their favorite pasta dish, hoping to break the ice between them.

Maria is busy in the kitchen chopping and sautéing, sipping on wine, when the twins saunter in. She greets them warmly, as if nothing has happened.

"I hope that you are hungry. I am preparing your favorite, linguini with pistachio and lemon. It is a beautiful evening. Shall we have our dinner on the terrace?"

"Mother, you can't just ignore us. Why did you make us return home early? Rosa and Luca can handle the business. You can consult with them on the phone. It is not fair to us," James speaks for both of them.

"Laura, help me with the lemons. James, set the table on the terrace. I gave the household help the rest of the week off, so we will need to manage without them. I know you are disappointed, and I am sorry, but it can't be helped. Life isn't always just the way you want it. It is not going to make any difference to complain. I will need your help at work this week, so plan to spend your days at the studio," Maria addresses them with authority.

Grumbling, the twins do as she has instructed. Dinner conversation is strained, and they excuse themselves as soon as they have finished their pasta.

Alone on the terrace, Maria sips the last of the wine and replays the scene with Lorenzo in her mind's eye. She examines the truth that she is still in love with him despite her determination to harden her heart. All of her efforts to focus on the business and the twins did her no good. She is angry at herself for allowing her emotions to rule. Maria acknowledges that she is deeply hurt by Lorenzo. It was so painful to see him with his wife and son. Tomorrow she will go to Santa Maria in Trastevere to light a candle and pray for strength. Before she sleeps tonight, she will take out the marigold chemise, slip it on, and evoke her mother and grandmother. It will comfort her. How she misses them.

Lorenzo settles back into his office. His wife and son will remain by the sea for a few more days. Yesterday afternoon, he had an appointment with a reputable DNA lab. The laboratory took his blood and assured him that they specialize in paternity tests and deliver the results promptly and confidentially. Taking his car keys from the tray on his desk, he summons his assistant and hands him the keys and an envelope.

"My car is in the garage. Drive to this address. There is a basket in the trunk. Take the basket and this envelope into the clinic and leave it with the receptionist. They will be expecting you."

His assistant takes the keys and envelope, nods to his boss, and departs.

He makes an appointment for lunch with his attorney for the following day. The two are old friends, and Lorenzo has faith in his legal talent. The attorney has managed to finesse Lorenzo's problematic situations over the years. Once he receives the results from the lab that he is expecting, he needs to have his attorney execute his plan. The twins are his, and he will not allow Maria to keep them from him. Signora Alberni will not be happy with this news, but it is not the first time she has had to deal with her husband's discretions. Money and status are more important to her than fidelity. His attorney usually recommends new jewelry, but the appearance of fifteen-year-old twins will no doubt require something more substantial.

Lorenzo is preparing to leave his office to meet his attorney for lunch when a messenger arrives with a document requiring his signature. When the messenger departs, he closes his office door for privacy. The document confirms that he is the father of James and Laura. He places the document in his briefcase and exits his building to meet the attorney.

The two friends greet one another warmly at the restaurant. They are regulars, and the waiter shows them to a discreet table in a corner of the dining room. By the time they have completed their lunch, the attorney outlines the document he will prepare for delivery to Maria. Lorenzo is prepared to take Maria to court and exercise his parental rights. He is proposing that the twins should reside with him until they reach the age of majority, eighteen. He will grant Maria visiting rights. The attorney is confident that because Maria kept Lorenzo's paternity secret for the first fifteen years of the twins' lives, the court will rule in Lorenzo's favor.

It is a busy morning at the studio on Via Margutta. Rosa responds to the bell indicating that they have a visitor. Through the intercom, a male voice states that he has a document that requires a signature for Maria Bianchi. Rosa lets the messenger in and goes to fetch Maria. Maria signs for the document and the messenger departs. She is curious as the envelope indicates that it is from a law firm. Her first thought is that one of her vendors must be upset about a transaction. Maria settles behind her desk and slits the envelope open with Orazio's ancient letter opener. She reads the document over three times before she begins to comprehend the viciousness of its contents.

Her voice is shaking as she implores Rosa to call her attorney and set up an appointment that afternoon.

"Tell him that it is an emergency," she directs.

Maria's rage soars with each step as she walks the mile to her attorney's office. By the time she is seated across from the stately old gentleman, she can hardly speak. She hands him the document over his tidy desk and watches his face as he reads it.

Finally, he speaks. "My dear Maria, it must have occurred to you that there might be consequences for not informing Signor Alberni that he had fathered your children. Under the law, he does have parental rights."

"But I have raised James and Laura by myself. Surely he can't take them from me," Maria implores her legal counsel.

"We will have to go to court to try to stop him, but you must prepare yourself that he will most likely prevail. He can't stop you from seeing them, but he has a strong case. You kept him in the dark about the existence of the twins for fifteen years." The attorney reaches across the desk for Maria's hand, his eyes warm with sympathy for her.

Three months later, the judge is presiding over the custody case. Maria has managed to keep this development from James and Laura. She considers taking the twins out of the country, but that is not practical due to her business. Sophie is the only person Maria has confided in. Sophie has patiently listened to Maria's fears and anger. She strongly advises her not to take the twins out of the country. It would only prolong the inevitable. Lorenzo obviously wants to be a part of James's and Laura's lives, and as he is their father, he does have that right. Her friend gently tries to convince Maria that the best thing she can do is to accept the verdict of the court. The twins are approaching their majority age soon, and they will learn who their father is. Maria knows that her friend is correct, but her heart is not ready to be peaceful with Lorenzo being part of the twins' lives.

The court has appointed a judge who is decisive and efficient in his rulings. Maria and her attorney arrive at the court and make their way to the front table set aside for them. She glances to her left and sees that Lorenzo and his legal team are already in place. He appears to be ignoring her. The judge instructs the parties about the parameters of the law as it pertains to child custody matters. There will be no jury. He will allow each attorney a prescribed amount of time to summarize their case. He has already reviewed their briefs and documents, including the DNA paternity report.

Maria is having difficulty concentrating. She feels as if part her is floating above the room. Her heartbeat is rapid, and her hands have turned ice cold.

Finally, the two attorneys have presented their summaries. The judge is ready to pronounce his verdict. Maria's attorney nudges her to pay close attention. She shakes herself to attention and sits taller in her seat, attempting to calmly focus.

The judge's voice booms and echoes off the chamber walls. "Signor and signora, I am ready to pronounce a decision in your case after carefully considering the supporting documents. Signora, you have been deceitful to Signor Alberni and to your children. They could have had access to a loving father, and you have deprived them of that. You have kept them to yourself for fifteen years. Therefore, I am granting Signor full custody of the twins until they reach their majority at age eighteen. You will be granted visits with them twice a month and for two weeks during their summer school break. The two young people will reside with Signor Alberni beginning in two weeks. This decision is final. There is no avenue for appeal of my decision. The court is adjourned for the day."

Sophia moves from her seat in the back of the room to the hallway. She is prepared to take Maria home and stay with her this evening. The twins will have to be informed of this momentous decision. Their lives are about to be upended. She feels strongly that Maria will need her support. She calls her husband and relays the news. He will have to manage the home front for her this evening.

Maria looks like a ghost as she exits the courtroom. Sophia takes her arm and leads her outside. Her car is waiting for them. Sophia directs the driver to take them to Maria's villa. They are silent as the driver navigates the Roman traffic, weaving expertly between the noisy mass of cars and motorcycles.

When they enter Maria's villa, she goes directly to her bedchamber and closes the door. Sophia decides to let her friend have some privacy. She makes herself comfortable on the terrace and waits.

She is startled by the chattering of young people as they step onto the terrace. James and Laura are startled to see Sophia relaxing on the divan under the wisteria.

"Ciao, Sophia. Where is Mother? Is she still at the studio?" Laura inquires.

"She is resting. She will be down in a little while. How was your day? Are you looking forward to the new school year?" Sophia asks.

"Why is she resting and not at work? Is she not feeling well?" James chimes in.

"We had a coffee together earlier, and she began to have a headache, so I brought her home. I thought I would wait for a while to make sure she was feeling better," Sophia lies.

"She will be fine. Mother never gets ill. We were playing tennis this morning. I need to go clean up. We will talk to you later." Laura smiles as she and James leave the terrace.

Once Sophia determines that the twins are in their rooms, she makes her way to Maria's bedchamber. She knocks softly on the door and lets herself in. Maria is lying on her bed wearing the marigold chemise. Her right arm is hooked over her eyes, bent at the elbow. She turns when she hears Sophia approaching the bed. Still shielding her eyes, she thanks Sophia for bringing her home.

"James and Laura have returned home from tennis. I told them that you started having a headache while we were having coffee this morning. They are cleaning up now. Maria, you need to tell them. The sooner, the better. You don't want them to hear this news from Lorenzo or his solicitor."

"Sophia, I can't do it. I just can't. I won't be able to look them in the eyes. They will never trust me again. I don't know what I am going to do. My heart is broken, and my courage has left me." Maria's arm remains over her eyes. She can't even face her dearest friend.

"Maria, I know this is horrible for you. But you are their mother, and it is your duty to inform James and Laura of the court's decision. If you don't tell them, I will." Sophia is firm.

"Then you do it because I won't," Maria replies.

Sophia returns to the terrace and waits. Before long, she hears the twins in the kitchen foraging for lunch. They are chatting happily about their tennis games that morning and gossiping about one of the young men they played with. He is cheating on his girlfriend, and she is sure to find out before the school year resumes. They bring their lunches out to the terrace and are surprised to find that Sophia is still there.

"Sophia, did you speak with Mother? Why are you still here?" asks Laura, noting the serious look on Sophia's face.

"Laura, James, please be seated. I have some important information to share with you." Sophia indicates that they should join her at the table. She takes a slow deep breath and clasps her hands together tightly on the table. Once she is certain that she has their full attention, she begins.

"I am afraid that I was dishonest with you this morning. Your mother was in court. There was a custody hearing involving the two of you. Your mother is deeply distraught about the decision the judge has made. She had an affair with a man named Lorenzo Alberni sixteen years ago. I believe you met him when you were on vacation and there was a birthday party for him. She was very much in love with him. It turned out that he was married, and they stopped seeing each other. It was then that she found out she was pregnant with twins, the two of you. At the time, she made the decision to keep the identity of your father a secret. Only Celia and I know the truth. Once you two were old enough to no longer require a nanny, Celia moved to other employment and vowed to keep your mother's secret. Your mother truly believed that she was doing the right thing.

"When Lorenzo saw the two of you with your mother at the party, he became suspicious and arranged for a DNA test to determine paternity. He took your mother to court. This morning, the judge awarded him custody of you until you reach your majority age of eighteen. You are to go live with him beginning in two weeks. You will see your mother twice a month and for two weeks during your school break. I know this is astonishing news. Your mother is so upset that she is unable to face it. I am sorry."

James and Laura are stone faced. They look into each other's eyes for a long moment. Then James stands and slams his fists on the table, sending the lunch dishes smashing to the stone floor. He turns to leave the terrace and Laura follows him. They burst into their mother's room to find her lying prone on her bed with only the marigold chemise on. She doesn't turn to acknowledge them.

Laura is weeping, and James is shouting. "You are a filthy liar. You had no right to tell us a lie about our father dying. We could have had a father all these years. How could you do this to us? Where is he going to take us? Where will we go to school? I hate you." He slams her bedchamber door, storming out of the room, Laura following.

The twins hop on James's motorcycle, Laura on back and holding tight as they speed off. He has no idea where he is going.

Sophia is drained. She finds Maria still in the marigold chemise and now lying face up.

"Thank you, my friend. I know it was my duty as a mother, but I am so grateful that you had the courage to do what I couldn't. I heard them leave on the motorcycle. I pray that they will be safe. They will return. You don't need to stay any longer. Please, go home to your family. I will speak with you tomorrow." Maria's voice is drained of confidence.

She stands and embraces Sophia. Their tears mingle until Sophia ends the embrace and prepares to leave for her home. Maria watches out her window as Sophia's driver helps her into the car and drives down the street.

Alone, she carefully slips out of the marigold chemise and places it in the muslin, returning it to the box at the back of her wardrobe. She takes a cool shower to revive her senses, dresses, and calls for her driver to take her to the studio. There is much work to do. Before leaving, she leaves a note for James and Laura advising them that she is at work but will return in time for the evening meal. She signs the note, "With much love, Mother."

The appointed day for Lorenzo to bring the twins to Milano has arrived. Maria, James, and Laura have barely spoken in the past two weeks. They have long telephone conversations with their father. He has arranged for their schooling in Milano. They will be living in a villa with a cook, housekeeper, and a tutor to supervise them. Lorenzo will be visiting them frequently. Stephano will accompany him as well. Stephano is already arranging plans for James and Laura to join his group of friends. He tells them they will love their new life.

7At first, they take the train from Milano to Roma to visit with Maria, but after a year, the visits cease. She speaks to them on the phone and sees them when she has events for the company in Milano. They make it clear that they remain angry and distrustful. Their home is now with Lorenzo and Stephano. Once they finish their secondary studies, they plan to work for their father. They tell her with excitement.

Maria and Sophia decide to take a holiday to Corsica. Sophia is lonely now that her children have left home and her husband is very busy at work. Maria concedes that she could benefit from a week of relaxation by the sea. The two friends enjoy themselves. They take hikes, shop, and enjoy long seafood dinners in restaurants overlooking the sea.

One day, they hire a driver to take them on a tour of the island. At the end of a lovely road lined with olive trees, they come upon a cottage overlooking the sea. There is a sign on the gate indicating that it is for sale. Maria asks the driver to wait. She climbs over the gate fence and proceeds to explore. Surrounding the cottage, she peers in the windows and peruses the gardens. The cottage appears to be in decent shape although in need of some attention. On the spot, she makes the decision. She runs back to the car and retrieves a pen, paper, and phone from her bag. She notes the number of the real estate company and snaps several photos of the cottage. Back in the car, she tells the driver to take them back to their hotel.

"Sophia, I am buying this cottage. I am going to make some improvements, and I am going to spend time here. Because of the new technologies, I can easily go back and forth from Roma and manage the business. Besides, it is time for Luca and Rosa to take on more responsibility. I am not getting any younger. You will visit, won't you?" Maria is beaming. She hasn't felt this excited in a long while.

"Bravo, Maria! Yes, I will visit so much you will get sick of me." Sophia is happy to see the old Maria back.

Part VI

Today will be an eventful one. Maria has summoned her son and daughter without their respective spouses to visit her at the island. They will be arriving late this afternoon. She needs to discuss her failing health and the disposition of her business and assets. Laura and James have not been apprised of the purpose of this meeting, and she is surprised that they agreed to make the journey to the island without the usual fuss about taking time from their busy, chaotic lives. Whenever she thinks about her children, she is astonished that they are her offspring. Sometimes she thinks that they are the devil's spawn. Once their father took over the twins up bringing, they transformed from delightful, happy children into entitled, selfish, self-absorbed obnoxious beings.

The vista from her bedchamber overlooks the harbor. Each morning, she performs her ritual barefoot, silk robe embracing her figure. She pads to the bay window and slides on to the cushioned window seat, tucking her legs into a comfortable position. She gives thanks for the events that have landed her here, in her cherished home on the cliff above the sea. She asks for wisdom in carrying out the duties in her business and to be kind but firm with her employees. To complete the ritual, she reaches for the mosaic encrusted cedar box that resides on a small table near the window seat. Reverently, she unclasps the lock and dons the pair of white cotton archival gloves resting on the muslin protecting the garment inside. She removes the garment from its muslin wrapping. The marigold chemise remains in remarkably decent shape, having been passed along to succeeding generations since the seventeenth century. Perhaps she will donate the garment to a museum, she muses, as she slowly rewraps the chemise and returns it to its box, since her offspring are disdainful of family history unless it is money in their bank accounts. It breaks her heart to think that the marigold chemise may never be owned by another Galvani or Bianchi.

Since moving to the island, she speaks to Luca each weekday morning. Luca has proven himself to be an invaluable business manager, and she enjoys their status meetings. They are perfectly in sync, shepherding the business to one of the leading designs and producers of fine lingerie in the world.

Today they are discussing the palette for the fall collection. There will be a charmeuse and chiffon bralette, silk slips, bikini briefs, and swimsuits. For inspiration, she has chosen lapis blue from Utah potash mines, the pale coral of a vintage slip, and the creamy white and phosphorescent purple of the petals of the anemone flower. She creates the palette with watercolor and sends the samples to Luca and Rosa. They work with the fabric dyers to create samples for Maria's approval.

"I spoke to the dyer yesterday afternoon. He promises to deliver the samples to me by early next week, and I will rush them to you. We need to make sure we have lead time in case there are delays in construction. Are you returning for the pattern design approval and to meet this year's models for the show?" Luca is a master at keeping to the production schedule.

"Luca, are you forgetting our last conversation? The doctor has not given me the approval for travel yet. How is Rosa coming along with the patterns? I have seen her sketches, and she may be ready to be designing the pieces without my input. You know, it may be time for a more youthful mind to work on our collection." She realizes that Luca is avoiding confronting the reality that she will not be around much longer.

"Don't worry, Rosa is on schedule. Maybe for the spring collection, we can look at some of her ideas." Luca isn't facing the fact that she may not be here for planning the spring collection.

"I will call when I have the samples, and we can discuss any refinements then. Give my love to Rosa and the team. We will have to have more conversations, you know. By the way, Laura and James are arriving this afternoon for a meeting. Wish me luck." She ends the call and starts thinking about her afternoon. But first, a nice breakfast to fortify herself.

She is preparing an omelet with fresh eggs from her neighbor's brood of Bresse Gauloise when her housekeeper Mireille arrives. Mireille has been to the market and is weighted down with provisions. She wants to have an abundance of local specialties and wine for the children's stay, as they won't be able to catch a ferry back to the mainland until tomorrow afternoon at the earliest. Mireille is a dear, and she embraces her, thanking her profusely for the extra hours she has been working, helping her prepare for the visit. Her husband, Gabrielle, will meet the afternoon ferry and drive Laura and James to the house.

Discarding outfit after outfit in a puddle on the floor of her closet, she realizes how anxious she is about the meeting with her children. They are so sure of themselves and intimidating. They are always furious with her. Enough! She chooses some slim black slacks and a black cashmere turtleneck. Emerald velvet flats and a simple gold bracelet, earrings, and necklace complete the look. At the mirror applying her makeup and lipstick, she gives herself a good talking.

"You are the mother. You have worked very hard for years to expand the business inherited from your dear parents, and it is your decision and obligation to place the business in capable hands. You will be a good steward to this legacy, and your children have had the opportunity to be involved and disdainfully declined. Be strong."

She hears Gabrielle's car approaching the house, gravel crunching as he brakes and retrieves their luggage from the boot. Voices raise in the foyer as she descends the staircase to greet her children.

James intercepts her embrace with a hand extended to shake, as if meeting an acquaintance for an initial introduction. Laura avoids her embrace with a swift step backward and an exaggerated air kiss.

"Welcome, children. Gabrielle has prepared your rooms. Perhaps you want to freshen up, and then let's gather in the sitting room. Would you like some refreshment?"

"Whatever." James and Laura shrug and roll their eyes in response. They ascend the stairs to freshen up. Maria feels her chest tighten with tension.

She goes to the kitchen and directs Mireille to bring a tray with lemonade and biscuits to her office where she will be meeting with James and Laura. Mireille hands Maria a glass of water.

"Signora, you look a bit pale. Are you feeling all right?"

"*Oui, oui*, I am just a little nervous about the meeting with my children. We need to have a difficult conversation. Thank you for the water," Maria replies.

Maria goes into her office and orders the files she has prepared for the discussion. She has arranged for her solicitor to visit next week to finalize her will. Mireille arrives with a tray of refreshments and sets it on the sideboard. Maria feels a bit light-headed, so she sits at the table where they will be meeting, choosing the side that has a view of the sea. She says a little prayer of gratitude for her life and especially this time on the island overlooking the sea.

James and Laura descend the stairs and make their way to their mother's office. They are curious as to why she seemed so insistent on meeting on the island. They enter the office, Laura leading the way. She sees her mother with her back to the door, appearing to be enjoying the view of the sea.

"Mother, we are here. I see Mireille brought lemonade. It looks delicious. I am thirsty from the journey. Shall I pour us a glass?" Laura directs her request to her mother's back.

There is no response from Maria.

"Mother, Mother, did you hear me?" she asks. There is still no response. Laura glances at James. James walks over to his mother, touching her lightly on the right shoulder. She does not respond. He indicates that Laura should join him. They move to face their mother. She is completely still, staring out the window. Laura shakes her mother at the shoulders, calling her name. There is no response. James checks her pulse at the wrist and the neck. Nothing.

"Laura, Mother is dead. She has passed away. Oh no, what are we going to do?" He looks terrified as he addresses his sister.

"Go get Mireille and see if Gabriel is in the garden. They will know what to do," instructs Laura.

Gabriel takes charge. He calls the local police.

"The authorities will be here shortly," he informs the twins.

A police car and an ambulance arrive shortly. The medics confirm that Maria has passed. They call the local coroner who will transport the body to the funeral home in town.

Gabriel tells James that he will drive him to the funeral home. He will need to make decisions.

James and Laura are in shock. Their communication with their mother has not been frequent in the past few years. They have no idea what she would want for a funeral. They agree that James should go with Gabriel to the funeral home, and Laura should begin a search to see if their mother left any instructions or a will. They are both surprised at the depth of their immediate sorrow and regret.

Laura opens the door to her mother's bedchamber and finds herself at the window seat overlooking the sea. She settles into the cushion, taking the same posture as her mother, tucking her legs underneath her body. Her eyes land on a mosaic encrusted box. Curious, she opens it. There are white archival gloves laying on top of a muslin. Laura puts on the gloves and carefully unwraps the muslin. She unfolds a marigold chemise.

"It is meant to be mine," she speaks to the sea. Memories of the stories of the paintings and the marigold chemise come flooding back to her.

"I am sorry, Mother. I love you so much, and I know that you love me and James. Please forgive us," she whispers to the marigold chemise.

The Ara Pacis the Lungotevere in Augusta is filled to capacity with admirers celebrating the life of Maria Bianchi. James and his husband arranged to have Alessia's paintings moved from his mother's villa to the Ara Pacis for the event. They have never been viewed by the public. Everyone is stunned by the work. The marigold chemise is incased in a glass frame with a beautiful history next to it.

Laura wears her mother's marigold slip dress and jewelry as she addresses the crowd, thanking them for honoring her mother. When she glances up, she spots Lorenzo in the back of the room. He smiles in acknowledgment and removes his handkerchief from his pocket, discreetly wiping a tear from his right eye.

The Bianchi villa is alive with family. James and his husband share the villa with Laura and her husband. They enjoy entertaining friends and love living with Alessia's paintings. Laura is the owner and creative director of *Maria*, the family lingerie business, choosing to work from Orazio's studio rather than move to larger headquarters. James is now chief executive officer of the Bianchi enterprises.

The twins and their spouses are enjoying a beautiful summer's evening on the terrace. Laura's husband pours wine for a toast.

"Laura and I have an announcement to make. This coming May, we will be welcoming our first child. It will be good to have a little one running around the villa, don't you think?"

Laura beams as James and his husband embrace her and slap her husband on the back.

"Well done!" they exclaim.

That evening, Laura dreams. She is seated on an elaborate chair in the center of the Tempietto. Cradled in her arms is a baby girl. Surrounding them are angels dressed in marigold chemise. One of the angels brings a marigold chemise and lays it gently on Laura's lap, partially covering the baby. The angel kisses Laura on the forehead and then floats away, the flock of angels following her.

La fine

The Marigold Chemise
Cast of Characters

The Galvani Family

Father: Luigi
Mother: Eugenia
Daughter: Lucida
Daughter: Brigida
Son: Luigi Jr.
Son: Giovanni
Daughter: Beatrice
Tutor: Ariston (Greek freedman)
  Son: Ariston Jr.
  Son: Luca
    Wife: Rosa

Salvatori Family

Father: Orazio Salvatori
Mother: Signora Salvatori
Daughter: Alessia
Art dealer: Signor Ruel
Gossiping collector: Signor Stassi

Bianchi Family

Father and mother: Signor and Signora Bianchi
Son: Niccolo Bianchi
Daughter: Martina Bianchi

Niccolo Bianchi's Family

Father: Niccolo
Mother: Lucida (Galvani)
Daughter: Cristina
Son: Antonio

Stratassi Family

Father: Pietro
Mother: Alessia (Salvatori)
Daughter: Lucia
Son: Piero
       Wife: Cristina (Bianchi)
       Daughter: Maria Bianchi
           Son: James
           Daughter: Laura
Businessman: Signor Reda
Prostitute: Adonna
Businessman: Lorenzo Alberti
       Wife: Signora Alberti
       Son: Stephano

About the Author

A native of the Pacific Northwest, Sheryl Westergreen is a writer and an abstract painter represented by the Seattle Art Museum Sales and Rental Gallery and Zatista/1stDibs. Her writing and paintings are inspired by memories of places or experiences. She lives in Seattle, Washington, with her family. This is her first novel.

CPSIA information can be obtained
at www.ICGtesting.com
Printed in the USA
BVHW080258230522
637770BV00001B/47